CONVERGENCE

PRAISE FOR CONVERGENCE

An Amazon Breakthrough Novel Award Finalist

"[A] smart splice of espionage and science fiction. ... frighteningly realistic. Well-drawn characters, excellent pacing, and constant surprises make this a great cautionary tale about technology and its abuses."

- Publisher's Weekly

"From the opening page of Convergence I was hooked. The dystopian world building is well done and the descriptions are vivid. The technology is imaginary and different...great characters and plenty of suspense/action."

- Nicholas Sansbury Smith, author of *Extinction Horizon* and the Orbs series

"Convergence is fast-paced, full of action and a thrilling ride from start to finish. There is violence, depth of feeling, explosions, car chases and tenderness. The book has everything and is perfect for those who like their SciFi gritty, edgy and realistic."

– J.S. Collyer, author of *Zero*

"A cyberpunk thrillride through a future America under Chinese rule. The conflict between the humanity of the main character, Jonah, and the things he has had to do to survive in this harsh new world makes 'Convergence' an absolute pleasure to read."

– SciFi365.net

PRAISE FOR EMERGENCE

"Hicks writes like Philip K Dick and Robert Crais combined, making for clean, exciting prose. He focuses on the story and never lets go."

- Lucas Bale, author of the award-winning Beyond The Wall series

"It has all the gritty cyberpunk of the first book plus a more fully-realized world in which to immerse yourself. Excellent."

- SciFi365.net

"Excellent, fast-paced thriller with fantastic world building. Mesa is a troubled yet strong heroine that captivates you from the first page."

- E.E. Giorgi, author of *Chimeras*

PRAISE FOR REVOLVER

"Wow. Just... Wow. *Revolver* aims at the world we live in and blows its head off."

- Edward Lorn, author of *Bays End* and *The Sound of Broken Ribs*

"*Revolver*... takes the 'shocking' gold medal. A classic example of social science fiction ... most gripping."

- David Wailing, author of *Auto*

"[A] truly gut twisting, heart wrenching, sphincter squeezing tale of lossand abandonment that stuck with me long after the last page."

- Anthony Vicino, author of *Time Heist*

"*Revolver* is a brave, powerful piece of writing... It's unapologetic, visceral, and the kind of story that would probably have sent the Clean Reader app into cyber meltdown. Give it a read if you like your stories to take you to the edge of your seat."

- Tommy Muncie, author of Shadow's Talent

"A lot of what happens in this story resonates with what we see and what we read in our very lives today. *Revolver* is a great story, bristling with tension, unflinching with its descriptions and thoughtful. I get the feeling that people who misunderstand this may need to perhaps take a long hard look at themselves in the mirror."

- The Grim Reader

"*Revolver* is a perfect short story/novella to read right now. The political extremists are gaining more and more power and they aren't easily ignored anymore. *Revolver* tells the story of what would happen if we let this extremism go too far. And wow was it good. ... *Revolver* is a big "what if" book that will leave you feeling raw and full of emotion."

- Brian's Book Blog

"Hicks has written a seminal political – psychological thriller that packs a massive punch in a short space. ... I think it's a piece of fiction that will stand the test of time."

- Steve Stred, Kendall Reviews

ALSO BY
MICHAEL PATRICK HICKS

DRMR SERIES
Convergence (A DRMR Novel, Book 1)
Emergence (A DRMR Novel, Book 2)
Preservation (A DRMR Short Story)

THE SALEM HAWLEY SERIES
The Resurrectionists (Book 1)

Broken Shells: A Subterranean Horror Novella
Mass Hysteria

SHORT STORIES
The Marque
Black Site
Let Go
Revolver
Consumption

CONVERGENCE
DRMR SERIES, BOOK 1

MICHAEL PATRICK HICKS

CONVERGENCE
Copyright © 2014 by Michael Patrick Hicks

Edited by Red Adept Editing
http://redadeptpublishing.com/

Cover artwork by Eight Little Pages
http://eightlittlepages.com/

This is a work of fiction. Names, characters, places, and incidents either are the products of the author's imagination or are used fictitiously. Any resemblance to actual persons, living or dead, businesses, companies, events, or locales is entirely coincidental.

Printed in the United States of America

ISBN-13: 978-1-947570-07-8 (paperback)
ISBN-13: 978-1-947570-08-5 (ebook)

To my wife, Maureen, for her constant love and support.

CHAPTER
ONE

MURDER IS EASY WHEN YOU wrap a cause around it, like a flag or a god—or money.

I was sitting in a car that wasn't mine. It had been given to me for the job, and when I left the motel lot, I would drop it off at a pre-arranged location, where somebody else would pick it up. I wore thin leather gloves to prevent leaving fingerprints and to save time on cleanup.

A light rain spotted the windshield. A young black woman in a too-short red skirt walked past, then up the stairs to the second-floor landing. She passed a row of dull-green doors with black numbers, then stopped and knocked on one about three-quarters of the way down. An Asian man dressed in boxer shorts and an undershirt answered. They exchanged a few words, but his mouth barely moved when he talked, and he didn't smile. She followed him into the room, closing the door behind her.

I gave them a few minutes to get down to business. I pulled a pistol from the center console, checked the magazine, and chambered a round. I screwed on the silencer and tested the heft. Like the car, the gun had been supplied by my employers.

The hit was fairly standard. Only thing odd was that the job had come to me via two employers, each with their own reasons for wanting the man dead: Alice Xie, whom I worked for often, and Jaime, a guy I occasionally did jobs for in exchange for favors. Both had taken an interest in the Asian man, and each wanted something different. One wanted his life, and the other wanted his memories.

Alice had her fingers in a lot of criminal activities, including prostitution, and she had provided the girl in the red skirt as a distraction. However, other factors ran beneath the surface of this small favor. For one thing, the street value of this particular combination of illicit sex and murder would be high. Black-market memories never came cheap, especially for snuffs; add on a taboo tax, and you were looking at some serious profit.

I pulled a balaclava over my head and face before I got out of the car. I went up the stairs to the motel room. The prostitute had been told to leave it unlocked, and when I turned the handle, the door swung open.

Both occupants of the room were naked, and she was kneeling on all fours on the bed while he took her from behind, his back to me. He grabbed her face and roughly twisted her head back toward him, causing her to cry out in pain. Then he pulled her hair until she screamed again. He swore at her in Chinese as he punched her in the back of the neck. He shoved her face down into the mattress, trying to suffocate her while he screwed her.

When I shut the door with a click, he turned quickly, pulling free from her, and gasped in surprise. She pushed herself away, wheezing. His eyes went wide at the sight of my gun. His words came at me in a rapid clip. I didn't know what he was saying, but I knew he was pleading for his life.

Then his hands shot out, and he grabbed the gun, pushing my arm away as he stepped toward me, trying to force me back. I popped him with a quick palm strike to the chin, rattling his teeth. He must have bitten his tongue because blood spurted through his lips. I tugged my arm away and drove my knee into his crotch. When he doubled over, I hammered the butt of the gun into the crook of his neck.

"Please don't," he said, over and over. Thin ropes of blood and drool dripped from his bottom lip, and he cradled his genitals in both hands.

The girl was scrunched up against the wall, bedsheets pulled tight against her with one hand, the other hand busy massaging her bruised throat. Half-moon shapes marked where fingernails had been pressed deeply into her breasts. Her mouth and cheeks were swollen. She was young, maybe sixteen, not much older than that. Given the hard nature of her working life, she could have been younger.

I pulled a small black rectangular box and a coil of wire from my pocket. "Turn your head," I told the man.

He did. I spotted the data port behind his ear and ordered him to plug in, while I fed the male connector into the box.

"Please don't." His mouth quivered. Tears ran freely down his face.

I glanced at the girl again. "Go in the bathroom."

She shook her head. "No way. I wanna watch."

"Go in the bathroom," I said again, my tone leaving no room for argument.

She sulked off. I could feel her eyes on my back, and I knew she was watching anyway.

Wanting the fresh memory, I hit record. I didn't care about whatever else he had in back-up. I was getting the good stuff—the fear and adrenaline. His heart and thoughts had to be racing. Synapses fired and fired and fired, creating huge chemical dumps, his pineal gland working overtime.

He kept begging. Finally, he shut his eyes as I raised the gun. I pulled the trigger. He knelt for a moment, a small bloody hole in his forehead. A spasm shot his eyes open. His bowel muscles relaxed, and he evacuated onto the carpet. Then he collapsed to the floor.

I ignored the smell and rolled him over onto his stomach. I unplugged him, and tossed the DRMR and its cord onto the bed. I pressed my fingers deep into the skin on the back of his neck, near the data port, trying to get a feel for where the wires ran, which wasn't easy through leather gloves. Latex gloves would have made this part of the job easier, but I didn't trust the thin rubber not to tear.

"What are you doing?" the girl asked. She was standing in the bathroom doorway with the sheet tied around her body.

"Go back in there." I dug my fingers into his shoulder blades and down the length of his spine. I felt around his scalp and hit pay dirt with a small protuberance near his hairline. That was why I'd used a .22—no exit wound. The bullet had gone in the front of his skull, shredding his brain, before being lodged somewhere inside there. No damage to the electronics.

I looked over my shoulder, into the bathroom. She sat on the edge of the bathtub, tears streaming down her face, snot running from her nose and around her open mouth. Bruises around her mouth and cheekbones darkened her mocha complexion from where the Asian man had laid hands on her. Finger marks ringed her throat. Suddenly, she seemed a lot older than sixteen.

A cracked mirror over a filthy-looking sink caught my reflection. My late forties bordered on late fifties, and a nose that had been broken a few times too many in recent years without ever being reset graced a face lined more with crags than wrinkles. More gray peppered my short hair than I remembered.

I pulled out a knife, grabbed a good handful of his hair, pulled as far as it would stretch, then stabbed the knife in and scalped him. A glint of steel grafted to his skull caught my eye. I unscrewed the cap with the blade of my knife and popped loose the memory chip. A lifetime of the man's memories. I stuck the knife into the chip socket and twisted, pulling it in all sorts of directions until the hole was large and disfigured. Then I did the same to the data port behind his ear, damn near tearing it completely out of his head.

I fired two more rounds into the back of his skull, just to be safe. I wanted to bring any chances of data recovery down to zero.

"Come here," I called to her. "There's a bag in my pocket. Take it out and open it."

She moved tentatively. I dropped the chip into the antistatic bag and told her to seal it. Her hands shook while her thin fingers pressed the silver material of the bag shut, then she carefully put it back in my pocket.

Once she finished, I said, "Get dressed. Get a towel from the bathroom and wipe down anything you touched."

She moved quickly, and the task didn't take her long. She'd touched hardly more than the doorknob and the bed. She wiped the bathroom counter.

"You leave first," I said. "You walk casual, but keep your face down."

She nodded, then left. We were finished with each other. The interaction was nothing more than a passing blip in one another's lives, hardly worth the mem space.

I'd been in the motel room for maybe five minutes. It felt longer, thanks to the adrenaline comedown.

The dead man's clothes were neatly folded on a small chair between the bed and the windows. I had noticed from outside that the blinds had been drawn and shuttered closed. They let very little light into the room, but I instantly recognized the pine-green Type 07 uniform and the patch on the shoulder. A red background with a prominent golden star set inside a circle. Pacific Rim Coalition. Epaulets decorated with two gold stars marked him a *zhong chiang*, or lieutenant general, in the PRC Army. The rank was a political appointment, if his pleadings for mercy were anything to go by. Somebody had granted him a lot of undeserved favor and attention to be promoted to such a high rank at such a young age.

I shoved the DRMR back in my pocket and did a quick assessment. If any of the girl's fingerprints were left, it would be hard to trace them to her. Motels as disreputable as this one enjoyed heavy transient traffic. All kinds of people, touching all kinds of things, over and over. It'd be damn near impossible to get a good impression. The *chiang's* memory core was in my pocket, and with his brain Swiss-cheesed and the core and data ports ruined, any chances for recovery were hopeless. I was sure no one would be able to identify me under the balaclava. The girl and I would be able to walk away and disappear into the ether.

I peeked out the window. Nobody was standing around in the lot. No new cars. I pulled the balaclava up and made a cap out of it. Less suspicious that way. I wiped the doorknob with the towel, used it to open and then pull the door closed behind me, and walked back to the car, casually, with my head down, like any other patron who frequented shady motels. Passing through the sickly yellow glow of the pulsing holosign advertising the motel's cheap hourly room rates, I quickly checked over my shoulder. I didn't see anyone peeking out from the doors or windows as I went. The lot and the street beyond were quiet, and I had no reason to suspect anybody was watching me or could tie me to the *chiang's* murder.

I dropped the towel on the floor well behind the driver's seat, then got in front and turned the keys. The car was an antique that still ran on gas. Miraculously, there were people that could still afford the gas and oil needed to drive these old heaps.

I drove to a parking garage, where I left the car. The gloves and balaclava went into a dumpster a few buildings over. I disassembled the gun, discretely tossing the pieces into garbage cans and down manhole covers and sewer drains as I went. I checked behind me for tails, committing the faces to memory and cataloguing them for reference, then crossed the street and walked in the opposite direction, to a bus stop, where I waited for the 704 to Echo Park.

Traffic was slow. The bus was crowded well beyond its capacity, and bodies were pressed tightly against one another. I started to feel claustrophobic. What little was left of LA's mass transit systems after the war was overburdened. The city didn't have enough shuttles in service to accommodate the population, and with much of downtown decimated and many of the major thoroughfares closed, travel was slow. Before the war, the Metro Rapid shuttle had run stop to stop in about twenty minutes. Anymore, with all the detours and random PacRim checks, the commute was likely to take at least forty.

A brief stop eased the constriction of the crowd as people unloaded. Mercifully, few got on. We shuffled a bit to make more room, and I briefly caught a glimpse out the front window. Ahead of us was a military convoy of Type 103 tanks protected by reactive armor and jeeps that were painted green, brown, and black over a gray background of urban camouflage.

The bus stopped a short time later for a PRC road check. I sighed, aggravated. Soldiers flanked the bus and inspected the wheel wells and underbody. They flitted through the crowd, barking rapid questions at random people. They took the driver away and, through a sliver of window between clusters of bodies, I watched as he was questioned. He gave short answers, shaking or nodding his head in response to the PRC inquiries. A guard came up the steps and looked inside, at the congestion of bus riders. He held a gun, but casually. No threats there. He looked under the driver's seat and gave the wheel well a quick once-over. His uniform was similar to the *chiangs'*, but he was of much lower rank, wearing green pants and a buttoned coat, a lighter green button-down shirt, a soft cap, and black leather boots. He looked around briefly, shouted something out the door in Chinese, then walked out after the bus driver pulled himself back up. Then we were off again.

I got off at Sunset and made the short walk to Tent City. That was what those of us who lived there called the refugee camp run by the PRC to house what were euphemistically known as the "war displaced." We'd once had homes and lives in Los Angeles. Then the Pacific Rim Coalition invaded and destroyed everything we knew, forcing us to live in tents that the UN had fought to provide for us. Echo Park was one of a dozen camps scattered across California.

I passed through a series of security clouds on my way to the check-in gate. The clouds were a thin fog of biometric analytic nanites designed to sniff out chemical traces and toxins indicating I either carried or had handled explosives. At the gate, the guard asked where I had gone and what I had done. We knew each other and had a certain understanding, thanks to a mutual acquaintance, Alice Xie. He didn't ask me questions about the DRMR unit or the memory chips in my possession.

He swiped my identity card and logged my return to the camp. I saw my record appear on the air display between us, listing my daily movements into and out of the camp, guard notes, and my photograph—which was the same as the one on my ident card. At the top of it all, my name, Jonah Everitt, was written in all caps.

"Why did you go into the city?" he asked.

"I was meeting friends at a restaurant in Century City."

"Refugees?"

"No," I said. "They live in Chinatown."

The guard nodded to me, and I nodded back, smartly deferential.

"Take off your shoes and socks. Go to Line Five for reentry."

I did as instructed. Line Five was long and slow moving. After twenty minutes, I passed through a metal arch and a denser cloud of security sniffers. Shoes and socks in hand, I walked barefoot to my tent.

Once there, I shrugged out of my coat and fell onto my cot. The day's work was catching up with me. I got up again, long enough to grab a nearly empty bottle of honey whiskey from my footlocker. It had been payment from the last job I had done for Jaime. Then I fished the DRMR unit from my coat pocket. I uncoiled the wire and plugged it into the data port behind my ear. I untwisted the bottle cap and took a quick hit. The thick, warm whiskey's heat was familiar and offered a bit of a bite against the taste of aged oak.

I remembered the jolt of adrenaline as I had walked into the motel room. My heart rate had spiked; my mouth had gone dry. I could have left, and a little remnant of instinct, of that fight-or-flight reflex, kicked in. But I had ignored it, clamped it down. The *chiang*, though—his emotions had been palatable, intense. I was excited to feel the moment of death from his perspective.

I took another slug of whiskey and held it in my mouth for a moment, savoring it. Then I swallowed and the let the odd chill and heat soak deep into my chest.

I hit play.

A grotesque electrical charge jolted through me, sparking neurons in my brain. A white light blasted through my cerebral cortex and optic nerves. Everything went blindingly bright for moments buried atop moments. An eternity of moments. This is how death feels. Invigorating. As my heart raced and pulse skyrocketed, my brain fought against the violent, foreign memory, against the shock, not knowing if it was alive or dying. A massive chemical dump, a deep, long aching undercut a sudden throbbing that stitched its way from my forehead to the crown of my skull. I could feel my hippocampus burning, like a ram's horn on fire in the center of my skull, feeling the flames, seeing the flames. Everything was amped way the fuck up. A building pressure spread a joyful ache through my groin, and I barely felt or heard the groan that escaped me before the sudden splash of wetness. This was death. This was life. Such beautiful pain, a cracking shot of noise and deafness. The whiteness slowly dissolved, then the walls of my tent snapped back into focus. My chest heaving, unable to catch my breath, I gasped for air. My winded lungs were sore.

Felt good. Felt so good.

Do it again. Hit play. The blast of white. My head throbbed under the searing heat and pain of shattered bone. My chest caught fire, heart racing so hard it felt ready to tear itself apart at the seams. My lungs were burning; each breath was agony. Beautiful pain. I screamed silently, my shouts lost to the buckling inside my skull. Throbbing and cracking, my bones shattered under the weight of memory.

This was death.

Cold eyes watching me.

A stranger's eyes.

My eyes.

"Please," I said. "Please don't."

Then the pitch tunnel staring coldly, as the gun is raised before me. A flash of light. Pain. Shock. Brutal. Short. Infinite.

I sat very still for a long time, trying to collect myself. I could finally breathe again, but I struggled to get my thoughts straight. I debated taking another hit and decided not to.

My arm was heavy as I reached behind my ear and unplugged the DRMR.

I was cold with flop-sweat chills. I couldn't shake the image of the hooker's fat, bruised lips, the trail of tears that had run down her face, or the impressions of fingers and nails on her neck and breasts. I raised the bottle to my lips and finished it.

I had to meet with Alice Xie the next day. The sun had set already. I was spent and hungry, but going to the mess hall, or to Jaime's for dinner, meant moving, and moving was too much work. I had noodles, but no fresh water. Both were too much work. I slipped the DRMR under my cot, then pushed my arms under the pillow as I rolled onto my side. I slept, and later, I woke up haunted.

I WAS CRAVING A HOT dog, which was a rarity in these times. Used to be, I could find them almost anywhere in Los Angeles, but not anymore. The PRC had upset the balance, upended everything.

Lunch was a bowl of yakisoba across from the wishing well in Chinatown. Having a Chinatown seemed redundant nowadays. Funny thing was, this part of town used to be known as New Chinatown. Old Chinatown, between Alameda and Macy, had been torn down back in the late 1800s to make way for Union Station. After the PRC arrived, almost everywhere along the Pacific became Chinatown.

American towns didn't exist anymore, not really, and not for a long way from the coast. Small pockets in the Midwest and along the Bible Belt, south of the DC ruins along the East Coast, clung to a dying heritage. Much of what was once the US had been co-opted between Canada and rival territories that had fought to carve out independent swatches of nation-states. The Northern Alliance ran from Maine down through the New York mainland and into Ohio and the southern regions of Michigan and Wisconsin. Their reach was extending farther west, with the aid and support of European and Canadian allies, but progress was slow, and some states had found they enjoyed their independence. Farther down the map, a group of Texan militias had carved out the Southwest Conclave, starting with Dallas and Fort Worth, and then worked their way up through the lower reaches of Oklahoma, creating a violent stretch of land that extended as far west as Phoenix and south of Chihuahua. The cartels in Juarez, along with the Mexican Army they largely controlled, hadn't reacted well to the Conclave's incursions and maintained a nearly constant state of war. Some states, such as Washington and Oregon as well as the upper reaches of Idaho and Montana became, or were in the process of becoming, Canadian provinces. The map had changed rapidly and left a lot of people without a nation.

I swirled the fried wheat noodles and chopped cabbage around a good-sized chunk of pork then dipped it in a small bowl of mayonnaise. Between bites, I drew a sketch on a small piece of e-paper. Before the war, I had been a small-time artist who taught art history at a local community college. I had carried paper and a digipencil at all times, to draft thumbnail images, jot down notes, or quickly compose scenes or ideas. The city, its people, its architecture—I drew all of it. Decades' worth of practice had constantly refined and honed my skills and techniques. I rarely drew anymore, and even though I hardly used the tools, I occasionally found myself carrying them with me, just in case. I embraced this minor return to my old life, the small feeling of normalcy.

A small girl leaning over a waist-high red brick wall threw pennies into the wishing well. The well was a decrepit mess of green paint chipping away to an ugly brown. Golden Buddha statues flanking the monstrosity were the only parts of the façade that were truly well maintained. I filled in the details of my sketch of her, getting the pose right. Her coins clinked off the metal cups. In front of the cups were white cards with blue lettering, identifying each—money, wealth, love, surety. She was wishing for one of everything. She couldn't have been more than twelve, with long shiny black hair that reached down between her shoulder blades. More coins went toward love, and I doubted her wishes would ever come true. If she kept spending coins on love, she would never accumulate wealth.

I thought of my daughter, Mesa, then about wealth, love, and money, and how tied up each are in one another.

I was losing my appetite. I ate a few thin slices of ginger to cleanse my palette, then checked the time.

I spent a few minutes roughly filling in the details of the well and the girl. I had a rough outline of the composition, mostly simple markings of the landscape and a skeleton of ovals and circles that would need to be refined and filled in to resemble the girl. Later, if I felt the need to continue, I could review the memories and draw it all in greater detail, with more focus, and give the image depth and clarity and really bring it all to life on the page.

I was lying to myself. The paper would be tossed aside, and the sketch, abandoned. I folded the e-paper and pocketed it, along with the digipencil. I had already forgotten the scene as I tossed the paper plate and the cheap, plastic utensils into a public garbage can.

A couple of PacRim soldiers came out of the Plum Tree. They said something to the girl that made her face redden, and she ran off, her head down and shoulders slumped. They gave me a hard look. As I walked, I checked out the reflections in the glass storefronts and saw the men were following me. I kept my pace moderate, not leisurely or lazy, but not fast, either. I turned down *Dai hok gai*. When I was a kid, too long ago, it had been College Street, with a few Chinese symbols below the English name. The English names were gone, stripped off all of the street signs. Maybe up in Seattle or Portland, maybe farther up the coast or deeper inland, street signs were printed in English, but not around here. Not anymore.

Behind me, the PRC turned, following me. Both were thin, but well-toned. One had dyed his hair a bright, unnatural yellow, but didn't care to hide the dark roots. The other was shaved bald. Their thumbs were hooked into their belts. Each had an assault rifle slung over his shoulder, a Type 56, similar to the AK-47s the Russians were fond of. I wasn't worried, just wary.

I slowed my pace a little, waiting for a reaction. Either they would slow, which meant they were interested in me, or they would walk on by. They slowed. I looked in the windows as I passed the storefront, pretending something caught my interest. They walked by, slowly, staring at me in the reflection.

Their gazes hovered over me as they passed. I noticed a distinct black freckling around their eyes, tiny dots placed at regular intervals encircling their orbits. I pegged them for battlefield enhancements, microcybernetic upgrades to provide feedback on battle conditions and enemy locations. They were probably analyzing my heart rate, pulse, and blood pressure, looking for any indication that I was a threat and not just some pathetic white guy in Chinatown. The blond said something that caused his partner to snicker. If they had picked up anything in my vitals, they apparently chalked it up to nerves and moved on. I stayed at the storefront, looking at an assortment of jade jewelry and wood-carved statues finished with a high-gloss red lacquer of elephants, dragons, and Buddhas.

I lingered and window-shopped until the PRC soldiers were farther down the block. Whites sometimes had problems after the war and occupation, especially if we were tagged as refugees. Blacks and Hispanics had it even worse and were often subjected to random searches, which typically led to beat-downs if they were considered to be belligerent or disrespectful. Sometimes, they were shot in the head outright. Los Angeles was a dangerous little corner of the DMZ for everyone, regardless of color. Most people didn't need a reason to kill, but for a lot of the old Americans, killing the Chinese was par for the course. Immense hostility was boiling beneath the surface, seeking an outlet. A lot of people were able to let it go, after a time. Some, though, some never could—and didn't want to. They found things to occupy their time, but thoughts of revenge were always curled up somewhere in their minds.

Red paper lanterns hung over the street, stretched between the buildings. A gentle breeze sent them bobbing and carried food smells from the many vendors and restaurants. The air was thick with the smells of frying oil, rice, meat, and vegetables, along with the crackling noises of fat and water hitting hot oil. Steam rose from the open-air kitchens while elderly men and women busied themselves in the cramped confines between hot ovens and stovetops. The thin wooden countertops were crowded with a shifting influx of the hungry and their lunch orders. People sat at small tables, alone or clustered in parties of two or three. Others ate while walking, leisurely scooping rice with their chopsticks or capturing chunks of bite-sized meat or fish. The square was crowded, but I stood out. Maybe that's what had captured the attention of the PRC. I was an old white guy, about a head taller than everyone else there, wandering after lunch, with no real purpose. As far as they were concerned, I should have eaten and left, or better still, never stepped foot in this part of town to begin with. Instead, I moved with no real direction, my head held high while those around me kept their eyes downcast as they moved quickly along the sidewalks.

An old man watched me. His face was coiled with wrinkles, the flesh paper-thin. A cigarette dangled from his lips, and his hands were busy prepping stir-fry at a chop station beside a steaming stove. The knuckles of his callused fingers were large and gnarly, twisted from arthritis. Dark bags hung beneath his eyes. His hair stood out from his liver-spotted skull in puffy, white tufts. He watched me, his butcher's knife quickly dicing onions, carrots, and garlic. Chop, chop, chop. Staring at me all the while. I nodded to him. He nodded back, then motioned me around the corner, to the alley beside his food hut.

I followed a shallow stream of water gurgling along the gutters in a fast current that spilled into a storm drain. A violent storm the night before had dumped rain and lots of lightning. In this alley, in this gutter, a lot of blood had probably mixed with the rainwater, turning this tiny river red. Fish blood, chicken blood—and people blood, too, more than likely.

About halfway between *Dai hok gai* and *Lei Min*, a black sedan was parked outside a Chinese restaurant. A pair of large cement lions guarded the restaurant's entryway— the statue feature was typical of this part of town. The lions always came in pairs, male and female. The male had one front paw resting atop a globe that represented the earth, while the female restrained a small cub. I had read that they were representations of yin and yang, a concept that reflects on the interdependency of polar opposites. Considering the damage Alice and I could do to one another if either of us were compromised, I figured the philosophy was about right. The lions also were a symbol of protection. I hoped that was right, too.

The driver's door opened, and a wiry man in a tuxedo stepped out. Hai opened the rear door and waved me inside.

"*Nî Hâo*," Alice Xie said. I returned the greeting with a perfunctory nod. Her bodyguard closed the door for me and climbed back in behind the wheel, where he was separated from us by a thick pane of soundproof glass.

"There were no problems?" she asked.

I fidgeted a bit, straightening my coat, trying to get comfortable. "Nothing unusual." I slowly reached inside my pocket and removed the antistatic bag and the small crystalline data chip inside it.

She smiled as she took it. "An entire life in the palm of my hand."

The cheap advertising slogan had become an even more tired joke. Nobody said that kind of shit anymore without irony, especially not Alice Xie, considering her line of work. Judging by her smile and the glint in her eye, it may have even been intentional.

Alice was a higher-up in the Bing Kong Tong, the Chinese mafia. She was slender and beautiful. When she turned her head, still smiling, to glance out the window, her long neck imparted a certain grace. She favored sleeveless blouses, to show off the toned arms she worked to maintain, and knee-length skirts or capris that displayed equally nice calves. Her beauty caused a lot of people to underestimate her. People like the *chiang*. And, as the *chiang* had learned, those who underestimated her usually wound up dead. If they survived, it wasn't without grievous injuries. Of that, there was no "usually."

Her long black hair was tied off close to her scalp and draped around the front of her chest. It helped to hide the breast she'd lost to cancer in her teens. She had never told me, but I had heard things. I had caught a glimpse of scar tissue once, through the armhole of a sleeveless blouse. The glimpse had been quick and casual, but she knew I'd seen, and that was enough. I'd heard she was also missing a toe because of a simple mistake she'd made at an even younger age. To prove she had learned her lesson later in life, the man who had taken the toe had lost his head.

"It's hard to believe," she said. "A person's entire existence on something so small."

The data chip was about the size of my thumbnail. I nodded agreeably, not sure what to say, itching to get out of the car. She seemed to be in a rare philosophical mood, and I didn't have the patience for it.

"You're not even going to ask what is so important, are you? Which memory he had that I would kill to possess?" She smirked and stared me in the eyes, daring me to ask.

I shook my head. I'd done jobs for her in the past and never asked about those, either. I figured those kinds of questions were above my pay grade, and I didn't really want to know why some people needed others killed or why they wanted it so badly they would farm it out to others. We'd done this dance before.

"Nope," I said, wishing I had a cigarette. I'd gleaned enough during my earlier playbacks to get the gist.

The *chiang's* offenses were many. He had a penchant for hookers and enjoyed snorting posh. Mostly, he was a power whore who believed that being of rank in the PRC put him above the Bing Kong Tong. Xie thought otherwise, but had briefly allowed the man his delusions. Acting against him directly would have drawn too much attention to her organization, and although they had many resources, the Tong could not sustain open warfare against the PRC. If they could find an intermediary, though... using a third party to solve their problem could draw official attention away from the Tong. Unofficially, those PRC soldiers who enjoyed the Tong's more nefarious offerings would also be made aware of the costs associated with betraying them. The small crackdown that was sure to follow the *chiang's* murder would be nothing that would break the tong, but it would at least allow the PRC to save a little face. In the end, everyone broke even.

The data chip disappeared into her pocket. She folded her hands in her lap. "And the girl?" she asked, quickly changing tracks.

The hooker and her bruised face. I could see her clearly when I closed my eyes. The *chiang* had preferred them dark, but he'd also liked them afraid and beaten. According to Jaime, the girl was one of the *chiang's* favorites, which made her somebody he could trust, as much as a *chiang* in Los Angeles could trust anyone these days.

"He beat on her some," I said, "but she'll heal."

"Will she be a problem?"

I pretended to give it some thought and scratched at the stubble around my chin. I was really thinking about the DMT rush I would get back at home in a few hours, reliving the *chiang's* death and a few other mems in my greatest hits collection. Being in Chinatown, watching the PRC sniggering at me, made me realize I'd been straight for too long.

I wasn't sure how much to tell Alice. The girl had been afraid of the general, and she had agreed to the job on the condition that she get passage out of the state and into Northern Alliance territory. We used a young Korean guy to help coyote some of our people into the northern reaches of Nevada. The massive influx of refugees meant they weren't exactly welcome in the old heartland, but she stood a good chance of a new life in Minneapolis or Michigan—if she survived the route through the Sun Belt and into the Corn Belt. That latter leg of the journey would be easier than the former, given the tentative alliances. The

Sun Belt states shared easy borders with the Conclave, and those Corn Belt regions were allied with the Alliance or Canada or, if they were wise and business-savvy, both.

"No, she won't be a problem," I said.

She gave me a hard look.

"We're working on getting her disappeared."

She smiled. She liked words like "disappeared." I liked her smile, so I said stupid things like "getting her disappeared." She had a nice smile and nice lips. Not too thin, but not too full. They gave her mouth a proportionate appearance. Her dark eyes were nicely slanted. Some guys were into that. I usually wasn't, but I would have made an exception for her.

"I trust you have already made your copies of his memories?" she asked, switching tracks again.

"I have."

"Then you have payment enough."

She operated on the "information is power" principle. The memories on that memchip would mean a lot to a great many people. I knew a couple buyers who would be very interested.

I nodded, and she smiled again. She gave a small nod, and the door opened beside me. Hai helped me out, gently putting his hand under my arm, then closed the door behind me with a soft click. He stood beside the car until I was far enough away to be safely deemed unthreatening.

A slow drizzle started as I walked down toward *Lei Min*. Flashes of light in the distance were followed by thunderous explosions. I sat at the bench near a bus stop and waited, watching thick columns of black smoke curl into the air over the freeway.

CHAPTER THREE

I MADE IT BACK TO the tents before nightfall. The PRC guards stationed at the camp's entrance gave me the usual pat down, wanded me, and then ran me through the security clouds. I was allowed to pass through the gate and the chain-link fence and into what used to be a rec center.

Traffic had been stop-and-go the whole way through. The explosions had shut down the 101, and vehicles making their way off the freeway had congested the surface roads after police shut down the on- and off-ramps and redirected everybody. Nobody was happy, and it didn't take long before motorists tried to find shortcuts and new routes, gumming up the works even further. The bus ride home had taken an hour and a half to get out of Chinatown and into Echo Park.

My eyes were tired and gritty, and my headache was

building up to a migraine. The dim lights were already too glaring, and I was squinting against them. I was moving slowly, and people swarmed around me as they made their way through the checkpoints. The line to get in had been long, and it only grew longer as curfew drew closer. The guards had quickly come to recognize us, but they knew not to become complacent.

Four months ago, a suicide bomber detonated herself while in line and killed twenty-six people. She'd waited until she was close to the cloud so that she could take out a few PRC guards, but the casualties were largely civilian.

Every security check was exactly the same—a long, methodical process that was sometimes slow, depending on luck of the draw. The guard's temperament that day and whether or not you were stuck behind a family or the elderly determined how random the random full-body searches were.

As I neared the final checkpoint, a fed-up guard got in my face and began swearing at me in Chinese. Nobody paid much attention. He cussed me out for several minutes, pausing intermittently to poke me in the chest with a bony finger, prodding me to nod along. A few of the other guards laughed, and after another brief round of verbal abuse to delight his audience, he pushed me forward.

Past the final gate, people milled around, deciding what to do next. A small cafeteria doled out rations of thin, greasy soup, or they could join up with the line forming at the opposite end of the rec center, to make their way into the camp and back to the tents they called home. I wasn't hungry, but I wasn't sure I was ready to go home yet, either. I figured, fuck it, and stood in line anyway.

The PRC was a fan of redundancy. That afternoon's freeway bombing had them on high alert, and I couldn't blame them. People were trying to kill them on a regular basis. People who lived there, in the tents. People like me.

People who remembered a life before the war and the way things used to be and resented the way things had become. People who would fight and die to reclaim a small piece of the past. So they had checkpoints at each entrance and exit. Getting out was barely easier than getting in. They checked people out, scanned ID cards, and scanned people back in before admitting them into the checkpoints in the rec center. Then the process started all over again to get out of the rec center and into the tent grounds. The line from the rec center to the tents was short, and it moved more quickly.

My head hurt, and the setting sun gave off a bright glare as I passed through the entrance. Outside were rows and rows of Quonset huts and tent shelters. The jogging and bike trails, palm trees, a man-made pond with a beautiful fountain, and the downtown skyline were all gone. The trees had been burned. The pond had been drained and used up. A series of carpet bombings had wiped out much of the skyline. What remained of downtown were ruined shells; once-tall skyscrapers stood like jagged broken teeth in a bloodied jaw.

The Echo Park neighborhoods were gone, and with them, the boundaries that had divided it between the 101 and the 110. The Heights were gone; Beaudry was gone. The only things the 110 divided anymore were the tents and no-man's land, where all the dead were buried in ruins of concrete and ash. All that was left was Tent City, a small camp where the survivors and their families were allowed to congregate and live.

Echo Park was a prisoner camp in all but name. Barbed wire was strung at the top of the tall fences, and guards patrolled the watchtowers at each corner of the camp. The efforts at visible security were for their protection as much as ours. Those of us living inside had no love for the PRC, but practicality had its place. Tent City beat living in the streets, trying to scrounge out a living among the gutters and sewers of our decimated city. The PRC did not treat the homeless well and automatically presumed them to be a threat. Often, they were shot on sight. Those of us in the camps had it a little bit better. We were issued day passes. We were allowed to leave and were expected to return before curfew. And we did, all the time, because these tents were all we had left. The camp was shelter, if not home. They were the last bit of normalcy we knew. The lot of us, we remembered four walls, comfortable living rooms, and kitchens that carried memories of family. We hadn't forgotten the beds we'd tucked our children into or the beds we'd made love in inside those four walls. But they had been replaced with tan canvas staked to the ground and zippered flaps for a door. Or we slept in bunk beds under a rounded tin roof with a hundred-plus souls crammed inside, where the bodies heated the room to stifling and the stale air was rank.

I had an old tent riddled with rough patches. It fit two, me and Mesa, but most nights, I was alone. The dual-separating zippers on the flap were locked together with a small brass padlock. Anybody who wanted to could have picked it or cut through the thin canvas. The lock was more for peace of mind than security. I fished out a key, unlocked it, then relocked the zippers from the inside. Small window flaps on each side of the tent were unrolled and let in enough light to see. I zipped those back up, trying to make the tent as dark as possible. I shut my eyes against the rest of the dimness. I lay on my thin cot, resting my head on an equally thin pillow.

I felt shitty. Too fucked up to get really fucked up. I slept, and when I woke, the sky was dark. Bugs smacked against the tent, tiny thuds in the dark. I was thirsty and couldn't remember when I'd last had water. I kept a small pot in the footlocker at the end of my cot, along with a couple glasses that weren't exactly clean, a worn-out, ragged toothbrush, a small, chipped mirror, and a few days' worth of clothes that weren't exactly dirty. My name and ident designates were stamped and sewn into the collars of my shirts, the waists of my pants and underwear, and the tops of my socks so that they could be laundered by the community service and returned to me by some kid who had been volunteered for the light labor duties until he was old enough to work the reclamation gangs. The DRMR pad was still in my pocket. A couple data/mem chips were hidden in the locker beneath a fake panel that none of the random inspections had been able to suss out yet.

I grabbed the pot and stood in line for water. The hour was late, and the line was short. I had missed the dinner rush, and the small gathering around me was getting their fill to prepare for morning.

PRC guards, a dark Latino man and a pouty-looking light-skinned black woman, stood on either side of the water spigot. TIMMONS was imprinted on her shirt; the stamping was dull and worn out. The Latino's shirt was so faded that I couldn't make out his name. She had her rifle slung over her shoulder and was responsible for rationing out the water, while the man held his weapon casually between both hands, relaxed but ready.

Timmons was sweating in the evening heat. The top two buttons of her shirt were unbuttoned and barely hid a string of numbers tattooed along her collarbone. A nine and sixteen were plainly visible, but the rest were hidden beneath the dark-green uniform top. The numbers corresponded to letters of the alphabet—a *P* and an *S*—which had probably meant she had been a member of the Crips gang in her former life.

The PRC had attracted the disenfranchised early in the war. They had unleashed thought-bombs on all the major urban hubs and poorer sections of the city. When the bombs exploded, they unleashed clouds of broadcast particles that quietly, but incessantly, whispered propaganda in the people's ears and flashed videos of promise in their eyes. Wind currents had carried the particles through the city, into businesses and homes. The messages had forced their way into people's heads like a catchy pop-rock song, impregnating minds with a future ideal more glorious than anything America could offer, calling for pacifism and offering food, clothing, and jobs. Evacuation efforts were focused on downtown LA, Hollywood, and Silicon Valley, where all the money was, where all the powerbrokers and campaign donors lived. The National Guard had been on hand to quell riots and ensure that the borders dividing the rich from the poor were maintained violently. For people in Compton, Inglewood, Echo Park, Watts, and Hacienda Heights, the thought-bombs had confirmed something they had learned a long time ago—their government would do nothing to help them. They were on their own. Allegiances shifted quickly.

I couldn't help but think that the winds of change would soon shift again. People would wake up to see what the new order was really about and get sick of how long reclamation and rebuilding was taking. Soon, they would want more than they were being given, and trouble would flare up again. Discontent would build. Those like Timmons, who had bought into the Pacific Rim's propaganda and traded one gang for another, were in store for an awful wake-up call.

I shuffled forward and put my pot under the spigot. Timmons turned the knob, and the water flowed, clean and cold. Sometimes, early in the morning, it came out rusty brown, and the guards decided to either to let it run clear or let you take it as it was or walk away with nothing. I tried to go later in the morning or evening whenever possible, figuring I would avoid confrontation over the rust. I didn't want to die over brown water.

I moved on, and the lady behind me stepped up. I was a few paces away when voices rose, turning heated. I turned back out of curiosity, in time to see Timmons punch an older black lady in the face. The old lady had cut her lips on her teeth, and she spat at Timmons' face. The Latino clubbed her with the butt of his rifle, sending her to her knees and taking the feistiness right out of her. She cradled her head, lying in a fetal position in the small depression of mud worn into the earth by feet and loose spray from the spigot. He radioed for back-up, and a terse response came back quickly. The line of people stood still. Everybody stared blankly at anything other than the woman and the guards.

When Timmons looked up, I made eye contact with her, and she strode forward. We weren't supposed to make eye contact with the guards because the Chinese viewed it as a deliberate provocation. A simple expression could be a death sentence, particularly with a former gang banger. She unhooked the leather guard on her holster and drew her pistol. She knocked my pot away from me, sloshing water over our boots as the pot hit the dirt. It bounced, landing upended, spilling the rest of the water in a fast deluge.

She stared at me, her gun hanging loosely at her side. Her nostrils were flared, and a violent patchwork of blackheads freckled the bridge of her nose and her cheeks, dotting the darker pouches beneath narrow eyes. Anger and hate were carved into her stony face, and beneath that were embarrassment, an abundance of pride, and a very strong urge to shoot me for no reason at all. I averted my eyes and let my head fall. My shoulders slumped, making my posture relaxed and non-confrontational. I was burning up inside, pissed off that she'd cost me my water, but I said—and did—nothing. I let her gaze burn into me for a hard, long minute. She turned to walk away, shaking her head. She didn't holster the gun until she was back at the spigot.

I picked up my pot, thought about getting in line again, and decided against it. Timmons was watching me, her eyes boring into me, making the line of people wait until I was gone, waiting for them to cast some of their scorn and resentment my way. The pot was flecked and streaked with dirt and dust, and mud was caked against the steel rim. I brushed it off with my hand as best as I could. I nodded to her as two PRC hurried past me and grabbed the old woman by either arm and hauled her to her feet. She was dazed and crying as they quickly took her away. I moved off, and the shock of the sudden violence wore off. People got back to normal. Just another day at the camp.

The old woman would be taken to solitary and locked up for a few days in a hot metal cage with no windows and merely a hint of ventilation. She probably wouldn't live through it. Thinking about her trapped and dying, slowly being cooked to death, I needed a drink of something stronger than water. One hand in my pocket, my fingers playing with the set of mem chips I carried. Jaime would be glad to have the chips. He ran a small makeshift bar and restaurant, a real DIY venture he'd scrounged up out of the earth, and I knew I could get food and a drink there. My dry mouth and rumbling stomach made my decision.

I made my way through the twisting alleys between the tents, shooing away mosquitoes. Curfew would be coming up soon, and parents would start rounding up the children playing nearby in small groups, kicking a beat-up old soccer ball back and forth. Voices were hushed, but the hum of conversations went on, filling the night air.

I wasn't in any rush to get to Fingerling's, even though I greatly welcomed the cool burn of a shot. When I made it there, the bar was getting crowded. It occupied a decent-sized lot not too far from the habitation zones. The PRC, by and large, did not prohibit the use and sale of alcohol, but they frowned upon excess, public intoxication, and disorderly behavior. Drinking too much and being an ass was a good way to get hurt or killed. A guard tower in the northeast corner overlooking the rec lot and Fingerling's kept the area well-lit for constant supervision.

Jaime had built the bar from scrap wood rounded up during reclamation runs. Even the small canvas tarp hanging over the bar was shoddy and riddled with small holes. What little liquor could be found in the bombed-out ruins of LA had been hoarded by those living out in the ruins or gathered by reclamation workers. Any booze that was found and sold to people like Jaime was slowly dispensed, but Kristoff had set up quite a microbrewery and distilled his own whiskey.

Tabletops were scarred and mismatched, and hardly any of the chairs came from the same set. The bench seat from an old Buick had been installed on some cinderblocks to provide additional seating.

I took a seat at the bar and put my pot up on it. I glanced around and nodded at a few familiar faces, then watched a few of the women dancing while I waited for Jaime. He knew what I wanted, which made ordering easy. He set down a tumbler filled with amber, and I took a slow, appreciative sip.

The whiskey, smooth and mellowed with a few drops of water, had notes of chocolate, honey, coffee, and oak. It warmed my chest, from the back of my throat to deep inside my belly. I savored it, then held the tumbler up away from the bar, ready for the next sip. People tried to slam Jaime's whiskey, but that was a total disservice to his craftsmanship. This was a sipping whiskey that should be taken slowly and enjoyed. Its taste was made for studying and appreciating.

"Hear you're on reclamation tomorrow, Jonah," he

said.

I nodded. I knew where this was going.

"If you find anything, could be worth some credits here." His arms were folded on top of the bar. He wore a natty denim shirt with the sleeves cut off. He had an old novelty tattoo animated by nanofilaments on his upper bicep. The tattoo was of a skull smoking a long, thin cigarette. The ash lit up orange and slowly died down as a cloud of smoke wafted from the skull's black nostril pits and drifted up his arm. It paused, then started up again, always with a small flicker between the playback cycles. Maybe he'd missed a software update, or the nanos were dying and cycling down. Soon, he would have a regular old tattoo, instead of a cheap parlor job that had gone out of style a decade ago.

"I'll look," I assured him. I always did. Sometimes, I even found stuff he could use—a bottle of Jack, maybe some wine. Most times, I struck out. Most of the liquor and convenience stores had been looted from top to bottom ages ago. Still, it never hurt to look.

"Alice had a friend here earlier," Jaime said.

It piqued my interest, but I knew what that meant. Her friend had probably "requested" that I make it into the reclamation sites.

Jaime confirmed my suspicion: "Said if you find any bodies out there, you should chip them. Said Alice would be mighty appreciative."

I nodded again. The reclamation sites, out in the ruins of LA, were never short of bodies. More often than not, they were wired for upgrades and memory back-ups. The dead were usually easy pickings. I wondered what Alice was searching for or if she was becoming an addict. She'd been taking an awful lot of chips lately.

Jaime had long salt-and-pepper hair that he pulled back into a ponytail. The light struck him in a peculiar way, and I was hit by how old he seemed. I knew he was in his late fifties, but suddenly the scars were older, the wrinkles deeper. His left arm and most of his hand was covered in a thick blanket of twisted, warped flesh. He'd said a deep-fryer accident from way back when had burned him all to hell, but it didn't jibe. A long, puckered scar ran across his face and under his cheekbone. I never talked with him about it, but I'd overheard him telling a customer about the burn once before.

He reached under the bar and came up with a small paper-thin tablet. Old tech, probably smuggled in from out east or way up north. A mess of cables was routed through it. The illegal hack job picked up the newsfeeds and infolines. It came to life at my touch, the screen filling with small text.

"Your handiwork got some press." A smile touched his lips.

The authorities had no leads, the news piece claimed. The article's source was a Sacramento feed. The PRC was attributing the *chiang's* murder to Liberty's Children, a terror cell based in Los Angeles.

The article was at the bottom, so I scrolled back up to the top, to the breaking-news banner and images of burning cars on the 101. A woman, her face smudged black and her hair a bloody paste against her skull and forehead, cradled a small boy who was maybe five or six. His head was canted at an unnatural angle, and a large blackened piece of shrapnel jutted from his neck. Her face was timid and placid, frozen in shock.

"So did yours." I turned the pad, slipping a copy of the mem chip I'd burned from the *chiang* into a data slot. The memories would comp me on the whiskey and food.

"We've had a productive couple of days then."

Fingerling's was Jaime's public face. His hidden one was more violent—and much more dangerous. He operated a cell of freedom fighters made up mostly of ex-American soldiers, Army guys who had gone AWOL after the United States officially withdrew from combat operations and declared California a lost cause. Although I lacked any formal military training, I'd found over the years that I could kill well enough, and Jaime had found uses for me.

We bumped fists, and I took another sip of whiskey. When the burn faded, I asked him for an order of his cheesy potatoes. Aside from the whiskey and craft beers, the potato dish was what he was famous for around here. The name of the bar came from the fingerling potatoes, cut into one-inch slices and fried in bacon grease, then smothered in a Roquefort béchamel and topped with bacon and green onions that he grew behind the bar. He grew the potatoes in a community garden, and somebody who must have been artisanal in a past life made fancy cheeses for him. In my past life, most of my cheeses had come wrapped in plastic sleeves or out of a spray can. Some of the park had been cleared out and reclaimed into farmland, with homegrown butchers selling beef, ham, and bacon from the imported cows and pigs they raised there. Civilization was on the rebound, some said.

I skimmed through the pirated newsfeeds, trying to get a grasp on the world around me. The final death count stemming from a shootout between PRC and militia forces near the Hollywood Bowl the previous day had risen by three. One was a PRC casualty; the other two were UN Peacekeepers who had responded to support the PRC and attempted to quell the violence. A UN spokesman offered up a sanitized quote about the emerging peace, how California as a whole was becoming a more stable region, and that peace itself was a constantly ongoing effort. PR fluff. A sidebar made brief mention of UN inspections of the state's various refugee camps and said those they had visited so far had received passing marks with minimal suggestions for improvement.

Smaller stories told about other UN Peacekeeping causalities in Sacramento, where insurgents opened fire on a squad of soldiers from Scandinavia. A schoolyard bombing at a PRC state-run facility had blown thirteen children to bits during their morning recess, and another twenty students and eight teachers had been injured.

An editorial that had been picked up from the *Times-Picayune* encouraged Los Angelinos, if they were reading, to move forward and embrace the future. The war was over, the New Orleans writer said, and after four years, the time had come to lay down arms, for what was left of America to rally together and join hands in the unity of brotherhood.

Fucking armchair quarterbacking without a single clue. The PRC had never made it as far east as Louisiana. Even with the support of their Russian and Iranian allies, they'd had their hands tied in Los Angeles and Beverly Hills, busy securing the offshore oil rigs that lined the coast from Long Beach to Santa Maria and seizing control of the Wilmington oil field, the third-largest oil field in the nation, so that they could export that oil back to the resource-starved China.

I refolded the tablet and slid it across the bar, back to Jaime. I'd read enough, and I worked hard at slowing my breathing, trying to quell the anger the newsfeeds had stirred. I was ready to go back to my tent and get fucked up again, but my stomach reminded me of other, more pressing, needs.

Behind me, a woman danced, her slender hips swaying back and forth with an easy rhythm. Long, sleek legs stretched out from a frayed denim skirt. Her arms were raised up over her head, her hands turning in waves and flicks of her wrists, her shirt lifting to expose a smooth, tanned belly and the lines of her hips.

Watching her, I was reminded of other, largely ignored

needs.

The music was loud, as always, but nobody complained, and the PRC didn't seem to care. Most of the PacRim soldiers felt as trapped here as we did. This was our home, and I suspected some of the troops even viewed themselves as our neighbors. A few—the younger ones, mostly—made attempts to be friendly. They hadn't been in-country very long and were dumb enough to think of this as an adventure.

A man joined the woman, and they danced together, their bodies pressed tight, hands roaming. I turned away, and a minute later, Jaime was sliding me a plate of potatoes. I ate slowly, trying to forget, trying to blank my mind.

A flicker of movement caught my attention as someone sidled up to the bar beside me, slender arms hugging the bar top. She noticed my glance, and her eyes quickly darted away from mine, back down to the bar. She brushed a loose strand of hair behind her ear.

"Hey," she said.

"Hi, Mesa." I slid the potatoes over. "Hungry?"

"No," she said without looking up at me. A tall, slender man with distinctly Asian features stepped up behind her, his hands going around her waist with an unsettling familiarity as he bent in to nuzzle her neck. Her hand came up to stroke the side of his face. "Hey." She gave him a quick peck on the lips.

"You coming home tonight?" I asked.

She at least had the courtesy to pretend to think about it, softly biting her lip. "No," she said, shaking her head slowly.

"And why not?"

"Because it's not home." Her voice held an edge of exasperation from the hundred, or thousand, times we'd had this argument before. "It's a fucking tent in the middle of a fucking park. We don't have a home."

"Hey, baby," the guy said, trying to soothe her.

"Shut it," we both told him. His eyes darted between us, not quite sure whom to be offended by. Quickly putting on the tough-guy façade, he shot me a deadly stare. But he must have seen the look in my eyes and thought better of it. He squeezed Mesa's shoulder and told her he would be over by a table that he pointed to, then went to sit down.

"He's too old for you," I said.

"He's twenty-six."

"You're eighteen. He's too old for you."

"What the fuck do you know?" she asked.

I shrugged. It was a good question. Maybe I used to know, but I wasn't quite so sure anymore.

"I know you ought to be at home," I said lamely. Still pissed, I added, "Instead of sleeping your way from tent to tent."

My reflexes were quick, and I grabbed her wrist before she could slap me in the face. I forced her arm down, and she shot me daggers with her eyes. If looks could kill... I took another sip of whiskey then offered her the glass. She took it, rifled the shot back hard and fast, then slammed the glass down on the bar, giving me all kinds of defiance. I signaled Jaime for another.

"Just one." I nodded to Mesa. "Water for her."

"I hear Washington's relaxing its borders," she said. "Letting people in through Walla Walla and Vancouver. People who want to be repatriated."

"People who want to be Canadians," I said. I wondered about the black woman from the *chiang's* motel room the other night. She should have made it into Nevada by that afternoon. She probably had a better chance of making it to the seasteads, but their immigration policies were tight, and breaking through naval patrols was a risky proposition at the best of times.

"I'm not asking you to go with me," she said.

"You don't owe me explanations. If you want to leave, you can try. Never stopped you before."

I speared a potato and ate it quickly.

She sat quietly, nursing her glass of water. Behind her, the woman danced on, oblivious to the pain around her, lost in her own daze and the music. Bored and dejected, Mesa's boyfriend sat at a table, scratching at the scarred Formica with his fingernails and picking at it.

"He PRC?" I asked.

"No. He was a grad student. Now he's just one of us."

Her voice trailed off, and she slid the glass back and forth across the bar, between her hands.

"We should go," she said. "Be like old times. A road trip." She smiled, still staring down at the bar top. The smile was weighted with sadness, though, and the hurt in her eyes stabbed painfully at my heart.

Mesa was older than her eighteen years. Her life had been hard, and she'd been forced into adulthood far too soon. Her ears were pierced. One was heavily and colorfully decorated with an assortment of studs and bars and costume jewelry pieces. The other ear had an old, thick, two-gigabyte USB thumb drive dangling from the lobe by a thin, golden S-hook. The red-and-black drive was a custom job. Rugged and unfolded, the shiny metal tip hung loose from a hard shell of shiny plastic. I wondered if it held any data or if it was merely a fashion statement. A maze of tattoos sleeved her arm in shocking bursts of color and tangles of black. A long Japanese dragon, its scales red and green, flowed from a cluster of golden tulips. Its large talons wrapped around a thick Gaelic cross. She'd had more coloring and detail added since I'd last seen her.

"It's nice," I said, surprised by how much I appreciated it. It spoke of her heritage, of her mother, and me.

"Thanks," she said, finally making eye contact with me.

"Will you come home tonight?" I worried I sounded

desperate, needy.

"Don't call it that. Please. It's not home. Our home had walls and a kitchen and a bathroom. We had a TV and radios and photographs on the wall and Mom's paintings and... This isn't home." She stared at me hard, urging me to understand a difficult foreign concept, imploring me to understand.

"Okay," I said.

She nodded, slowly, as if I were stupid. "I'll think about it."

I'd heard that before, and it never meant what I wanted it to.

"Okay," I said again, not knowing what else to say. Realizing I didn't have anything else to say kind of hurt. So I said okay again and ate another potato smothered in a cold glop of congealing cheese.

She took a potato, too. When I looked at her, she giggled the way she had when she was younger, when I would catch her stealing food off my plate. Maybe it was a peace offering, a common ground rediscovered. She kissed me on the forehead, keeping her hand flush against the center of my back.

"You should sleep," she told me. "We're going up the hill. There's a concert there."

She was already moving off before I could say anything, before I said something stupid and caused another fight. My anger died, leaving me tired and desperate.

"Kids, huh?" Jaime said.

I shrugged.

"Wash your pot?" He pointed at the smudges of dirt and mud.

"Thanks." I pushed my empty plate toward him. He took it and my pot and went to a small washtub to clean them.

I missed the feel of Mesa's hand on my back. I missed

how I used to carry her when she was a tiny girl, her arms wrapped around my neck, and how she had found so much humor in life, so many things to laugh at. I wasn't sure how long ago I had last heard her laugh. A few years, at least—probably longer. She had her mother's long jet-black hair. The slant of her eyes had been softened but not extinguished by my Irish blood. I could still hear her mother's laugh and feel the press of her lips against mine and the way her hands felt on me. I knew I was lost down dark roads I should have avoided, and suddenly, I was angry again.

Four years had passed since Selene's death, since the blackout, and since the end of my world. I'd spent much of my last night with her being an asshole.

The irritation over small things had built up over a few days—things like picking up the morning newspapers from the driveway, bringing in the mail, and putting dirty dishes in the dishwasher. She couldn't be bothered with these small tasks. She was content to run over the newspapers with her car on her way to work and then run over them again as she pulled into the garage at the end of her day. Mail and dirty dishes would accumulate for days on end, to the point of overflowing, before she could be bothered with them. She would remind me that "we" needed to clean the house over the weekend, which inevitably meant I would be the one cleaning the house. Or "we" needed to mow the lawn and spruce up the garden, but I couldn't remember the last time she'd ever done anything even remotely resembling yard work.

I'd grown sick of it. I was tired of the accumulated weight of all these tiny chores and annoyed to walk in the house to find her sitting on the couch, watching TV. I'd had an attitude when she finally uncurled herself from the sofa to greet me, and it must have been radiating from me in thick, heavy waves. She'd asked me what was wrong, and

I'd said something stupid, out of anger, and one thing led to another. We tossed bitter accusations back and forth until I wore her down and berated her to the point of tears. And then I made a simple pasta dish for dinner, but the act of cooking fueled my resentment and left me wondering why, again, I was the only one who ever contributed.

The irritation kept rising, and we fought again. I was loud and belligerent when angered, quick to accuse, and fast to find her fatal flaws and pick at her quirks. I'd wanted my words to cut deep, and I was willing to settle for tears.

I ate quietly, wrung out from the fighting, both physically and mentally. Her pasta sat on the plate, growing cold. She stared at it and picked at the food with her fork but didn't eat. She tried to speak a few times, stammering out a word or two between lengthy pauses before finally giving up. Her whole body deflated as tears cut swaths through her makeup. I tried to make small talk rather than apologize, but she was on lockdown, afraid that whatever she might say would trigger another vengeful rant. I was almost proud of the way I had reduced her, but I was also disgusted with myself, and eventually, I shut up and let the tension simmer between us, feeling guilty and ashamed.

Then the blackout happened. The riots started. The explosions. The spreading panic.

We didn't know about the attacks on Hawaii or the EMP blasts in Seattle, Tacoma, Portland, San Francisco, and Sacramento. We had no idea how coordinated and organized the attacks were. We never saw it coming. And I'd wasted the last few hours fighting with the love of my life, unaware that we were on borrowed time. Such an oblivious idiot.

I shot back the whiskey, letting the burn choke me. I grabbed my pot from Jaime and left before I lost all my credits getting drunk, intent on punishing myself by getting fucked up again.

In my tent, I let the memories crawl over me, jacked into the DRMR, my anger tempered by loss, sadness, and hate. I relived the old days of Mesa's birth, her first steps, and her first words. I relived my life with Selene, her mother, remembering the better nights. I felt her touch again, remembering her fingers brushing through my hair and the feel of her lips against my mouth and kissing her way down my chest and stomach. All over again, I felt her taking me inside her and driving away all the pain and horror, thrusting against me, her hot breath gasping in my ear as we came. I was crying, and we were fighting again. Then she was dead, Mesa was gone, and I was lost and damned... And, at some point, the sun had come up again, and I hated myself when I disconnected, tired and covered in cold sweat.

Mesa never came home.

CHAPTER
FOUR

THE MASSIVE DUMPS OF SEROTONIN left me faint and exhausted. The memories clung to me and made me feel dirty. I missed Selene, and my nerves were raw. I wanted to cry. My eyes burned, but no tears came. My ears felt hot, and my cheeks were flushed. I had wanted to get fucked up, but not like that. I had made no particular plans to revisit that old life, but the chips were there, and I promised myself I would use only one of them. The addict's motto: just one, then I'll stop. It never works out that way. One always led to one more and then another one and another.

I was still wearing yesterday's clothes. In the footlocker, I found work gloves, a hat, goggles, and a scarf. I slipped into my work boots, the leather stiff, wrinkled, and worn down.

My empty pot sat on a small Bunsen burner. I remembered my mishap the night before and swore. I took a canteen and got in line for the spigot with the rest of the reclamation crew. No guards were at the spigot yet, but the people waiting weren't helping themselves. This was not a self-service station, and a man in the watchtower glared down at us.

I knew the guy in front of me but said nothing. His clothes were stained and wrinkled, not too different from my own. He turned around and nodded. Hafiz. I didn't know his last name.

"You're looking pretty shitty, Jonah," he said.

I nodded back. "Couldn't sleep." The words were a thick paste in my mouth.

When a guard finally came, the water ran rusty from the spigot. It stunk like a foul egg, but seeing the water reminded me of how thirsty I was. Last night's whiskey had dehydrated me, and a dull ache twitched and throbbed behind my eyes, promising to get worse.

We shuffled forward to get our canteens filled. Another guard ordered us to form a line for morning roll call, then we were led through the security checkpoints and into truck beds for the drive downtown. Most of us were quiet and tired. One guy yakked incessantly while everybody ignored him. Our disinterest didn't stop him, though. He chattered away, talking to himself but occasionally seeking confirmation from the others.

"Am I right?" he would ask, making it sound like a single word. *Amiright?*

I shrugged, not feeling in any shape to judge. Right or wrong, who I was to say?

He asked again, "Amiright?"

I shrugged again, giving him a half-hearted I-suppose-so nod.

"My man!" he said and gave me a gentle fist to the

shoulder. Then he went on to talk about something else, but I paid no attention. His words were lost on me. My brain was fried. I was good and truly fucked up, but I didn't really want to be anymore, especially not with the day's work ahead of me.

The bumpy ride jostled us against one another. Bombing runs had rendered the Pasadena freeway impassable, so the driver took Sunset Boulevard to Figueroa. The truck stayed to the cracked and shattered road as best as it could, but eventually, the road ended at a crater, and the driver had to off-road it. The ride wasn't much different.

The PRC employed contractors to make headway with the repairs, but they were slow leviathans riddled with bureaucracy. They gave Sacramento and the Chinatowns to the contractors, who got those areas rebuilt and back up to speed pretty quickly. Los Angeles was different, though.

Los Angeles had pockets of snipers and gangs who fancied themselves freedom fighters. They were itching to take on the PRC and the contractors who worked for them. Most work crews going into LA were met with violence, and rumor had it that the PRC had lost more soldiers after the war than during it, thanks to the resistance's guerilla attacks throughout the area. Liberty's Children operated fiercely but discreetly. Usually, they recognized a POW work crew and met them with discretion, maybe even tried to free them. Not always. The violence had led to a dramatic slowdown in the reclamation work, but both sides persisted in their efforts, creating more damage and more dead bodies.

Men unloaded from the trucks. PRC gathered at one end of a truck bed to set up a few cups and thermoses of coffee and ice water. A cooler carried sandwiches for each of us for lunch, probably made with hard bread and old meat.

I scanned the ruins and checked the skylines.

Skyscrapers had once been there, but few were still standing. Most were husks, their walls shattered to reveal broken patchworks of steel girders. The US Bank Tower and Wells Fargo had been decimated in the first wave of attacks. One and Two California Plaza were broken stubs of exposed metal, loose wire, and chunks of concrete. Odd, shiny glints of broken glass dotted the surface.

I tugged on my work gloves as dump trucks pulled up to the work site, and we formed a line, went through another headcount in case someone had fallen off the truck after leaving Echo Park, and waited for our duty assignments. I was put in a group with three others and waved off down to Hope Street, off Third. One of the dump trucks followed us, inching forward slowly, debris cracking and popping beneath its large wheels.

I shifted blocks of concrete and brick, lifting with my knees and twisting to dump the loads into the wheelbarrow next to me. Hafiz gripped the wooden handles and pushed it across the uneven ground, back to the truck, where another man helped him unload. I dug at something hard and yellow, shifting the dirt away to expose part of an *M* from a McDonald's sign. Half-buried was a curved piece, but I couldn't tell what letter it may have come from—*C*, *D* or maybe an *O*. Whatever. It didn't matter. Just something small to puzzle over, to keep my brain working through the dull labor. I tossed the broken signage into the wheelbarrow, along with some busted chairs that had once formed an outdoor seating arrangement at The Court outside of the Wells Fargo Center.

We pushed, lifted, and hauled debris. We sweated and swore. Hafiz traded duties with me after a time, giving me a bit of a reprieve while he tackled some of the harder work.

"What the fuck do you suppose this is?" He held up a piece of broken wood with odd lumps. I took it and turned it over in my hands. I swept away some of the gray dust, revealing a smear of green that time and rot had dulled considerably. My fingers brushed against a hard protrusion on the front. Loose flaps of brittle leather hung from the back of the board. I couldn't help but laugh, recognizing the object.

"*Caress of a Bird*," I said.

Hafiz raised an eyebrow at me. "Huh?" he said, as if I'd lost my mind and were speaking gibberish.

"It was a sculpture inside Wells Fargo," I said. "Joan Miró."

He shrugged. "Dunno. Never heard of it."

After another minute of digging, he asked, "How you know about that?"

"I'm a historian," I said. It was a private joke, but he nodded, taking me seriously.

A soldier sat atop a hill of crumbling steps, his back resting against a half-wall—the remains of what must have been an office at some point. Beyond him were other walls that had been blown apart, lined up like chipped dominos. Cracked and broken desks were covered with chunks of drywall, plaster, and curls of pink insulation. A rough semicircle of ceiling had survived the collapse when the upper floors caved in. Our guard was uninterested and bored. He smoked and rested while watching us work.

I remembered sitting on those steps with Selene and Mesa, long before the war, eating kettle corn from a food truck vendor that always parked nearby. The Bank of America Center was a ruin. Calder's *Four Arches* sculpture towered over the remains. Covered in a thick layer of grime, nicked and dinged, the swoops of its arches were slightly cracked and weathered, but it had fared surprisingly well.

As the war dragged on, the arches had become a memorial for lost loved ones. A collection of faces and frozen smiles, photographs, their colors faded by time, curled and browned from exposure to the elements, were plastered around the sculpture's red legs. A small boy enjoying birthday cake. A toddler whose face was smeared with pasta sauce. Dogs and cats. Grandmothers, uncles, and aunts. Group photos of friends and families. Hand-lettered signs, asking in large, bold black blocks: HAVE YOU SEEN HER? Old pictures and lost lives.

I helped Hafiz lift a large, heavy chunk of asphalt. My arms and wrists sore, I gritted my teeth under the strain. Sweat had soaked my shirt, dampening the carpenter's coat I wore over it. I was covered in gray dust from head to toe, my face slick with perspiration. We heaved it into the wheelbarrow, and I rolled it to the truck, where three of us handled it a bit more easily. When I got back, we moved a few smaller blocks, taking it slow and easy.

The sun was harsh, and I caught a glint of metal. I dug around a bit, tossing fist-sized pieces of road and plaster into the wheelbarrow. After a few minutes, I had unearthed a small, feminine hand. Thin fingers of rotting flesh wore a wedding band and long, broken nails. I pushed more debris away, exposing her forearm. Scooping up dirt, pebbles, and rocks in my cupped palms, I found an elbow. Seeking help with another large hunk of rock, Hafiz looked over, saw the remains I had unearthed, and forgot about it. He started digging, too.

She was fairly well preserved, all things considered. Decomposition had started and settled. Bugs had found her and feasted, taking away patches of skin for supper. She was dirty, her crusty hair matted and filthy. Her skin was dried out and stretched taught.

Behind her right earlobe was a small metal port. I probed the back of her skull, where it joined the neck. I recalled Jaime's message of the previous night, from Alice, to chip any bodies I found.

Hafiz grabbed her forearm, trying to pick her up. The skin pulled away, loose and crinkly, and it reminded me of tissue paper as it tore at her elbow and slid down to her wrist in a clump. He fell back, coughing at the sudden stench.

"You okay?" I asked.

He nodded.

"What's the guard doing?"

He stared past me, over my shoulder. "Nothing. I think he's asleep."

I turned around to steal a glance. He was slumped up against the wall, a lit cigarette dangling from his lips. I could hear him snoring, even over the grunts of lifting from the other crew members.

I prodded roughly at her skin but couldn't feel much through the thick hide of the work gloves. I pulled one free, then went back to my search. Her skin was pliant and thin. My stomach lurched at the touch. Bile rose in a burning wave along the back of my throat. I turned my head and buried my face in my shoulder to breathe through my mouth. I gave myself a few seconds to regroup then resumed my explorations of her body. I was hunting for a circular mound of calcification, similar to the hard nub buried beneath the flesh of my own neck.

"What are you doing?" Hafiz whispered, leaning close to me. His breath stank, and his body odor, baked under the day's heat, was worse than the smell of the corpse I was poking at.

"Looking for something," I said.

A jagged edge of vertebrae scraped against my index and middle fingers as I pushed through the rot and struck the bone of her spinal column. Thin strands of nerves and stringy muscle sloughed away, and I kept digging, my stomach heaving and threatening to revolt as I pushed upward, to the underside of her skull. My fingers fell into a sharp and jagged crater where the back of her head was missing. Her brain had rotted away, been eaten, or dried up under the rubble ages ago. My fingers brushed against the thin wire filaments patched into the inside of her skull. They fell away in loose bundles. I pulled back, hooking my thumb and fingers around the data port behind her ear. I tugged it away easily, a thin collection of cords coming with it. I swore under my breath, then pressed hard against her thin skin, working my way back around to the underside of her skull and the back of her neck. I pressed hard and found nothing. Down farther, maybe?

This was taking too long. Worried that the guard would wake and catch me, I was racing against an invisible clock. My forehead was soaked in sweat, and dark, wet circles were growing out from my armpits. I poked around her shoulders, pushing my fingers beneath the collar of her blouse, and found something hard against her shoulder blade. My fingernails tore into the flesh, tracing the outline of a squarish deposit soldered to the bone.

"What's he doing?" I asked. Opening my mouth gave my stomach its cue, and I fought back a convulsive heave, a thick wad of bile lodging in my throat.

Hafiz looked at me quizzically, then looked down at her and back up at me.

"The guard," I said, a twinge of anger creeping into my voice.

"Nothing, nothing," he said.

The metallic square was hard and wafer thin. I found a small bump at the edge of the device. Around a slope of calcified mineral deposits on the bone was a collection of nanofilaments that would branch off toward the spine and ride up into her skull, networking the data entry port into her brain and the small storage device on her shoulder. A small latch kept the unit sealed, and I had to jam my thumbnail into the crevice to pry it apart. Inside was a tiny data chip, smaller than the fingernail on the woman's pinkie. I carefully dislodged it, turning back to check on the guard.

Still asleep. Nobody else was paying us much attention. The crews working in small clusters, spread out in zones, were focused on their own work, not me and Hafiz. I pocketed the chip and replaced the lid. I could do nothing about the damage I'd caused to her flesh, but with the pattern of injuries etched across her back and head, what I had done was hardly discernible.

A loud crackling noise from the radio woke the guard.

I wiped my hand in the dust, trying to lose the gore as best as I could, then wiped it on my pants and replaced the glove. It felt funky and damp.

I threw more chunks of concrete into the wheelbarrow, and Hafiz followed my lead.

"We good?" I asked him.

He nodded. "Sure."

I didn't think I would have to worry about him. "Body!" I hollered out and waved to the guard. He came over to inspect then radioed for the meat wagon. The flatbed took a few minutes to grind its way over to us, and when it did, Hafiz lifted her a bit more gingerly, working his hands under her arms, while I took her ankles, hoping the squishy skin of her legs didn't suddenly loosen and puddle against my grip. We heaved her into the truck. Four bodies had already been collected from the other sites.

I looked up at the sky, trying to gauge the time by the sun. It had to have been close to noon, if not past. I sponged away the sweat with the forearm of my coat and thought about ditching it. We'd all heard stories about some poor bastard who'd scraped his bare arm at a clean-up site and got an infection bad enough that his arm had to be amputated. I'd never met anybody who actually knew the guy, but what difference did that make, really? So we all wore our coats, sweated our balls off—and kept our arms, legs, toes, and fingers.

My hunch about the time was confirmed a few minutes later when the guard announced our lunch break. We lined up, went through another head count, and accepted the rations handed to us. A cup of water, a stale sandwich, and an apple.

I wandered back to the steps and sat near the *Four Arches*. I'd always enjoyed it there. Even after so long, I could smell the fresh popcorn and the hint of lemon in Selene's perfume. Her black hair would have shined under this sun, glossy and waxy smooth. She would have sat next to me, our knees touching and arms brushing as we ate, and made small talk. She would have been wearing a skirt for work, and I would have lingered over the curve of her calves and the lines of her legs beneath the dark fabric. She would have accused me of ignoring her as she talked about her day, and then I would be lost in the deep green waters of her eyes, only half-listening. Mesa, so small and her skin untouched by the stab of an inker's needles, would be a few steps below, interrupting us with incessant strings of questions. Selene would smile and answer, always so patiently, with the love pouring off her. And a part of me would realize that I didn't belong there, that this should not be my life. I would feel guilty or depressed, and she would pick up on it instantly. If she asked me what was wrong, I would lie with a forced smile across my lips.

I wanted to shove those memories away, but I couldn't. After the previous night's DRMR session, they were still too fresh and opened too many old wounds.

I tried to eat, but the dry sandwich was dusty in my mouth. I'd lost my appetite, even though I hadn't had solid food since the night before. I forced myself to eat the rest and drank the water, feeling dehydrated and dizzy. All it did was make me thirstier, so I went back down to the truck to refill my cup.

"Ten minutes," the guard mumbled in a thick accent.

His English was broken, and he spoke as if he had cotton in his mouth. His words lacked enunciation and were jumbled together. *Tamits* it sounded like.

I crossed the street, back over to the Wells Fargo Center, where I climbed over and around the debris then up the steps. There used to be life there, shopping and dining. But the entire block was bare, skeletal, and dirty. A part of a wall remained, along with a sign that said Nick & Stef's Steakhouse. Selene and I had eaten there a few times, usually before catching a show at Ahmanson Theater— ages ago, back when we were dating and I was still trying to impress her.

I remembered the perfectly grilled dry-aged New York strip from there. I could nearly taste the hints of mesquite and oak in the flame-licked meat. My mouth watered, and I couldn't remember the last time I'd had steak. Or a nice, smooth, dry red wine.

The restaurant was a shell. Broken, upturned tables, and shattered chairs. Cracked slate floor. Broken wooden beams. The walls were covered in black mold and stained from water damage. The bar was in ruins and cracked in half. Exploded bottles that had once held thousands of dollars in liquor littered the floor. I saw nothing I could take back to Jaime, and certainly nothing I could idle ten minutes away with.

I got back to work, sick of the past and the discord of memories. My hand was tacky and uncomfortable in the glove. I drained my cup of water, tossed it into the wheelbarrow, and loaded that with as much as I could. When I lifted wrong, I felt a sharp pop in my back. Muscles seized up, and I sat down, sore, throbbing, and angry. I gritted my teeth until it passed, and Hafiz sat with me, nursing a cup of water.

"You okay?" he asked.

"My back," I grunted.

"Take a few," he said. "It's all good."

He went down for another cup of water and brought me back one. The pain was subsiding, but the rest of the day was going to be rough. I could work through it, but the next day was going to be worse. He passed me the cup, and I gave him my thanks.

The soldier's radio crackled, and he clicked a button, said some words, got another crackle, and said something else. He blew his whistle, and we reformed for another headcount. Hafiz helped me to my feet. His grip was strong, but I shrugged him off when he tried to help me down the steps to Hope Street, where we all stood at attention. Never making eye contact with us, the guard did his count, making little ticks on a piece of paper on his clipboard. He said something, followed by a grunt of approval, and put us back to work.

The afternoon sun bore down on us. I wiped sweat from my scalp; the gloves were gritty against the stubble. We worked hard, and the knots in my back began to bunch up. Every square inch of me hurt.

The radio squawked, interrupting the quiet labor, and a rushed string of gibberish came through the speaker. The PRC responded, his face screwed up in confusion. I couldn't make out any of the words, but something in his eyes and the way he held himself meant trouble. A new knot twisted, this time in my stomach, its claws working into my chest. A worker from another crew shouted something at him. Hafiz turned to see what the commotion was about. The guard did, too.

The crew had found another woman buried under a light pile of debris. Things were happening quickly. A buzz in the air made the hairs on the back of my neck stand up, causing my skin to crawl.

One of the workers, a young guy, probably still in his teens and new to the labor, bent to pick her up. He hooked his hands under her armpits and lifted with his knees. The explosion tore out from under her. Shrapnel buzzed by, a hot sting slicing through the bridge of my nose and cheek. I fell to my knees, burying my head under my arms, watching between a slit of skin.

My eyes struggled to piece together the horror. Screams. Limbs disconnected from bodies. The boy who had found the corpse had taken most of the blast, but it hadn't saved the rest of his crew. A face, split down the middle by a long, jagged strip of metal. Half a leg, tipped over, the sole of his work boot smoking, a gory stump where a knee had once been. A coil of intestine had slopped against the piles of plaster, wood, and concrete in a wheelbarrow. One man sat, dazed, watching blood pour from his elbows, where his arms used to be, while he bled from the nose and ears. His shock-glazed eyes moved back and forth between each gushing wound, struggling to figure out what had happened and where his arms had gone.

The PRC guard hadn't been close enough to the blast to take any damage. He looked back at me then came toward me. His mouth opened, and then his jaw exploded off his face while he was mid-step. It pushed him back on his heels, but he kept walking, painfully oblivious because it had happened so quickly. Not even a second later, a small crater punched into his forehead, blowing his brains out the back of his skull. I heard the dim dual bangs a moment later, realizing my eardrums were probably gone.

I scrabbled for cover, hooking my fingers into Hafiz's collar and dragging him down. He followed me, moving quickly in a half-crouch, searching desperately for shelter. His nose and ears were bleeding. Pieces of concrete were pebbled into his face and neck like tiny pieces of buckshot.

"Snipers," I said over the buzzing whine that filled my ears. His mouth was moving, but his words were leagues away.

We crawled behind a thick concrete pillar that had fallen across the steps outside the Bank of America. It offered thicker shelter than the *Four Arches*. I risked a quick glance, hoping to catch a peek of a sniper, but the bank was too squat to offer any really good vantage points. Over my shoulder, the buildings were taller, but not incredibly so. All the high-rises and skyscrapers had been reduced to stubs. Could be a few good spots, though. I hoped for a glint of sunlight catching off a scope but saw nothing.

My face ached, felt wrong. I brushed at my cheek, found something hard, and fought to get a grip on it. I pulled and was rewarded with a sharp, searing pain. Pinched between my fingers was a long, rough sliver of bone that wasn't mine.

Hafiz was scared, near panic and in total shock. I smacked his arm, pointed toward the bank. We could maybe find shelter in there. He shook his head, obviously afraid to move. I understood, but being stationary was not an option.

The whine was lessening, and I could clearly hear volleys of gunshots. Snipers were killing the other crews, cleaning up, making a nice little massacre of all this.

"The gun," Hafiz said, his voice breathless. He pointed to the guard.

I shook my head.

"It's only a few yards," he argued.

"We have to go," I said, but Hafiz screwed up his face into an angry expression.

Apparently, he didn't understand that heading down meant certain death and that I was trying to save his life. I urged him to his feet, taking his hands in mine. "C'mon, goddamn it," I yelled.

I hauled him to his feet, and he worked his legs to help me out by getting his boots under him. Blood splattered across my face and chest, and I was blinded by gore. I stumbled back in shock and fell on my ass. My gloves were rough, too hard to clean the muck from my face. I pulled them off, palmed away thick puddles filled with hard pieces of bone, and forced my eyes open. Part of his skull was missing; an eye had been blasted away. Some of his brain had splashed onto my chest, mottling my carpenter's coat with gore.

Half crawling, half trying to stand, ignoring the sharp, painful protests riding up alongside my spine, I bolted toward the half-wall and, staying low, jumped over it, into what used to be the building's lobby. A bullet broke the floor tiles ahead of me. The second sniper, unused to chasing prey, had led too far ahead. I zigzagged, making each step unpredictable, a crazy sort of dance. Bullets came faster, and their strikes became as erratic as I was trying to be. My foot lifted, but I stumbled in pain. There was a hole in the back of my thigh and another coming out the front. I thought the bullet had missed the bone, but it hurt like a motherfucker. I rolled, but even that was a struggle. I dodged the next bullet, preventing it from going into my head. I had become easy prey, ready to be taken down, but I didn't want to make it that easy. I slid behind a squat, thick leg of a plastic office directory.

My heart was racing, and I was trying very hard to ignore the throbbing pain in my leg.

The countertop above me exploded. Flying plastic stung the back of my head. The sniper had resorted to taking potshots, trying to rattle me out of hiding or maybe get lucky and tag me again.

I didn't have many places to hide. A bank of elevators went nowhere. If I tried to make a break for the offices, I would end up dead before I got anywhere else. I was trapped, and a cold sweat broke out across my face and back, either from the pain or the fear. I had to do something, but I had no idea what.

I could stand up and take the bullet, let it pluck out my heart or tear through my head. End it all. Fuck it.

They came in cautiously, but swiftly. Guns pointed forward, tucked close to their bodies, they rushed in on each other's heels, spreading out to cover the angles of the room and protect one another from attack. Their entry was well-practiced, from years of tactical training. They came around the directory, clearing the room, making sure I was alone. A quick once-over deemed me a non-threat. Weaponless, bleeding, and crippled, I certainly didn't feel very threatening. I was more woozy than anything else. I smirked.

"What's so funny?" one asked, his gun pointed at me, ready to use it.

I almost couldn't help but laugh. He stepped forward, onto my injured leg, and ground the tread of his boot into my skin.

"Just that mop top of yours, tough guy."

He smashed the butt of his Beretta into the side of my face. It hurt, and it loosened a few teeth. But he stepped off my leg, and the pain instantly lessened. While I was bent over, waiting for the ringing in my head to dissolve, he slapped something against the side of my head, and my skull buzzed with the familiar tingle of electronics mating. The buzzing pushed deeper into my head, even as the pain of the pistol whipping dissolved, and the neural net wrapped around my brain went dark.

All of the men wore urban camo, and each carried the distinct weight of military bearing. They even had American flag patches stitched on their shoulders. Could be some unit that had gone AWOL after the fall and stayed behind enemy lines to carry on the good fight. Could be a militia who fancied themselves freedom fighters and had raided an army surplus store or ripped off a defunct supply caravan or military depot. Could be a bunch of assholes role-playing.

A tall black man with close-cropped hair and thick stacks of muscle stepped forward, put a hand on my guard's shoulder, and eased him back, making him step away. He waved over another man, who knelt beside me. I realized he was a medic with a small black box of field dressings and long needles.

The medic took a pair of sharp, short scissors and cut away my pant leg above the wound, then jabbed a needle in above the gunshot. Morphine plunged into my system with an icy rush that made my eyelids heavy. His movements were rapid, but precise. He wrapped my leg in gauze to staunch the bleeding then moved away.

"You the last of them?" the black guy asked, his eyes and chin indicating the dead men outside.

"Guess so," I said. The fact of the matter was, I really didn't care. If he was going to kill me, he would have done it already. Probably wouldn't have had my leg wrapped, either. "Let's get this over with."

A smile flickered across his face, and I guessed that was a hard thing for him to come by. He had a gruff voice and stony hands that cinched around my wrists with the strength of a vice when he helped me to my feet.

"There you go," he said.

I stood on one foot, gamely, not daring to put any weight on my other leg. One of the soldiers shoved thickly gloved fingers into my pockets and extracted the small collection of memory chips I carried with me.

"I'm with you," I said, my tongue thick and heavy, slurring my words into an incoherent jam.

Something that wasn't exactly confusion crossed his eyes. Even under the morphine spell, I could tell something was not right. His urban camo was new, crisp, and clean. I tried to commit this fact to memory.

My brain was mush, and the world was fading quickly. I was groggy, whipped beyond exhaustion. I welcomed the collapse.

Then he said, "Bag him up." And the world went dark.

CHAPTER FIVE

MEMSEQ0500015789

ANGER STEWED ACROSS THE TABLE between us, its thickness fouling the air. The darkness was almost a relief when the lights went out. Power outages in Los Angeles weren't exactly new, and neither of us thought much of it. We had bigger problems—mostly each other.

The energy crisis had been going on for five years, and rolling blackouts left a couple million households without power at any given time. Oil shortages had sent prices through the roof. Because of that, our ever-growing debt, and annual theatrical displays of government shutdowns, the US dollar was worthless. In four or five hours, the lights and air conditioning would click back on, after some pressure on the grid was relieved.

Or so we thought, anyway.

The tension between Selene and me was interrupted by a piercing rumble that was too close overhead. The noise pulled me away from the table, to the window, and then outside, as if that could change what I was seeing. The noise grew louder as a jumbo jetliner passed above us, flying far too low, but missing our neighborhood. It disappeared behind a rise of land, but the cataclysmic results were thunderous. The acrid stink of burning rubber and scorched metal clung to the air. Thick black plumes of smoke rose in the distance.

The lights never came back on.

A few of our neighbors had PetHuman droids that they used for yard work and household maintenance. The droning sounds of lawnmowers and weed whackers had dropped off into nothingness, and the robots stood or crouched where they had died, silent, synthetic sentinels of a now-dead age.

"Where's Mesa?" I asked, my voice still tinged with bitterness.

I stood on our country porch, leaning against the rails, watching the smoke. Neighbors were starting to gather, their curiosity not yet turning to the fear that this was the end of their world. But the change was quickly catching up to us all. Many pointed skyward, following the white contrails in the dying light as it led to the pillar of smoke rising from the ground.

"I'm not getting any signals at all," someone said, prompting others to nervously fidget with the data entry ports behind their ears and on their forearms. Some were disconnected for the first time since birth and were starting to panic from the sudden, strange sensation of isolation.

Selene's fingers moved between mine, her hand tightening. I could feel her fear, which mimicked mine. The air felt haunted, and I sensed that something was deeply, strangely wrong—a horrifying otherness that went beyond a mere power outage. In between heartbeats, the world had changed.

"Where's Mesa?" I asked again, my annoyance with both of them curdling in my gut.

"At a friend's," she said. The worry in her eyes was growing. Her body curled against mine, her hands clinging around my waist. I put my arms around her and kissed the top of her head.

A few hours before, I had been bothered by her mere presence and started a fight. With the end of the world blooming around us, I couldn't even remember why I'd been angry with her.

The growing confusion and worry worsened as night fell. Whatever disquiet had grown between Selene and me, whatever fractures I may have introduced to our marriage, were suddenly mundane and unimportant. I didn't know what was happening, but I told her everything would be fine.

"Everything is going to be okay," I said, hoping that it would be. Then I told her that I loved her and held her close, hoping Mesa would have the good sense to come home soon.

She was getting rebellious, going out late, staying out late, and walking out on us in the middle of talks with her because she'd decided she didn't need to hear whatever we were saying. Telling us to fuck off. Trying to figure out how far she could push things. Trying to take it further and further each time. She spent most of her energy being angry, yelling, and telling us how she was an adult, so we couldn't stop her. We'd caught her smoking and drinking. She'd left condoms lying around her bedroom, still sealed in their packages. They'd been given to her by her school administrators who wanted her to be safe. She got off on torturing us with it, putting it on our face, and rubbing our noses in it.

"I should try to find her." I untangled myself from Selene. A part of her—the needy part—looked wounded. I went to the car, slid into the driver's seat, and pressed my thumb to the small black plate on the dash. It did nothing. I sat back in the seat, realizing the car's unresponsive biometrics were fried. I brought up my commNet. The retinal display filled with local server errors and host-unavailable messages. No car. No power. No connections. No communications.

"Who was she with?" I asked.

Selene was distracted and didn't answer for a minute. "Macy," she said uncertainly.

"We'll have to walk. Car's dead."

"What's happening?"

I didn't have any answers. I took her hand and started walking. We crossed the street, heading two blocks north, over to Macy's. We knocked on the door, but nobody answered. No answer at Linda's or Jennifer's. Her boyfriend, Tom, answered when we came to his door, but he hadn't seen her. He told us they'd fought two nights before and hadn't talked since. She wouldn't take his calls and had refused his attempts at messaging.

"If you hear from her, call us," Selene said. Then, looking at the darkened houses around us and apparently remembering her unresponsive commNet, she must have felt stupid, and her face flushed. "Yeah, I guess you can't do that, can you?" She gave him a small, half-hearted laugh, and he closed the door, sullen.

The absence of a working commNet was growing into a palpable void. We couldn't raise Mesa and had no way of contacting her friends other than by foot, and that was getting us nowhere.

"Maybe you should go back home," I said. "One of us should be there if she comes back. I can keep looking."

We knew a couple other friends she hung out with, but they were all in the opposite direction. We would be passing our house anyway.

We were walking down Burbank, to get to White Oak and back home, when a clopping noise rushed up from behind us. A mounted police officer rode up beside us.

"There's a curfew in effect now folks. We ask that you get inside immediately." He'd used cop-speaking, saying "we" even though it was only him and his horse.

Selene and I were still a mile and a half away from our house on Kittridge, and I told him so.

"Get inside as soon as you can."

"Please, we're looking for our daughter," Selene said. She stepped toward the horse, and it whinnied, taking a step back. She reached for the officer's arm in a mother's plea.

"Please step away, ma'am."

She didn't. She moved forward, crying and grasping. Her panic unraveled as she tried to make him understand the urgency of our plight. "Help us, please. You have to help us. Our daughter is missing!"

The horses of the mounted unit were used for crowd control and had been trained to deal with noise, like gunfire and shouting, as well as smoke and rowdy demonstrators, so they were used to people. But the Arabian was unsettled by whatever vibe Selene was giving off and was trying to get away from her, but she kept getting closer, aggravating it even more. Despite any kind of training, an animal always has a basic instinct that can never be overcome, and this horse sensed something in the air, something that had it spooked.

I tried to pull Selene away, but I was a step too slow. She

got a hold of the officer's arm, invading the horse's space, making it rear. The cop tumbled off and hit the pavement hard. The horse was on its back legs, kicking with its front, its hooves getting dangerously close to her face. I grabbed Selene around the waist, yanked her away before she got kicked.

The cop was getting his feet back under him, his expression equal parts dazed and pissed off. "You crazy bitch," he said.

Selene was struggling in my arms, crying and panicking. Her small fists pounded my chest, ordering me to let her go. She slapped my face, and it surprised me, made me relax too much, enough for her to break free. She ran to the officer, but he had his hand up, ordering her back.

"Please," Selene was screaming. "My daughter, we can't find her."

"Step the fuck back. Now!"

"You have to help us!"

"I'm not warning you again. Step back and lay down on the ground."

His voice hitched. His horse was screaming, rearing up on its hind legs, and breathing loudly, its hackles raised. Selene was too distraught to think straight, and none of us had any fucking clue what was going on.

Gunfire rang out in the distance, and fresh smoke rose into the air.

"I told you to get back!"

She stumbled forward, tears lining her face. "Please, listen. You have to listen."

Stepping forward, he told her to get back again. He pulled himself taller, squared his shoulders, and pushed his chest out, the promise of a threat in his eyes. His hand went to his belt and pulled out a stocky black device with yellow striping. He fired, and she screamed, jerking away. She fell to the ground, but he kept his finger on the trigger, sending jags of electricity through the Taser wires and into her body. Fifty thousand volts, nineteen pulses a second, punched into her.

"Get down, on the ground," he yelled at me.

I raised my hands, slowly lowering myself onto my knees.

"Down!" he yelled again.

People were lining up on the street, watching the spectacle. We knew some of them from PTA meetings, neighborhood garage sales, and block parties. They stood there, whispering and watching, hands over their mouths. Nobody dared move or speak too loudly.

I flattened myself on the street, my arms spread out, head hooked at an odd angle so that I could see what was happening. Selene's body relaxed then stayed still. The horse had calmed down since the threat of violence was past. I waited for my wife to move, but she didn't. She made no sound, no groans of pain, no whimpers, none of the crying I had become used to over the last few hours.

I kept waiting for her to move. The officer rolled her onto her stomach, straddled her, pulled her arms back, and handcuffed her. He only had the one set and seemed confused about what to do with me. No car. No handcuffs. No radio to call for back-up.

He tried to pick her up, but she was dead weight. He thought she was being funny or trying to resist. "C'mon," he told her and dropped her. He checked her pulse, his mouth opening to a tiny *O*. Then he looked at me. He had a funny look in his eyes—confusion and maybe sympathy, but not all the way. He was young, probably new to the force, but not so new that he was unhardened or shocked.

He uncuffed her, and slipped them back on his belt. He rolled her over onto her back again, surprisingly gently. He didn't know what else to do or how to handle the situation. Far off in the distance, the first faint sounds of gunfire rang out, the single reports of pistols and the rat-a-tat-tat of automatic weapons fire. He stared at me again before mounting his horse. His mouth opened, closed, and opened again. Then without a single word, he rode off.

I stayed on the ground until I no longer heard the galloping of hooves on concrete. Selene's body was still, and I crawled to her, on my hands and knees. I was sobbing, yelling at her to come back to me. I cradled her, rocking back and forth with her corpse held tight against me.

She had died from what was euphemistically called "excited delirium." It sounded a lot better than it actually was. It used to be a cute legally and medically aesthetic way to say somebody had overdosed on cocaine, but it had grown into a catch-all phrase used in autopsy reports for people who were Tasered to death. Selene's panic had ratcheted up her catecholamine levels, and her blood pressure was high. Her fight-or-flight reflexes had increased her heart rate as she tried to get the officer's help. Those things never mixed well with the introduction of sudden, intense jolts of electricity, and they combined to trigger cardiac dysrhythmia. She had gone into cardiac arrest and died.

That was when it all started to break down, when society started to crumble around us and the world changed. In the days and months that followed, reports trickled in, carried by word of mouth, about the lives lost in Hawaii in the first waves of the attack and the US carriers that were sunk off Pearl Harbor.

Downtown, a small sleeper cell had detonated a non-nuclear EMP bomb. Power went out, cars died, and people were trapped underground in immobile subway cars. The civilian infrastructure screeched to a halt. Internet servers went off-line, although the cybernetic implants in our heads and some of the newer peripheral devices were shielded well enough that they remained undamaged.

With nothing to connect to, though, the chunks of metal and strings of wire were useless.

But all that was noise. For me, Selene was the first loss, the first victim. The world fell apart with her death, and the world was inextricably different because she was gone.

T HE BURLAP BAG WAS ROUGH and itchy. It stank of sweat and copper and made my skin crawl. When they pulled it from my head, the sudden brightness stung my eyes. My eyelids closed in painful reflex, and purple shadows shot up against them. Brief people shapes, the glow of light, and shapes I hadn't had time to process and recognize danced around me.

Slowly, I opened them, adjusting to the dim light. A single bare bulb hung overhead. I could hear the hum of a generator. The walls were bare drywall, chipped and stained.

My shoulders ached. My hands were cuffed tightly behind me, and the chain link had been woven through the slats of the chair's back. My leg hurt as the morphine started to lose its grip. I'd bled through the gauze, and all the moving I'd done over the last few minutes had reopened the holes on either side of my thigh. Blood beaded and dripped, making little smacking noises on the concrete floor.

The man who had taken the sack off my head was already exiting, slamming the door shut behind him. It hit the frame with a heavy clang followed by the tinny click of a lock latching.

My back was to the door. Not a situation I particularly enjoyed. I wanted to see what—and who—was coming at me. This was part of the process, though, a way to amp up the anxiety, charge up the fear, and make me wonder.

The room was small. Not much to see. Not much to do but wait.

We had driven for maybe an hour, but that estimate was useless in determining where I was. They had driven in circles, changing up their route, and doubling back. We could have been back at the Bank of America for all I knew. But I figured that was a bit too humorous and a bit too ironic for these guys.

The dampener jammed into the side of my head had started chattering away during the drive. Somebody had been pinging my brain wirelessly, checking for traps, mining as much info out of me as they could. It had taken them awhile to crack the firewalls and memshells and work on defusing the digimines that checkered my neural weave. They were well trained and proficient, and their hard work overcame the technology and my patchwork security. They plundered as much as they could. They were no doubt busy reviewing and piecing together the data trove while I sat chained to a chair, guessing at what they knew or thought they knew.

The message was pretty simple. Lying was pointless because they'd siphoned off my entire life during the drive. The downloads wouldn't be enough to prevent what was coming, though. Memory was subjective and deeply layered, but some finely tuned questions and proper motivation could work together to create new angles on interesting answers.

They were waiting for the morphine to wear off a bit more before they got down to questioning me. They would want me pliable and in need, willing to barter information and answers for painkillers.

I knew the ploy: dope me up, get me feeling good, and get me to forget about the pain and used to feeling numb. Then they would let it wear off, let the pain come back in, and make me hurt. They would ask me questions, find ways to make me hurt in other ways or other places, and ask me the same questions in different ways before promising me more morphine and asking me more questions.

The interrogation would give their techies time to piece together the data dumps and work on comparing it against my answers, and then they would question me even harder, believing they had a more complete, but not quite full, picture from which to pry loose more information and more truthful answers. Then, maybe, they would reward me with a shot of morphine and start it all over again.

The walls were thick, but muffled screams made their way toward me from somewhere down the hall. The scare tactic didn't work too well because the noise was blunted and dull. I could hardly hear it. Closer but still barely audible, voices came through the door. Their conversations were muted and indecipherable.

I wondered about this unit's military bearing. The clean, fresh battle fatigues their commander wore struck me as strange, out of place. Where would militarized insurgents stuck behind enemy lines for years get fresh uniforms? Whoever they were, they weren't local.

A number of active cells hiding out in the wastelands and demilitarized zones routinely threatened to topple the peace. The Northern Alliance, their allies, and the PRC were mutually agreed that these rogue factions were terrorists. Once upon a time, they might have been called heroes, before the war degenerated into the usual politics.

The politicians in charge, the ones who claimed they were solely responsible for spearheading the war against the PRC in the fight for California and much of the Western Seaboard, had quickly grown fatigued. The war took up too much bandwidth, and the constant reports of violence desensitized the public. Americans were quick to turn their fear and anger into confusion and apathy. Nobody had the patience for sustained combat. Not after the first year, definitely not after the second. Nobody had been satisfied with the slow campaign, and when the Pacific Rim Coalition found themselves unvanquished after days, weeks, and then months of fighting, much of America had given up hope. Our leaders had promised a swift resolution and a quick victory.

That didn't happen.

A war-weary nation and its handwringing politicians quickly turned on its own people and chalked up California as a loss. The liberals cried and pointed fingers, refusing to believe they bore any of the fault. Tea Party conservatives shrugged off any responsibility and blamed Los Angeles for the PRC invasion, saying that the state's liberal attitudes had angered God, and this was punishment. The porn industry and scores of violent TV shows, movies, and video games that had for so long corrupted and plagued American children, they said, were the cause for our exile. We were too liberal and too weak. We had been more concerned with having abortions and legalizing drugs, DRMR, and prostitution than with resisting the enemy.

Indifference became a national pastime, but it did not stop the war. It didn't save New York or DC or halt the millions of deaths across the eastern front. It didn't stop the militia uprisings. The PRC and their Russian and Iranian allies burned the White House to the ground. Their minor dictatorship wasn't able to stop domestic terrorists from smuggling backpack nukes into the nation's capital and wiping it off the map.

I remembered reading in high school that the average lifespan of a democracy is two hundred years. By the time America fell, the country had been well overdue for change. It had been even longer since a foreign army had set foot on US soil. Maybe we were overdue for a lot of things. Chaos reigned, and nobody knew who the enemy was. Militia groups struck out against the police, the Army, the National Guard, and the PRC along the western fronts. Terrorist cells and minor factions rose up to join the frenzy. UN Peacekeepers constantly found themselves under attack.

The military was ordered to pull out of California. The disorganization of their hasty withdrawal was infused with bitterness and disbelief. Entire units went AWOL, ignoring the winds of political change. They stayed behind to fight, to carry out the orders of a country that had given up and ceased to be.

The state's borders were redrawn in a cordial agreement between the PRC and the Alliance, the de facto recognized government of choice. The governments reached mutual decisions, while many of the people did not. People like me, and those of us living in Echo Park, were remnants. We had no country, no homes. We were displaced exiles with nowhere to go. We could try to brave the DMZ that separated California and a pocket of Oregon from the rest of North America and maybe die in the desert, either from exposure or the military and militia groups that patrolled it, keeping the nation-states secure.

Plenty of organizations fancied themselves freedom fighters. Could be one of them that had me handcuffed to a chair with a bullet hole in my leg. I wasn't quite convinced of that, though. So far, a certain level of equality had been present in the proceedings. Not exactly kindness, definitely not respect, it was at least a professionalism of sorts. Militias were more down and dirty. I didn't think a militia would have bothered to wrap my leg or waste precious morphine on me. I wasn't convinced they would have taken a prisoner.

No, these guys were military. This was all part of a technique. They were softening me up or trying to. But the real brutality would come soon, the kind that would put even the militias to shame.

The voices outside grew closer. Their words, while still muffled, became more pronounced. I could pick up syllables and emphases, but not the conversation itself.

The door lock clicked again. Its hinges were smooth and oiled, but the weight of the door carried it open and sent it thudding into the wall. The men who entered were quiet, and I had no idea how many were sneaking up behind me.

"Jonah Everitt," one of them called to me. "I'm Sergeant Kaften."

A face caught up with the voice, stepping in front of me. I recognized him from the bank—the big black guy that I had pegged for being in charge. Nice to know I was right about something.

I nodded to him curtly. "Hey, Sarge."

He was dressed a bit more casually than he had been earlier, his torso covered in a brown military-issue T-shirt instead of the combat jacket he'd worn at the bank. His left arm was a robotic prosthesis, a gift of the once-great United States. It seemed to work as well as his organic right arm and had full range of motion. The midnight-blue color of the thick Kevlar shell and the heavily reinforced joints and points of articulation gave it away as military.

Under the Kevlar was a complex mess of wires and EMP shielding encased in tough plastic. The limb was well-crafted, but inhuman. Like his real arm, the prosthetic was controlled by neural impulses so slight that he never really had to think about how to move it. As good as the real thing, but probably better in a lot of ways.

He grabbed my jaw between one large mechanical paw and turned my head roughly. The robotics gave him an incredible degree of strength. This was him trying to be gentle. He held my head at an uncomfortable angle, his fingers, cold and rough, poking at me painfully.

"That's a nasty cut you got there."

His thumb dug into the gash. The bullet wound to my leg had made me forget about the pain in my face and the shard of bone I had pulled out of my cheek.

He snapped his fingers and held out a hand. Somebody behind me handed him a brown bottle and a wad of cloth. He jammed the cloth against the mouth of the bottle, upended it, then jammed the cloth against my cheek. The cool burn was antiseptic, and the strong stink of alcohol invaded my nose. I winced, felt liquid trickle down the side of my face to pool between my neck and shirt collar before evaporating in the still air.

"How's your leg?"

"Not well enough for your hospitality. Check back later."

He slapped my cheek, but not hard. The gesture had a hint of joviality to it, as if we were old buddies, and he smiled. He took a chair from another man behind me, opposite from whoever had handed him the bottle. He sat across from me, crossed his ankles, and tucked his legs under the chair as he leaned forward. The gesture was oddly prim, but I figured, don't ask, don't tell.

"Tell me about Samuel Hodgson."

"Who?" I asked, genuinely confused. I didn't know

anybody by that name.

"What about Jaime Kristoff?"

I knew the game here. It wouldn't matter if I answered truthfully or not. This was just an opening volley, and they would ask me the same question a thousand times in a hundred different ways before this was over. I knew my role here. I could tell him and then keep repeating myself over and over. Or I could deny, which was probably what he expected. Either way, I was in for a beating.

"I don't know Jaime Kristoff." I smiled to let him know I knew how this game was played. If I was right, he'd already had my memories vetted for traps and downloaded. He knew what I knew. But he was at least smart enough to doubt it—and too smart to assume that because he'd found them in my head they were automatically vouchsafed and valid memories.

"All right," he said, sounding disappointed. He puffed his cheeks then blew out a strong, disgusting huff of breath into my face. He nodded, his eyes darting over my shoulder.

Behind me, something cool wrapped around my index finger at the first joint, just past the nail. There was a quick, tight pressure, and then it released. Stomping my legs, I screamed as the pain flooded through me.

Kaften tore the bandage from my leg, and the man behind me handed him the piece of finger they'd cut off. He jammed it into the bullet hole without ever breaking eye contact with me.

This was bad. Not at all what I was expecting. Worse. A gorge rose in my throat, and my stomach pinched and twisted painfully. The pointed edges of my ex-fingernail dug into the raw flesh of my wounded leg, twisting and turning. Perversely, the word "thumbscrew" popped into my head, and I wanted to laugh through the agony. Instead, I spat up water as my stomach heaved. My face burned, and little dots of sweat broke out against my forehead and temples. More water splashed out of me in a thick sheet of liquid and phlegm dribbling down my chin.

"I'm not fucking around with you, Everitt. You answer me, or we cut some more, shorten a few more fingers. Then I'll let the medichines put you back together and start over, 'less you start getting smart here."

I grinned through the pain, the world tilting crazily around me. I was hunched over as far as my arms would let me go, spitting between my legs, but I looked up and found his eyes.

"I don't have medichines, you asshole."

That one got me a punch—a hard one. No pull on his cybernetic patch job this time. Loose teeth popped free, and I tasted copper.

"That's too bad," he said. "You struck me as a medichine man for sure."

I laughed, honestly amused. He was referring to an old advert from years ago, back when medichines had been new.

Daedalus Industries had promised to cure mankind's ailments with a vaccine of nanomeds that would boost the immune system, slow aging and cellular decay, and improve cellular recovery. Cuts and bruises healed in no time. The adverts showed brief glimpses of policemen, firemen, and military professionals in the course of an average day. They all said the same thing, to a T. "I'm a medichine man." Then it closed in an operating room with a brightly lit woman dressed in surgical garb, saying, "And I am a medichine woman." It earned Daedalus a tremendous amount of popular support.

I'd never bought into it. I avoided the nano boosters the same way I disregarded annual flu shots. I was beginning to regret it.

"So, tell me, what do you know about Jaime Kristoff?"

"He runs a bar, grows his own potatoes, makes his own

whiskey. It's good."

"Uh huh."

"For those of us in the tents, he's a nice little corner of the way things used to be. Somewhere we can go and feel normal."

"Even with all those guards looking down on you? Fucking with your water?"

He caught my eye and winked at me. My run-in with Timmons was a recent event, a surface memory that would have been easy for them download, loaded with emotion, and kept close to the heart. Truth be told, I was still pissed off about it.

I tried hard to settle in the chair and find a more comfortable position. It wasn't easy, and I was dizzy and lightheaded. My finger ached with each pulse, and a coppery taste tainted my mouth. I spat again, noticing all the old discolorations on the floor around me.

"He's like you guys," I said. The air around me changed, and something told me that was not the right answer. Instinctively, I braced for the blow. I was trapped under a flurry of punches as the men behind me took shots to either side of my head. My ears rang and something inside my skull popped. Kaften was yelling, but not at me. My shoulders were hunched, my head down, chin buried in my chest. Everything hurt. Nose broken. Had to be.

"Get out," he said to the men, his voice calm but hard. A wordless moment passed before the door clicked shut again.

Cold fingers pried at my chin, pulling my head up.

Jaime, what the fuck did you get me into?

Cybernetic fingers pinched my cheeks hard, forcing the skin between my teeth. "You and Kristoff. You ain't nothing like us. We clear? And we sure ain't nothing like you, you understand that?"

I tried to nod but couldn't with my face trapped in his

grip.

"Look man," I said. The words were thick, clumsy and slurred. My lips were fat and swollen. "We do our part. We try. The war... it's over. We take potshots where we can."

He looked at me with a degree of pity and a shade of sadness. He slid down the wall and sat.

"You live with them," he said. "In the tents. You eat their food, drink their water. You don't do shit except kneel, and you say you're doing your part? That's bullshit, man. You're weak. And you're a fool. You're being played up and used, and you don't even know it."

"I fought," I said, desperation creeping into my voice. "I took lives. I know what that's like."

"Maybe," he said. "Maybe once, before. But I know you, Everitt. Who you are now. You're a fucking junkie. You kill for the mem, for the rush. DMT, right? You're a dreamer, nothing more."

"No, that's not—"

"Shut up. Quiet down for a minute. This is how it's gonna go. You've taken shelter with the enemy, you and everyone else in those fucking tents. You turned your back on us, on your country, on your homes. We got your memories, as much as we could, and we'll splice 'em into a nice little story we can easily follow and forensic the shit out of. And then I'm going to put a bullet in you."

Neither of us spoke. The air was still and quiet.

"You defiled that girl," he said. I must have look confused, because he screwed up his face and made a small angry ticking sound with his tongue and teeth. "The one you found during clean-up. The one whose gore is all over your hand there, from tearing out her back-up."

Jaime. Alice Xie. What the fuck did I get into?

I hated his self-righteousness. "Better to hide bombs under them, right? Kill whatever innocent fucks find her?"

"Ain't none of you innocent," Kaften said. "You're

colluding with the enemy—all of you. You're cleaning up the mess those chinks made, handing our cities right over to them."

"We're not colluding." I tried to say more, but he wasn't having any of it.

"You slaves then. That it?"

"Your hands aren't clean, either."

"No, mine ain't at all. But at least my head is. I'm not some washed-up whore needing a fix. But what about you? That how desperate you are?" he asked. "Defiling dead girls now? Looking to get high off the war kills?"

"It's not like that." The words were a hollow lie. The truth was, I would have burned copies, played them, and passed them off for credits or favors. I would have lived her life, licking my lips in anticipation of her death and that white, burning rush of death's chemical dump. I would have played it over and over, until euphoria turned to unconsciousness.

"Nah, sure. You molest them for the money."

I couldn't deny that. A small degree of shame sank in over the truth of his words, but I was already feeling beaten.

"It's why you killed that general, right? Little Alice, she's got her hands in a lot of pots, too. What do you suppose that's all about?"

"I wouldn't know."

"Course you wouldn't," he said. "So. Jaime Kristoff. What do you know about him? I mean, what do you really know about him?"

I thought about it and about what I knew, remembered Mesa asking me what the fuck I know about anything. Everything hurt. My vision was limned with red, and each heartbeat brought pain. He asked me if I wanted more morphine. My finger throbbed, cascading waves of torment that tickled their way through my whole body.

"He leads a cell, or at least, I think he does." I hated myself for this. Talking. Spilling secrets. "He was responsible for the bombing on the 101. He lost his wife in the war. We both did. After the US gave up on us and pulled out, we were on our own. We had nothing left. Not a single fucking thing."

"And he never told you nothing, huh?"

"Hey, you've got all my memories, man. There's not much else I can add."

"We think we have your memories. Some surface ones, sure. But deeper down, who knows how reliable it is? Especially with your jacked-up brain. How many mems you'd say you've done now? Hundred? Thousand? You even know which are yours, buried in that skull? Which ones are reliable? You got any suppressant software in there? Anything maybe your subconscious is electing you to forget? Any wipers in there? Maybe reformatting your shit?"

I didn't know how to answer. He wouldn't believe any arguments from me, and I didn't have any I could sell credibly. Not while I was crying and bleeding all over the place. I was a shell, and he was picking me apart one piece at a time. The few defenses I did have had been hacked through far too easily for my liking. My thought bombs and mem-mines had proved impotent.

His questions about Jaime made it clear he knew things that I did not, and he was aware of it. He was plumbing for information, but his mind was already made up. He had passed judgment on me long before speaking with me, maybe even before the download on the ride over.

"Tell me what you know about Samuel Hodgson," he said.

Again, the name threw me. I didn't know what the hell he was asking me.

"Whatever it is you're looking for, I can't help you," I

said.

He pushed himself to his feet and walked out. I wondered how long it would be before he came back and we did all of this again.

My vision faded, the red going black. The touch of fingers roughly pulling at my wounded hand tore me back to consciousness. A young voice told me to straighten my fingers. A rough piece of wood was jammed between my teeth, and I bit down, bracing myself for the pain. But bracing for it was impossible. They said nothing. Their silence was punctuated with the hiss of an igniting flame. I howled as they cauterized the stump of my index finger. The rubbery smell of my cooking flesh was acrid and nauseating.

The cuffs had worn oozing rings into my wrists, and my arms were numb from immobility. When I tried to shift my weight, a blaze of pinpricks traveled up and down my limbs, and they felt heavy with sand. Everything hurt to varying degrees, some a dull ache, others a throbbing soreness, but each wound was vivid in its pain.

The light above me died, and I was abandoned to the darkness, left alone and broken.

I didn't know how many hours passed. I slept poorly and with no recollection of having fallen asleep. When I woke, my neck was sore and stiff, and all of my other pains had multiplied. Muffled screams lulled my eyes open. I had to piss so badly, it hurt.

The door opened. Harsh light spilled in, shocking my eyes after all the hours of blackness.

"I'm undoing one wrist. Just the one, though," Kaften said. "You're going to stand up and allow yourself to be re-cuffed."

With that done, he gripped my arm and led me out of the room. The screams grew louder, then softer as we passed, distancing ourselves.

"What's happening?" I asked him. My mouth was dry, and the words cracked.

"Seems you got a benefactor. We're through here."

"Who?"

The only answer I received was a small push forward, up the steps. My legs were weak and tired, and I was ready to topple over. Kaften stayed close enough behind me that his breath warmed the back of my neck. We went down a long, wide corridor. Guards were positioned on each side of heavy metal doors that were chained and padlocked. Kaften was apparently quite security conscious and had a thing for chains. Didn't want anybody getting in or out. His little fiefdom was far less porous than the refugee camp at Echo Park, which made me question the nature of his beliefs and how high up his moral high ground truly was.

Outside, the differences dividing Kaften and his regiment from the PRC grew thinner. If there had been a line drawn in the sand, it had eroded severely. The daylight revealed rows of canvas habitats and dirty, grimy people, fewer than those at Echo Park. For some, their clothing was nothing more than thin shifts of fabric. Children were hungry and thin, their faces long and hollowed out, making their round eyes appear too large and alien. Ribs poked through papyrus flesh above distended bellies. Armed guards—well-fed, muscled, and healthy—were a far cry from the gaunt wraiths living around them. They had been given purpose by the guns they carried, while everyone else seemed lost and sad.

This was not an outpost of freedom fighters, nor was it the last bastion of a dead America. The people here had no country, no objective. They lived merely because their bodies were too stubborn to die. Kaften had built up a dominion of rulers and their weak subjects. Even after all the wars, all the fighting, and all the death, Kaften and his inner circle had learned nothing. They fell back instantly on the ancient instincts of survival. I wondered which version of the American dream he was really fighting for.

"At least you're free, huh?" I said, feeling bitter. Animosity welled up out of nowhere, and I suddenly felt a lot less pity for myself. Rage burned inside me, along with hatred for the hypocrisy.

He didn't seem to appreciate my contrary tone, even as his eyes wandered over what I had seen, maybe trying to see them from my perspective. He said nothing. My pace lagged a bit, and he shoved me forward again, intent on keeping me moving. The eyes of hungry strangers dogged my every step. I couldn't tell if they were jealous, piteous, or just empty stares.

Small clumps of grass grew among weeds tucked into the cracks of broken sidewalks. Before the war, this had been an industrialized area. Everything was crumbling and rusted, an ill-maintained haven for broken souls. The remains of a massive metal crane towered over the site. Metal shipping containers, abandoned and forgotten, were stacked three or four high. The ground-level ones had been turned into a squatters' nest, home to a dozen people, if not more.

Kaften helped me into the back of a jeep, clearly a military relic, open to the air. He sat in the passenger seat, while I rode in back. Our driver's was not a face I recognized. A second jeep carrying four people followed ours.

The drive was neither slow nor fast. The batteries that ran the vehicles were silent. The tires kicked up dust all around us, turning our skin gritty and chalky. The men were silent, except during brief radio communiqués, and those were mostly to confirm that the people ahead of us were in place and the rendezvous was clear.

We drove for maybe an hour. The sky went from blue to orange, but I did not know what day it was. My seclusion in the dark, along with having slept, had deprived me of any sense of time. It could still have been the same day. I could have worked on the reclamation site that morning, and the world was only just giving way to dusk. It felt as though more time had passed, though. A day at least, but when I asked, I was ignored.

I watched the city slide by, remembering how it had looked before the war. The fighting had turned it into a dilapidated graveyard that stretched for miles. Nature had begun slowly reasserting itself, blurring the landscape with subtle greens from plant life that had found incongruous methods of supporting itself.

Ahead, a pair of lights flashed on, off, on, off. We slowed, and a garbled voice came over Kaften's radio once again. First the outlines of figures began to resolve, then people more distinctly. I recognized the lanky man standing in front of the plate-armored hood, dressed in a slimming black suit, a white button-down, and a thin black tie. The shine of his shoes had been lost to the cinders he'd walked through.

Kaften helped me from the jeep, mostly by stopping me from falling on my face as I half-tripped, half-jumped out of the vehicle. His patience and assistance were odd after all that had happened earlier. I looked at the skyline, knowing he had installed spotters well before this arranged meeting. I could practically taste the distrust in the air. If snipers were secreted away in the unfinished skeleton of the Alcyone Towers, they were well hidden.

He walked me forward, staying behind me, but pressed closely in a manner that suggested a degree of intimacy neither of us felt. From the way his body hugged mine, I was clearly a human shield. His movements were close, tight, and unsubtle, as his arm moved behind me. The cold, hard metal of a gun pressed into my back.

My breathing turned shallow and a pit opened in my

belly for my balls to crawl up into. My mouth was dry. I sucked a scab loose from the jagged stumps of missing teeth.

We stood patiently for a moment while the driver examined us. Hai walked around the vehicle's hardened shell, to the rear driver's-side door, and a pair of shiny black heels stepped onto the earth as shiny black hair rose above the doorframe.

Alice Xie turned to me, studying my cuts and bruises as if she were taking inventory. She saw my torn pants, the pucker of skin, and thick clots of blood from where I'd been shot. Her lips were pursed in disappointment, but when her eyes met mine, they were unusually soft and tender.

I hadn't been sure who my mysterious benefactor was, but when I saw Alice, I wasn't all that surprised. Even though our relationship was often one of employee and employer, we shared a mutual respect and, if I squinted hard enough, maybe even a degree of camaraderie around the rough edges.

She stood alone, ahead of the car, halfway to the space that separated us, while her driver hung back. Hers was the lone car on the far side of the imaginary divide separating us, and she and Hai were woefully outnumbered by the soldiers flanking my rear. I wondered if she had taken precautions similar to Kaften's. She seemed unconcerned and cool to the whole affair.

"He recovered a memory chip."

"It's in his right hip pocket," Kaften said. His voice was loud in my ear, but his body pulled away, and he whispered, "I'm going to uncuff you. Keep your arms at your side, your hands away from your body."

He nudged me forward, and I could still feel the gun pressed into my back. My body would hide it from view for several paces, and I knew its presence alone would bore into me every step of the way. I had a hard time walking. Unbalanced and uncoordinated, my feet shuffled forward as I limped painfully and over-favored my good leg. I probably resembled a penguin, wobbling toward an invisible line.

Alice urged me forward with her eyes. The rest of her body was motionless, coiled tight, and waiting to strike. I nodded to her.

I was still close enough to hear Kaften's soft voice, intended solely for my ears. "I forgot to tell you. We finished splicing together all of your memories. Remember that promise I made you?"

I had no time to turn, no time to question it.

The gunshot boomed in the still air, driving me forward. I stumbled and fell to my knees, coughing up gore as white-hot pain blossomed in my chest and back. Bullets stitched the ground in front of me, driving Alice back to her car. I was deafened. The sound of automatic weapons fire sounded dull beneath a high-pitched whine in the center of my head.

I tried to crawl forward, but the pain was too immense, and I couldn't feel my arms. My legs kicked uselessly at the ground. My eyelids grew heavy, and the world swam out of focus, leaving me with a deep yearning for sleep. My heart was beating too quickly, pushing far too much plasma from my body.

Black shoes rushed forward. Bare caramel-colored ankles and smooth shins kneeled before me, and I watched Alice's lips move, but I couldn't hear her over the ringing in my ears. My eyelids were heavy. I didn't want to close them, but I did. I tumbled into a void of silence and darkness, feeling nothing, even as I coughed, wracking my body, purging myself of fluid. The darkness was a cool invite, but it promised warmth, and I could deny it no longer. I fell in whole and knew that I was damned. My eyes fluttered open briefly. Red lips floated before me. Impossibly delicate, they parted to reveal white, impossibly perfect teeth. And they swallowed me into the darkness.

CHAPTER SEVEN

Gunfire sounded in the distance, loud enough to pull me from my stupor. I needed a few moments to collect myself and remember where I was and why there might be gunfire. The sound was no longer foreign to my life.

I untangled myself from a thin, moth-eaten blanket and pushed myself up from an equally thin cot, gripping the metal frame for support. Rifle reports echoed in the air, and I recognized the familiar cadence of target practice.

The cot across from mine was empty. I pushed through

the tent, surprised by how early the hour was. The sun was slowly ascending, and the grass was wet with dew.

The smell of coffee pulled me toward the reservoir, and people sat in lawn chairs beside their RVs, eating and drinking. Our little group had picked up three newcomers—refugees heading north from Chula Vista to escape the Mexican gangs and militias fighting over border claims. The plan was to head east, into the Sun Belt.

My exhalations turned into gray bursts of vapor, and I stuffed my hands deeper into my wool-lined coat pockets. I nodded at the few acquaintances Mesa and I had made, my mouth watering at the plates of venison being breakfasted on, even though the meat was too gamey for my taste. Not feeling particularly personable, I filled a cup with coffee and moved off toward the shooting area.

Staring intently though the scope, Mesa had a rifle stock jammed against her shoulder. A man in his mid-twenties stood close to her, his hand pressed low and flat against the small of her back. I didn't much appreciate the familiarity of the gesture. In the still moment, my footsteps crunched loudly, and Jacob took his hands away from my daughter and stood at a more respectful distance as I approached.

"Morning," I said. He nodded hello.

Mesa said nothing, as was often her way these days. She stared down the gun sights, centered it, and fired. The bullet pinged through an old soup can maybe thirty feet away, knocking it over. She watched it all though the scope, and when she was satisfied that the can was going to stay down, she relaxed and lowered the rifle. She looked at me quickly before pretending to ignore me. It was what passed for acknowledgement between us. She gave the rifle back to the boy and sulked off.

"How's she doing?" I asked him.

"Good. She's a good shot."

"Any funny business between you two?"

His face reddened and the denial that stumbled out was a lie.

"She's too young for you," I told him. "She's just a kid."

"Yeah," he said. "okay."

"Unless you want to end up like that soup can, you'll listen to me. You stay away from her."

"Yeah, okay," he said again, but his whiny, high-pitched tone told me otherwise. I didn't expect him to listen to reason, even as I hoped nothing worse ever came of this.

I made sure he saw the resolve in my eyes and made sure he broke eye contact first.

He said, "Yeah, okay," again, then pushed past me, muttering beneath his breath.

"Fucking kids," I said. The coffee was too bitter and burnt. I flung what little was left toward a clump of dead trees. Something rustled a bit deeper in the woods, drawing closer and moving quickly. We'd seen bobcats a few nights before, and the few deer we'd come across, we'd killed and butchered for meat. I found the grip of my gun at the same time a small child burst from the trees, smears of dirt and blood on his face. Charlie, thirteen years old, maybe. One of the scouts who had gone out the other day, but three others had been with him.

"Get out," he said, panting heavily. "Go! They're coming."

The words struck me dumb with terror, but I turned on my heel and chased after him, back up the slope. To each cluster of people he passed, he said the same thing, breathless and wheezy: "PRC! PRC! PRC!"

Everyone was bewildered and dazed. We'd expected it, of course, but that didn't make it easier.

Mesa was having an animated conversation with another girl as I ran toward her.

"C'mon," I said. "We gotta go."

"Go where?" she asked. I grabbed her hand, making

her run with me. "Hey, let go, goddamn it! Where are we going?"

I shoved her through the tent before me, dug the rifle up from beneath her cot, and handed it to her. I could see the terror in her eyes and tears standing on the surface. She wouldn't take the rifle. I shoved it against her, forcing her to take a hold of it or drop it.

"C'mon," I said, grabbing my own rifle.

I led her up the trails, to a nice perch for us to take aim. Through the scope, I watched mothers and their children being pushed into the RVs. The men stayed outside, shoving the doors shut after them, then banging on the side, telling them to go, go, go. A few clusters of single women with guns joined the party.

"Everitt, you up there, man?"

"I'm here," I said.

One of the men in our camp, Kevin Mason, was a communications engineer and had found a way to jury-rig a local system for our neural commNet. That was him inside my head.

"You see anything? What've we got?"

"There's a squad coming through," I said. "Count eleven strong."

I suspected that our scouts had reduced their numbers. Most PRC squads were composed of fourteen men. They'd met up with our scouts, one group stumbling upon the other, and shots had been exchanged. Of the four who had gone into the woods, only the boy had returned. The squad could have been out there for a training exercise or as part of a mission. Any reason at all, really. Maybe PacRim satellites had picked up our heat signatures from orbit, and they had come to check it out.

They'd engaged our scouts and would soon be coming upon our small, but armed, band. They would have transmitted word back to their base that they'd come under fire. If satellites hadn't found us before, they would be searching for us now, and the datastreams would be feeding information to them about our locations, our weapons, our numbers, and the terrain. Back at their base, reinforcements were no doubt being prepped for support, and choppers would be winding up to come in hot.

There were maybe twenty of us. Not many, but enough to hopefully do what we had to do and get the fuck out.

Mesa and I had been practicing with the rifles for a little more than a month. We were rank amateurs, and we knew it. We had to pull our weight, though. Our little commune didn't have much use for a community college art history instructor. Despite that, it had turned out that we weren't all bad, and even Mesa seemed to have a small bit of natural talent for shooting. Jacob, our tutor—if you could call him that—had lived in Michigan for a time. Then the plant he had worked at was shut down, and he'd found himself heading west. He'd been young enough to be able to get a fresh start somewhere new. He had served in the Army for a single tour, but he'd learned most of his shooting skills from his father and uncle. They had spent long weekends in the woods, hunting deer, and much of the advice he gave us had once been passed down to him. He seemed to have a knack for teaching.

Through the scope, I watched the squad taking careful, measured steps. They were alert, their eyes scanning across the potential battlefield before them. They moved with assuredness, but also with a subtle hint of nervousness. You could see it in the eyes of the younger soldiers, and they fought to clamp it down, Adam's apples bobbing as they choked their hearts back down into their chests. They were spacing themselves out as they moved, consciously making many targets instead of one large group that could be brought down more easily and quickly.

They were silent, their mouths still, no hand signals

since they were glued to their guns. Any communications to one another were being done through neural nets. Their combat armor was devoid of rank in an effort to better camouflage the commanding officer. I looked for the minor tells that would give away the squad leader, hoping a newbie would shoot a glance over to whoever was in charge before moving forward.

I found a candidate in a markedly older man. He was graying at the temples, and crow's feet crinkled the corners of his eyes. A glance passed between him and a younger man, along with almost a nod, which told me he was in charge.

"Do you see him?" I asked Mesa.

Her grip tightened around the rifle stock, and her lips were parted in a small O. She licked her top lip and nodded. Her nervousness came off her in waves. I could almost hear her heart racing with fear.

"Shoot him," I whispered.

"Uh huh."

"Do it."

"No."

"Mesa, c'mon. Shoot him."

Her lower lip trembled, and a glassy sheen coated the surface of her eyes. She shook her head.

"It's like the deer. Remember? You can do this, hon."

"Just shut up." Fear edged into her voice, tight and whiny, with a bitter dash of anger. She had hate in her eyes.

"We don't have time for this," I said. "I need you with me on this. It's like we talked about before. We both need to take down a target. I have mine. You have yours. We have to do this."

"I can't," she said. Her mother's stubbornness reared its head, a steadfast refusal steeled with the conviction that nobody would ever change her mind.

"Goddamn it, Mesa."

Her tears ran freely, but her hands were still tight on the rifle. She still gazed through the scope, following their movements. My gut was tightly coiled, a cold ball the size of my fist. It threatened to lurch its way up my torso, and a cold sweat broke across the nape of my neck.

I left my rifle and crab-walked across the rocky ground to her. The cold earth dampened the front of my clothes. I hugged her with my body and pushed a finger through the trigger guard over hers.

"Do you have a target?" I asked her.

She snuffled, her throat thick with snot. She wiped it away with her wrist then palmed away the tears. "I can't do this."

"You have to do this." Something painful pulled through my heart with the delicacy of barbed wire. I hated myself for what I was asking of her. But these were the new rules. This was our new life. She had to survive, and that meant making painful choices and awful compromises.

I followed the line of the rifle barrel. Her finger was cool beneath mine, her hand clammy. I kissed the side of her face, tasting tears on my lips, and whispered, "Everything's going to be all right."

I pulled the trigger with her. So close to her, I could hear her gasp, even over the sound of the gunfire, as a red mist exploded from the man's head.

The soldiers paused in reflex, looking around them as if an intruder were in the field with them. I slid back to my rifle as their eyes started to scan the horizon, looking for us. One man got excited and forgot about the commNet, pointing up at the mountain pass where Mesa and I were, shouting in Chinese. Eyes and guns turned toward us.

I pulled the scope close, trying to find my previous target—the older man with the weathered look. As I found him, the ground around me jumped where bullets landed, kicking up dust and rocks. Something hot scraped my hand, but I ignored it, centering the target in my crosshairs.

We'd found a deer the previous week—the first time I had ever killed something. I had felt tremendously guilty, watching its dull, dark eyes. It had not known I was there, up in a tree blind. It had been content and at peace. Sharp intelligent eyes scanned its surroundings. Seeking potential threats, its ears twitched at the strange sounds of the woods. I had taken a slow deep breath, not wanting to pull the trigger but knowing that I must, because our survival depended on it. We needed meat. We weren't killing for sport. I rationalized it and eased the trigger back. A wash of guilt swept through me—along with power, an assertion of control, and dominance. It felt right; it felt natural. And that made the guilt worse. But it also made the second time, and the time after that, easier.

When I pulled the trigger and turned the soldier's face into a messy crater, I had no remorse. I watched a man die instantly through the center lines of my scope, comfortably at ease.

Mesa was crying, and I knew how frightened she was as the bullets landed nerve-rackingly close.

"Two down," I said, seeking out a third target.

"About time," Mason said.

The soldiers were moving quickly, seeking cover behind loose scrub and felled trees that the winter thaw had carried down from the mountainside. Some retreated to the edges of the woods and hid among the branches.

Gunfire echoed from the canyons below as our guys stepped up to meet the enemy.

"Mesa? How you doing, honey?"

"I don't want to kill anymore." Her voice sounded numb and distant, and that awful barb ripped through me once again.

"I'm sorry, sweetie," I said. "I really am. But if we're

going to get out of this, we need to fight. This isn't going to be easy." My bravado was gone and I was an idiot for having thought that this could be easy or that because we had better numbers, it meant victory.

We weren't soldiers. Jacob was the closest, but even he had never seen combat. Much of his military experience consisted of filing away personnel records at a base in Germany. We weren't even a militia. We were painters, bakers, construction workers, teachers, and crossing guards. No training. No battlefield experience. We were in way over our heads.

Mesa's face was pressed tightly to the scope, and she clung to the rifle as if she were drowning. But she would not fire. She would not take a life.

One soldier risked a glance over the fallen tree trunk he'd tucked behind, rising high enough for me to chance it. I fired, but he was already ducking back down, and the bullet crashed into his cheek. He fell back, writhing on the ground, both hands pressed tightly to the wound.

"Stop it," Mesa cried. I thought she was yelling at the screaming man below. She rushed at me, falling to her knees as she skidded toward me. She pounded my face with her fists. The eyepiece of the sniper's scope cut me above my eye. I rolled onto my back, my hands up in defense, but it left my belly exposed, and she started punching away at my ribs. "Stop it," she yelled, over and over. "Stop it!"

I grabbed her in a bear hug, pulled her to the ground, pushed myself on top of her, and suffocated the fight out of her. Mesa's outburst had surprised the PRC. It had surprised everyone, and the battlefield became dull and quiet in its wake. Then I heard the nearly silent thrumming of a helo's twin-drive screw engines, felt the warmth pulsing from its large, black body as it descended. Demanding submission, pairs of gunnery sergeants hung from each side of the large insectile aircraft's carapace.

Mesa yelled at me, but her words held no shape and were mashed into angry noises. A thick rope of saliva hung between her lips, and she was breathing so hard and raggedly that snot bubbles burst in both nostrils. Eventually, she grew still as the fight drained out of her.

Below, heavily armored soldiers were rounding up the people I had come to consider friends and leading them to the helo. A half-squad was making its way up the trail to us as Mesa grew still.

I hugged her, and she hugged me back. Her body curled against mine, and her arm snaked around my neck as she held herself against me.

"I want Mom," she said in a half gasp.

I was suddenly struck by how young she really was. For the last few years, she had hidden behind a thick shell of teenage angst, with attitude to spare. She smoked, drank, and denied all of it. She had an old soul, though, and often acted years beyond her actual age, her rebelliousness aside. She was emotionally strong, strong-willed, and independent to the point of seeming indifferent.

But red-faced and crying, her breath coming in ragged puffs of fog, the façade had broken down around her and she buckled beneath the weight. She was a child, a girl in need of her mother, in need of a comfort and warmth beyond those a father could provide. She was an innocent.

"I know, sweetie. I do, too."

The fight was entirely gone from her. She was my little girl again.

I listened to the crunch of earth beneath heavily soled boots and felt hands grab me roughly, pulling Mesa and me apart. She went limp as she was dragged away, and neither of us struggled against the restraints. We had no need to.

Our war was over.

CHAPTER EIGHT

OPENING MY EYES WAS A struggle. They felt gummy and unyielding, and it took a moment before I could see, another for the blurriness to pass. A warm breeze brushed my face, and when my focus finally snapped into place, I found myself outside, half-reclining in a hospital bed on a spacious wooden deck.

The sky was clear, and the expanse of ocean was a rich blue green. A figure, too far away to be distinct, moved within the calm water.

I was confused and disoriented. The scene before me did not jibe with my last memories of blistering pain. I remembered Kaften, but he was nowhere to be seen. We were meeting Alice Xie, and I vaguely remembered her coming to my aid while I lay bleeding.

I was dressed in a terry cloth robe, but was naked

beneath that. An IV had been run into my left arm, and a drip bag filled with clear fluid was suspended from a tall metal rod beside the bed. No one else was around, so I pulled the robe apart. A fresh pink scar marked my right thigh with slightly puckered skin. I poked at it with a finger, but it felt fine. On my chest, another fresh scar. I found its twin on my back, barely within reach, but the skin felt smooth beneath my fingers. The tip of my index finger was still missing. The scar tissue there was a lumpy mess, a glaring disfigurement, though my other scars were not.

There were two possibilities for how my wounds had healed so quickly. One was better than the other, but I didn't care much for either of them. The most likely was that somebody had given me a medichine boost. I could have been in a coma, but somehow that didn't feel right, and I rejected it as a possibility.

My body was stiff. Not quite sore, but leaden. Guardrails were raised on each side of the bed. Using the rail for leverage, I pulled myself up and scooted toward the foot of the bed, past the guardrail. I swung my legs over the side. It took me awhile, and the exertion left me exhausted, but I hadn't even made it out of bed yet.

I pushed myself forward until my feet touched the hot wood below, and then I stood. My legs were weak. Small tremors jangled the aching muscles. I took small, carefully measured steps, holding onto the IV stand for support. The wind kicked at the loose robe, and I pulled it shut around me then tied it off, feeling slightly embarrassed at my nakedness even though I was alone.

A long flight of wooden steps led down to the beach, but the trek down would have been an ordeal on even the best of days. The deck was large and roomy, although the bed I had lain in clashed with the spartan decor. A hibachi grill doubled as a long table, and metal-frame chairs with thick cushions were arranged around it. A robe similar to my own was draped over the back of one chair. Tiki torches dotted the deck railing at regular intervals.

I walked to the railing and leaned against it. I was tired, and when I looked down, waves of vertigo rushed over me. I'd never been comfortable with heights, and the open spaces so far up put me on edge. Still, the view was beautiful, better than anything I had seen over the last few years.

Below, Alice Xie swam. Her naked body, long and slender, flitted beneath the water's surface. The sea was calm, and she glided easily. Her limbs and muscles seemed accustomed to the well-practiced movements. She was a strong swimmer. Watching her was calming and hypnotic, and I wished for something to draw this vista with, but my tools were still at Echo Park. The water, the way the light hit it, and the shadow of her figure beneath the surface—I committed it all to memory. She went out to a point, then dove again, her slender legs doing a brief scissor kick in the air. The ocean was clear, and her lithe figure twisted so that when she resurfaced she was facing me. She looked up and waved. She swam toward the shallow water and walked in toward the beach.

Alice was naked and unflustered when my gaze lingered. I watched her climb up the stairs, and she smiled as she approached me. She was trim, and her muscles were delicately defined. One breast was small. The other was absent. The tight skin was a patchwork of scars making a mess of folds and dimpled flesh from where her chest had been stitched together. She went to the chair to retrieve her robe. Her black, shiny hair was a stark contrast to the white terrycloth.

"It's good to see you up and about," she said.

"How long has it been?" I asked her.

"Three days."

Three days? Hours, I could believe, but not entire days. Fuck.

"How do you feel?" she asked.

"Tired."

She nodded. "Do you want to lie back down? Or sit?"

"I'm not really sure yet," I said.

She took my hand in hers and wrapped her other arm around my waist as she led me to one of the chairs. We moved slowly, and the short walk took me awhile. The bed felt miles away. When she helped lower me into the seat cushion, I wasn't sure I'd be getting up again.

"Do you want some water?" she asked.

I was surprised by her warm bedside manner. The degree of care and warmth coming from her was unusual given our past, brief encounters, and the stories I'd heard about her. Too many things were not matching up with my expectations lately.

"Water would be nice," I said.

She passed through an opaque sliding door, leaving it open behind her. The room was as spartan as the deck, with cherrywood floors, a large black leather sofa, and a fireplace. No photographs or any other mementos. If she lived here, she lived alone and kept few reminders of her life or her experiences. I listened for voices, but heard only Alice, whose soft voice was indistinct, and the small sounds of the surf below. She was gone longer than she should have needed to get a glass of water, and brief pauses punctuated her muffled conversations, but no other voices filled the gaps. After a few moments of quiet, her voice picked up a sing-song quality.

I closed my eyes, tilting my head back to absorb the warmth of the sun. The heat felt good against my face, scalp, and the stubble of my hair.

Her singing grew closer, and I recognized the foreign-language lyrics of a popular Muzyakimo Aki synthpop grinder ballad. She smiled, suddenly self-conscious, as the tune died away. She carried a tray of sandwiches and large tumblers filled with ice water.

"I didn't know you sang," I said.

"I don't," she said. "Not really. You should eat."

She sat and crossed her legs. The robe parted and fell away some, revealing a long expanse of toned thigh.

The sandwiches were simple—pita shells stuffed with slices of cucumber, spinach leaves, sprouts, carrot shavings, and thick, creamy arcs of avocado. Pickles gave it a nice bit of tartness. I was surprised by how hungry I was.

"Who were you talking to inside?" I tried to keep my voice casual, but I needed information. I was starting to feel paranoid and trapped. I wasn't sure how much to trust her.

"Your doctor," she said. "He'll be coming over soon to check up on you. He's glad to hear you're awake."

"What happened?"

She was weighing how much to tell me. I could see it in her eyes, her trying to judge which bits of intel were important and what I should be allowed to know. I wanted answers and honesty, and it angered me that she apparently was going to be less than forthcoming.

"We have things to talk about," she finally said. "I want the doctor to look you over first."

"I've been out for three days. I need to find my daughter."

"I understand that, but you are not in any condition to go anywhere. Not right now. Mesa is safe, and you need to get your strength back."

"What happened?" I asked again.

"How much do you remember?"

I told her about working with the reclamation crews, about Kaften's attack on us, and his interrogation of me. I explained how they had shot me, cut off my finger, then driven me out to meet her. I told her I remembered being shot again, but that part was fuzzy, and I pointed to the scars on my chest.

She watched me soberly. She took a long drink of water to wash down the remains of her sandwich then brushed the crumbs from her fingers.

"That's good," she said. "You remember a lot. We were worried there may have been brain trauma from the blood loss. The doctor needs to run tests, and he's going to ask you questions. I can't tell you very much because it may interfere with his exam. I know it's upsetting, but please be patient."

"Why are you doing all this for me?" I asked.

She squeezed my hand, and her eyes went to the uneaten half of my sandwich. "Eat. We'll talk more later."

She stood and primly adjusted the robe around her, cinching it tighter at her slender waist. She took her empty plate and glass inside, closing the door behind her this time. I was left to study my reflection in the black glass, and I didn't care much for what I saw. I looked as old as I felt. My face was weathered and lined, my eyes dark and heavy. A shadow of beard was growing. More salt than pepper, it still had a few streaks of color. My hair had grown in some, but was still short and crisp. The gash in my jaw had been reduced to a thin line. I was hungry, but my appetite was gone. I forced myself to eat anyway, knowing that I needed the energy. Halfway through, I fell asleep for a time.

A man dressed in faded jeans and a white T-shirt lured me back to wakefulness by shaking my shoulder. My eyes opened easier this time. His skin was ruddy, and his nose, bulbous. He leaned in close, examining my eyes with a penlight.

"Good, good," he said in a thick Indian accent, then held up a long, thin finger and told me to follow it with my eyes. "Good, good," he said again. He introduced himself as Sanjar Hashmi, and we shook hands. Although he was old and seemed frail, he had a strong grip, and his hand was warm but powder dry.

"Do you remember your name?" he asked me.

"Jonah Everitt."

"That's right. Good."

The man was a broken record, and I was getting irritated. Doctors ranked right up there with heights in terms of enjoyment. He checked my pulse at my wrist, then jammed his fingers beneath my jaw, around the sides of my neck, and behind my ears. He told me to open wide and say, "Aaaaahhhhh."

He fished a coil of wire from his pocket then plugged one end into the port behind my ear and the other end into a palm-sized tablet reader. He tapped some buttons, watched the data scrolls carefully, then disconnected me.

"Blood pressure is good. So is your heart rate. How do you feel?" He slipped his hands beneath the robe. His fingers dug into the bullet wounds at my chest and back, and although the skin had been knitted shut, the flesh was still sensitive and tender, and he pressed hard.

"Sore," I said, wincing.

"Move your arm," he said. "This way." He swung his arm in a circle, up over his head and back down, as if he were swimming.

I followed his lead, but more slowly. "It's stiff," I said.

"Mmm," he said. "It will pass in a day or two. Keep working your arm. And your leg?"

He opened the robe, impassive to my nakedness, and pressed at the edges of scar tissue. "Extend your leg as far as you can. Rotate your foot. Good. Keep moving your limbs, you will be fine."

"Alice said three days have passed."

He met my eyes, and I got the impression, for the first time, that I was suddenly more than a specimen for him.

He pulled a chair over and sat in front of me.

"I kept you sedated, and you needed the rest. Your body had been under a tremendous amount of strain. Your vitals were very low, very weak. You had lost a lot of blood."

"It's kind of odd for a couple gunshot wounds to heal in three days, don't you think?"

I knew what they had done to me, and I wasn't really surprised by it. I wanted to hear him say it.

"I injected you with medichines. If I hadn't, you would have died."

"So you're a medichine man, huh?" I laughed, and so did he. I couldn't help but think of Kaften, though. My laughter died in my throat, and I curled my ruined hand into a fist to hide the damage.

"I am surprised you did not have them already. Usually, for a man with modifications such as yours, tech augments are hardly a surprise. When they are missing, though... that is surprising. Especially nowadays."

"I like staying connected," I admitted. "The health industry was never for me, though. I figured when it's time for me to go, I'll go. Didn't really need or want the medichines."

"It's interesting," he said, "how selective some people are. You have no problem tampering with your brain and your nervous system, conjoining them with artificiality and cybernetic enhancement, perhaps to live a better life, no? Yet you are still a bit cavalier about that life, no? And besides, medichines were free, so..."

"Nothing's free, Doc." I looked down at my hand.

"Without them, you would have surely died. The amount of fluids you lost—the medichines were required simply for replication procedures, to synthesize new compatible blood cells and to close your wounds."

The bullet had punched through my back and chest at a high velocity. Much of the damage that had been done to my internals was the result of concussive forces and bone fragmentation. The sucking chest wound had collapsed a lung, and the bullet and its kinetic energy had shattered ribs.

I could feel the tackiness of the adhesive patch the doctor had applied over the wound to help re-inflate the lung. Keeping me alive while they waited for the medichines to kick in had been a struggle, he said. It had taken almost a day before the nanos started working on tissue repair, and Hashmi had to rely on old-fashioned know-how to keep me stabilized.

"You are lucky I am a good doctor," he said, adding a warm smile to show he was being modest.

I thanked him for his efforts, and he asked me to stand. He braced me with one arm, and we walked around the deck until I said I was getting tired and had broken a sweat from the exertion. He and Alice rolled the bed back inside, turning what I had thought was a living room into a makeshift bedroom for me.

I was still confused by her goodwill, but I found myself lacking the energy to question her again. I wondered if the doctor's ministrations had been an effort on her part to keep me sedate, to wear me down, and avoid confronting her motivations.

She helped me into bed and adjusted the sheets, tucking me in with a sort of maternal affection. The doctor said good-bye, but I was already fading. When I closed my eyes again, Alice was sitting in a chair, her feet tucked beneath her, a datapad resting on her lap.

I slept long and deep, but my dreams were troubled with nightmare images of Mesa being brutalized by Kaften. His cybernetic hand plucked off her fingers, one by one, as she screamed my name, begging me for help and cursing me. He made me watch, but I was nothing more than a torso, suspended from the ceiling by chains and hooks. My arms and legs were missing; even my teeth were gone. I could not move. I could do nothing to help my daughter. Selene stood over me, sheathed in white, but she said nothing, and her eyes were hollow black pits. I choked out guttural screams, but I wasn't sure if the sound came from the physical me or the me inside my dreams.

"It's okay."

I needed a second for my eyes to focus. Alice was holding my hand.

"You were dreaming." She wiped away the sweat on my forehead. "It's okay," she said again.

I relaxed, easing my head back down to the pillow. Her hand rested on my shoulder. She was tired, and her hair was mussed. She wore cotton shorts and a pink top. Dawn was breaking outside, and the opaque door was clear.

"What time is it?"

"It's early. You slept all day yesterday."

"I need to go to the bathroom."

She helped me up, and I trudged along beside her with the IV stand while she showed me the way. The house was as spartan as I had thought. Nothing ornamental, except for a few empty vases that stood on a recessed shelving unit in the hallway. No photographs, no artwork. The house was beautiful, but as desolate as the ruins downtown. Whatever comfort it provided was artificial.

After I urinated, she asked me if I was ready for a shower, if I was strong enough.

"I don't think I need this, either," I said, holding out my arm and the coil of tubing that led to the IV. She found some cotton balls under the sink, then tore the tape away from the crook of my elbow and withdrew the needle. She pressed the cotton against the tiny wound, and I held it in place, leaning against the counter. The small needle hole closed after only a few seconds and left hardly a drop a blood on the cotton.

She turned on the shower and waited for the water to get warm. "That should be good," she said, testing it with her fingers. Steam started to build up against the frosted glass. "There's soap inside, and shampoo. I have clothes you can wear, as well."

She left me, closing the door behind her. The hot water felt good, and it helped to restore me. When I stepped out of the shower, a fresh shirt, pants, socks, and underwear awaited me on the counter, along with a pair of shoes on the floor. The shirt was a size too big, and the sleeves were too long, but everything else fit well. After dressing, I followed the scent of eggs and potatoes to the kitchen. It felt good to be walking on my own, although I was still stiff. I rotated my arm and flexed my fingers, trying to work out the kinks and the pain.

"Do you feel better?" Alice asked. She was sitting at an island in the center of the kitchen, reading from her data pad.

"I do, actually." I sat, and we ate. I was starving, and I washed the food down with eager gulps of fresh-squeezed orange juice.

"Do you think you'll be up for a trip this afternoon?"

"To where?"

"You asked why I am helping you. Do you remember that?"

I nodded, unsure of where, exactly, this was going.

"I want to show you why I am helping you."

"You can't just tell me?"

"It would be better to show you, to let you fully realize what I am about to ask of you."

I waited. The potatoes turned to a cool lump in my mouth, and I had to force them down.

"I want you to kill the man who killed my family," she said.

I nodded, starting to understand. Her next words

shook me to my core.

"He has Mesa."

CHAPTER NINE

"WHAT DID YOU DO BEFORE the war?" she asked me.

We had been driving in silence, coming down from the hills, heading back into Chinatown. I felt as if I'd been away for more than a few days, and I realized I was steeling myself, as if the world had been overturned in my absence.

The tinted windows cast Los Angeles in dark tones and deep, sinister shadows. Mesa was out there, somewhere in the ruins, and for a long moment, I struggled to pull myself away from the depressing scenery. Alice had no idea where Mesa was, although she assured me, again, that she was safe.

Alice sat beside me, dressed in a business suit, which was the sort of attire I was used to seeing her in. Gone were the cotton shorts and T-shirts of that morning. A double-breasted suit jacket hung loose over a dark, sleeveless blouse. She wore a gold tie and loose slacks, as well as matte pumps over bare feet.

I was dressed similarly. Polished black tassel shoes. A white shirt with too much starch in the collar. A wide black tie. I hadn't been dressed that well in more than a decade.

"I was an artist," I said. "And a teacher."

She raised one well-manicured eyebrow. "Really?"

I detected hesitancy in her voice, as if she wasn't quite sure I was serious.

"Really," I said. "I taught at City College. Had a few of my drawings published, but nothing big. I was putting together an exhibit at the Da Vinci Gallery before the invasion. I was using DRMR to chronicle memories and the passage of time."

"Using your memories?"

"Some, yes. Some were from friends and family, and some were from students who volunteered."

The exhibit was meant to be a display of the human experience. Birth and death. Perceptions on race and culture, prejudice and hate and anger, compassion, and sex. A full-sensory experience. The mems were all raw, unedited, and uncensored life. Visitors would have become intimately familiar with total strangers, vicariously lived numerous lifetimes, and experienced a multitude of moments.

"You were going to put human memories on display for everyone to share in? How would that have been any different than what corporations were already doing?" She tempered her criticism with a soft smile, but it did nothing to quiet her dismissive attitude.

"Cheaper admission fees. Not as watered down and sanitized as MemSpace."

She wasn't interested in my deflection, and her gaze

persisted, waiting for an authentic answer.

"I wanted it to be instructive," I said. "I wanted people to know where it came from, to think a bit more about what this technology is, what it can do, to be aware of what exactly it is they're sharing with strangers."

DRMR began as a military application developed by DARPA. Its goal had been to create better soldiers with better adaptive protocols, through cybernetic implants and bio-regulated software that would control natural neurological responses.

The Databiologic Receiver of Mnemonic Response captured and decoded the brain's signals as it responded to stimuli. The DRMR recorded visual reception, cognitive and emotional responses, flight-or-fight reflexes, brainwaves, blood pressure and pulse rates, digestion, and respiration. Built from a series of complex neural nets and bionano interfaces, it tapped into the thalamus, hippocampus, and the intraperietal sulcus, the part of the brain responsible for binding multiple stimuli into a memory.

DRMR turned human soldiers into ground-based biological military drones, allowing command centers to survey and monitor a fighter's responses to conditions in the field. By linking a combatant's standard medichine deployment with DRMR, command could regulate the body's hormonal responses, delay the onset of shock, and nullify pain receptors. If a soldier was about to panic, his or her superiors could note the biological alterations and take preventive measures to protect both that individual and the entire combat squad.

DARPA's corporate sponsors and academic researchers recognized the potential for DRMR in the public sector, particularly in law enforcement, public health, and entertainment. Soon enough, DRMR was adapted for civilian use. As with GPS, the Internet, digital photography, and the microwave, DRMR entered the public sector as barely a blip on anybody's radar. Slowly and progressively, it built its audience as large, multinational corporations sought ways to expand and exploit it. After surviving a few years on the fringe, the technology exploded across the globe and became a mainstay in everyday use.

"Were you born with it?" she asked.

"No. I didn't get implanted until I was in college."

Her smile grew larger. "Ah, a late bloomer."

"Young and dumb," I said.

Her fingers moved lightly across my knuckles, tracing the line of a vein along the back of my hand.

"I was born with it," she said. "First generation, implanted in vitro. I've never known a life without the tech."

In another twenty years, it was estimated that cybernetically enhanced individuals would outnumber those without it. Already, entire generations, mostly in Asia, were growing up in a constant state of connection, thanks to fetal implants. Some embrace it; others protest its vast potential for misuse.

"I remember what it was like," I said. "Before, I mean. We didn't need all this technology, this invasive constant connection, always on. Now everybody thinks we have to have it, that we're out of touch without it. Everybody's one thought away, retinal displays, recordable memories. We're machines now."

"You don't like it?"

"Some of it's good." I thought about tripping on DMT, the rush of death and the psychedelics it produced, the adrenaline and dopamine, and the colorful vivid high of expiration. Then I thought about playing back memories of Mesa, of Selene, and of our past life. It left a hollow void that I was quick to push away. "But if I had the option to do it over again, I don't think I'd let myself become this."

I could feel the phantom weight of the cybernetic port behind my ear, and I fingered it impatiently. Suddenly, it made me feel dirty.

"It's a culture shift," she said. "The old versus the new. It's always been like this, though. Buggies versus cars, print versus digital."

Staring deeply in my eyes, she reached behind my ear to pull my hand away from the port. "This is the new normal."

"People still have a choice."

She shrugged and looked out the window at the blur of destruction that slid by us. "Maybe somewhere else that's true."

My thoughts turned back toward Mesa, and I hoped for her safety. My fingernails worried at a small knot of fabric on the thigh of my pants, picking at the tiny, raised imperfection in the otherwise-smooth plane of cotton. I dug at it, trying to work the knot out to keep myself from going crazy with worry. I needed to fix something, anything, and that was the closest thing I could get my hands on.

"We're pulling up to a checkpoint," Hai said. His voice was tinny through the intercom, and we were separated from him by lightly tinted soundproofed glass. The car began to slow. Traffic was reduced to a long single lane, but the PRC were efficient and quick. They worked in groups. A soldier appeared at the driver's-side window and exchanged words with Hai. Two other soldiers walked the length of the car on each side, examining the wheel wells and underneath the car. The trunk released with a noisy *clunk*, and I watched it open then close a moment later. The guards waved us through a short time later.

"The checkpoints have increased steadily since the bombing a few days ago," Alice said. "Attacks against the PRC have been growing. It has them nervous."

"It's good to see you're not," I said. The checkpoint had caused a spike of nerves in me. They always did, but it dulled quickly as Alice covered my hand with hers.

"My business has brought me into contact with several members of the PacRim Coalition, and I've made friends both here and abroad over the last few years. I have little reason to be nervous."

"Is that how you found me?" I asked.

Her relationship with Kaften had been nagging at me, and I was annoyed by her lack of answers. After goading me into this trip by bringing up Mesa, she'd said very little. What she did say was cryptic and maddening. We'd spent most of the afternoon on opposite sides of her stilt house. She'd meditated while I fumed and worked myself up into an ever-increasing state of aggravation. She had promised answers, telling me I would be able to see it all for myself soon enough.

"I had learned of Kaften's attack on the reclamation sites—"

"Which you had me assigned to, through your little network of friends."

She shifted in her seat, crossing her legs. "Yes."

"I hope her data chip was worth it."

She broke eye contact. She actually seemed sad. "In some ways, yes. In others, no. I had hoped for more, but her memories were still an important recovery."

"What does that mean, exactly?"

She ignored the question, continuing with her earlier train of thought. "After the PRC was able to figure out who had been killed and who was missing, they—"

I interrupted again. "Kaften took others?"

"Two men from another site. Three of the work sites were attacked simultaneously. When I learned you were missing, I put out some feelers and learned that Kaften had been responsible."

"Does the PRC know he was responsible for the attack?"

"No. They've had a difficult time establishing credible intelligence on his group or where they operate out of. They're blaming the militias. Liberty's Children is even taking credit for it."

"He asked me about Jaime. He never asked me about you, though."

She said nothing.

"Who is he?"

"A soldier. Beyond that, I don't know much about him."

"Bullshit."

She sighed and plucked at the knee of her slacks. "I am a businesswoman, Jonah. I conduct business with multiple agencies, and I have a broad, diverse list of clients."

"You play everybody."

"You could say I'm a middleman."

"You could say I don't trust you."

"You could say I saved your life." She smiled, with a hint of a chill. She was enjoying the sparring and was at ease. I relaxed too, a bit.

"He's not militia," I said. "Who is he?"

She stared at me for a long while, assessing me. "He's corporate. Private army."

"Which means he's not from here. He came in from over the border. He had help."

"I'm sure he did, but you know as well as I do how porous the border really is. How did you know?"

"His clothes. His behavior. The way he treated me. Things he said."

She looked at my shortened index finger.

"What did you give him?"

"In the past, I've provided him with weapons and armaments, food, fresh water, supplies, and munitions."

"And where do you get all those?"

She shrugged. "As I said, I have a diverse list of clients."

"You also said you're a middleman."

"You are unusually questioning today, Jonah. I can't help but feel that our arrangement has shifted."

"Feel whatever the fuck you want. I want answers."

She shrugged again. "I already promised them to you."

I shrugged, too. "So give them to me."

She took a deep breath, reevaluating me. "I provided Kaften with long-range sniper rifles with subsonic sound suppressors, recoil dampeners, and visual acuity upgrades."

"Was that for me or for the chip you wanted?"

A quick stab of pain flickered across her eyes, but the truth had a habit of doing that to people. "Both. You were a package deal."

"Why? Why do that for me?"

Alice took my hand in hers and tugged at my fingers. I loosened my fist, and she ran a finger across the top of my shortened index finger.

"Because I know what he's capable of." She squeezed my hand and met my eyes. "And because I like you Jonah. I do consider you a friend, for whatever that may be worth to you. You've been loyal, and I appreciate your services to me."

I'd never seen her more heartfelt. She was a woman who casually used words as weapons, but this had been honest and tender. She squeezed my hand again then gently released it and refolded her hands together on her lap.

"How long has Kaften been here? What does he want?"

"Several months. And you already know what he wants."

Jaime. I sighed heavily, through my nose. "What was on the chip?"

"You will see soon." She laughed to soften the

aggravation those words brought. "It was a life. A woman's life. Her name was Ann Cornell, and she was from Des Moines."

"But that's not what you wanted."

"It was, in some ways."

"But not in others."

"No, not in others," she said. "I believe, in that regard, that I had already found it, thanks to you."

"The answer to who killed your parents."

"Yes," she said.

What she did next surprised me. With one simple movement, she completely disarmed and unnerved me. She slid closer to me, enough so that I could feel her warmth. Her movements were surprisingly comfortable, but the degree of familiarity she had presumed in taking my hand, and by sitting closer to me, put me on edge. Thanks to her, medichines coursed through my body, monitoring my vitals and overall health, making any necessary corrections. What else had been done to me while I was sedated? Alice could have picked apart my brain and studied my memories. Maybe she was attempting to play off familiar associations from my past.

I stared out the window, telling myself I was being paranoid. I watched her reflection in the glass, and she glanced at me every once in a while. It sent a shiver up my spine.

The faces that flickered past as we drove into Chinatown grew increasingly sad and somber. The people who lived there usually wore stoic expressions borne of hardship. They'd faced war and racism. Some had been held at gunpoint, shot, or beaten because their skin was too yellow or their eyes too slanted. In the time following the invasion, I'd seen the people there shift through the streets with blank, down-turned faces, but I'd also seen happiness. The people outside appeared haunted. Some were dazed or shell-shocked. I'd seen these expressions before, too many times.

"The market was attacked two days ago." Her voice was whisper soft, close to my ear. She was leaning over me, following my gaze. Safe from their eyes behind the tinted glass, we watched slack faces and hollow eyes.

"A suicide bomber came in the morning, early, while the crowds were thick. Thirty-seven people were killed," she said. "Another sixty were wounded. The attack was bad."

"Who's claiming responsibility?"

"The same group that attacked the 101."

Jaime. I said nothing, but her eyes searched mine, seeking some sort of confirmation, as if I shared responsibility for this attack.

"I lost two of my chefs," she said.

We were pulling up to her restaurant, one of many side businesses she engaged in. The Tong's reach was deeper than I had realized, based on what she had been willing to trade to Kaften for my release. The guardian lions reminded me again about yin and yang, about polar opposites. What did that make Alice and me?

"They were buying fish for that evening's dinner," she said.

I wanted to apologize, but stopped myself. I didn't have anything to be sorry about; it hadn't involved me. I had been far away, recuperating beside the ocean in her safe house. And she knew that. But still she expected me to take some of the blame, to share in her sorrow, and to feel contrite. It pissed me off.

"Were any chips collected?" I asked.

"We were able to gather a few. Not many."

"I'd like to experience them."

"I will include them with the others."

"Great," I said.

Her eyes narrowed briefly, as if she were passing judgment upon me. Whatever closeness had connected us in the car evaporated and was replaced by a sudden gulf.

I patted a lion on the head as we walked past. Inside, the dining room was dark and mostly empty. It took a moment for my eyes to adjust. We ignored the hostess—who was seated behind a small desk decorated with a calendar from 1966, an ancient white rotary telephone, and a small circulating desktop fan—and moved deeper into the building. A few tables had couples. One held a group of three, and another held four. Two people at the bar, one on each end, were drinking sake, separated by four small bowls of crispy wontons. Aside from a few robotic PetHuman servers dressed in ill-fitting green uniforms resembling 1960s People's Liberation Army attire, complete with green hats and red arm bands, that was it for the post-lunch crowd.

The restaurant was a classic take on China's Red Restaurants, and the themes of the Cultural Revolution were redolent and excessive to the point of mockery. Along the back wall was a large red-toned mural, a rendering of an old propaganda poster of Mao Zedong standing above a group of PLA soldiers, holding a little red book in one hand and an assault rifle in the other. Framed posters were hung between tables. We passed a print of a Red Guard standing over a pile of crucifixes and Buddha statues, ready to deliver a crushing blow with a sledgehammer. The only color in the black-and-white image belonged to Mao's red armband and the cityscape of the then-new Red China behind him.

Around us, red brick walls fought their way through white plaster, as if a bomb had gone off, exposing the underside of the revolution. Red Chinese paper lanterns hung from the ceiling, along with several large red Soviet hammer and sickle props and framed pictures of important communists such as Lenin, Marx, Castro, and Tito. Their imagery was miniscule compared to the rife displays of Mao.

"On Saturdays," Alice said, "we do shows. We have the PetHumans programmed to reenact stories from the Cultural Revolution, and customers come in to sing and dance. You should see it sometime."

I nodded, but said nothing. I watched a man eat dandelions, raw cucumbers, and a small plate of shrimp that would have cost more than fifty dollars before the war. His partner was enjoying a pork dish with a red-bean curd.

The kitchen was quiet. The PetHuman chefs made precise and swift movements as they prepared the lunch orders and readied the ingredients for the dinner crowd. Alice ignored them, and they paid no attention to us in return. I followed her through the prep area and the storeroom, to a metal door with a retinal scanner and palm pad.

"Your chefs, huh?" I said, unable to keep the disdain from my voice as I recalled her attempts at plying sympathy or guilt from me over her loss of personnel during the marketplace attack.

"I do have some human staff," she said, chafing at my words. "My executive chef and his sous chef were murdered at the marketplace."

"Why didn't you send the robots to pick up the groceries?"

"They lack olfactory programming. Not very useful for when unscrupulous vendors try to pass off rotting fish to robots who don't know any better."

I arched an eyebrow at her, unsure if she was making a joke.

"It's happened," she said. "Not to me, but to others. So I use humans to purchase foodstuffs."

She pressed her hand to the wall-mounted pad, and the

gizmos verified her optic coding, scanned her palm print, and came back as a match. A soft click released the door, and we went down a flight of creaky stairs to the basement. The security measures clearly meant this was not simply another stock room. They protected more than Alice's surplus of bok choi and snap peas.

LED lighting cast white, sterile light over a long row of access terminals, data storage bins, and digital pads. A group of fifty, mostly men—but I saw a few pockets of women, as well—busied themselves at the terminals. All of them were plugged in, and each had large collections of memory chips at their stations. I almost laughed in disbelief, shocked again at the reach of this Tong's fingers and of Alice's personal involvement.

"You're a memorialist," I said.

The look on my face made her smile. The gulf between us closed as she took my hand in hers, and I wondered how much of it had been my imagination, my paranoia. Our hands fit together nicely. She giggled, revealing her inner youth, how she must have been as a child filled with hope and promise, and I wondered when, exactly, it had all started to go wrong and what it had taken to make her the woman standing beside me.

"I'm a historian," she said, full of good cheer.

Our private joke.

I had told her that line some time ago because it sounded better than telling her I was a DRMR addict and a death fiend who sometimes needed the rush of DMT to stop myself from going crazy. She saw through it. She knew what I was.

I moved slowly down the aisle, watching the methodical work of chips being slotted into the physical media players, which weren't much different from the one I had, and plugged into data tablets for download and analysis. Once the security scans came back clean and the data was dumped, the workers unplugged the DRMR devices from the tablets and plugged the players directly into the data ports on their bodies. They had multiple levels of storage, each one a redundancy for back-up. The bioorganic machines inside their skulls could hold a virtually unlimited amount of information, but natural limitations imposed on how readily accessible that information could become. To make things easier, the same data was also recorded to cloud and nanoether storage as well as physical servers containing a host of yottabyte drives.

The memorialist movement had begun overseas, back when DRMR was still a largely underground technology and protested by the religious right and lawmakers who didn't understand it. A small collective of French data enthusiasts had taken it upon themselves to upload mem records on a nightly basis, always from different locations and with masked transfer protocols to avoid pings and trace-backs from the authorities. What began as a counterculture meme quickly grew into a world-wide following and birthed a technocratic movement that was religiously zealous in its perseveration of memory and the sanctity of the present.

Even after mem-sharing became a standard part of the daily grind, memorialists were fanatical in their devotion. They downloaded everything they could then organized and cross-referenced it through keywords and tagged data points. They searched for convergences of moments and lives, from deep, meaningful relationships to casual acquaintances and the interaction of random strangers in random situations. They hunted constantly for an answer to a question so intricately complicated that humanity had no words to ask it with.

I had once heard it explained that they were seeking the societal version of the grand unification theory—the answer to everything. The more religious members adhered to the simple maxim that God was in the details, and they believed that was what they were searching for. God. The invisible hand. The hidden force guiding every life and bringing one person into contact with another.

They were voyeurs and collectors, obsessed with the lives of others. The few memorialists I had met struck me as strange, cultish followers with an unhealthy degree of interest in other people's lives and actions, and not enough interest in their own. They were shy, socially inept, and prone to loneliness and isolation. They were troubled and psychologically damaged.

And I had found myself in a room full of them.

Nobody had exchanged words, not even a glance, with Alice and me, or even one another. They were lost in their own little worlds built from the existence of people they had never met or interacted with.

A tiny clock inside me was ticking down to zero. My heart ached with the realization that I was on borrowed time. If I didn't find Mesa soon, she would be lost to me forever. She could be anywhere, with anyone.

He has Mesa, Alice had said to me earlier. And whoever he was, she believed he had been responsible for the death of her parents.

All of the work stations were occupied, but Alice found me a chair, and I sat. She gave me a tablet, an outdated, one-Exabyte model that was nearly full. I pushed the data spike into the port behind my ear, felt the customary electric chill as the electronic receptors flared to life, and accepted the connection. The tablet felt heavier than it should have. It carried the weight of answers. The weight of knowledge. The weight of lives.

I pressed play.

CHAPTER
TEN

I FOLLOWED NEARLY A DOZEN datastreams, examining the most recent memfeeds first, from the previous two days—the marketplace bombing. The convergence web was incredibly complex and deeply layered, composed of fifty-nine solid data points and over five hundred null-void sectors. Ninety-seven people had been caught in the blast. Thirty-seven were killed instantly. The fifty-nine data points accounted for the memory stacks that had been harvested from the dead, the wounded, and witnesses who had allowed their memories to be shared. The null voids, buried between the verified data points, were a minor convergence web in their own right. Each void was a link in the larger web based on the implied, but unrecovered, observations of the people present at the market. The data points were organized and coherent enough to present a faithful recreation of events, but the system AI presented the voids as markers for missing information and extrapolated statistical data from the surrounding clusters.

Official estimates said that seven hundred people had been at the market within an hour of the explosion, but that figure didn't account for post-explosion crowds that had gathered out of curiosity or to help. The high number of visitors accounted for the many null voids processed by the AI. Visitor estimates were calculated from statistical records that averaged the traffic trends of visitors to the marketplace over the last decade and took into account local population counts, deaths during the war, weather fluctuations, fishing and crop yields, social trends, and the number of vendors and purchasers.

At the center of this web was a seven-year-old girl. She was four feet tall and weighed approximately fifty pounds. Her brown hair, which matched her eyes, was pulled into pigtails. She was a cute child, and according to the mathematical speculations two hundred and seventy-six people had seen her. She was wearing a small yellow vinyl backpack, scuffed sneakers, faded jeans that were worn thin at the knees, and a light-pink jacket that was zipped to her neck to hide the vest of explosives beneath it.

She held her head high, in a sort of odd defiance that was unnatural for a girl as young as she was. The war had made everyone older than their years. She carried herself with pride, and she made eye contact with several people, curtly nodding her head in acknowledgement. She stood at the center of the market, a large open parking lot with vendor stalls set up for the weekend, and waited.

People passed in thick clumps, bumping and jostling one another, but somehow steering clear of the young girl in their midst. She was a jetty in a sea of shoppers. A few brushed up against her. A large Asian woman almost knocked her over, apologizing brusquely as she shoved past, though she was clearly not at all sorry. The girl's face flushed with anger, as if she'd had enough.

The explosives she wore weighed almost a quarter of her body weight. Her backpack was loaded with nails and small ball bearings. When she detonated, shrapnel arced away from her body and into the crowd around her. The violence was sudden, loud, and horrendous.

None of her memories could be recovered. The explosion had vaporized her body.

I watched the turmoil of her actions through a composite filter. Fifty-nine memories merged by their commonalities presented a seamless view. The safety protocols were active, lest the adrenal dump of fifty-nine emotional sirens kill me. I doubted my brain would survive all of the conflicting physiological inputs—fear, horror, shock, adrenaline, flight responses. Pain receptors fired as I relived the trauma of shrapnel and the evacuation of hormones at the moment of death as I lay bleeding on the ground, squirming and in shock. I watched the dazed survivors, their eyes glassy, try to collect themselves, trying to comprehend what had happened. A few had nails sticking out of their arms, chests, and faces. Ricocheting metal had turned the face of the man next to me to hamburger. My ears buzzing, deafening me.

I didn't need the complete sensory dump to be set on edge by what I had witnessed—a girl so young and haunted, capable of taking her own life and numerous others. The conviction in her eyes had been frightening. She hadn't been angry until the fat woman ran into her, but even that had quickly been replaced by... almost docility, but that wasn't quite right. The calmness of assured purpose had soothed her and given her the power to obliterate herself and those around her.

The next datastream was another labyrinthine web of mnemonic episodes collected from the 101 bombing.

Traffic had been heavy but was stalled to a halt by a car crash. Confusion was a predominate theme of the memories, which had come from drivers caught at the edge of the blast zone or survivors who had witnessed the chaos or had been peripherally involved.

After multiple explosions, it became clear that the crash and the subsequent explosions had been coordinated. The lead vehicle had initiated the crash and caused a pile-up of thirty-some vehicles before drivers were able to stop. Traffic quickly grew congested between the exits, and three vehicles had smartly positioned themselves to block other motorists from exiting. The ramps onto the 101 were blocked by traffic attempting to merge, unaware of the problems on the freeway.

The lead car and all three cars blocking the exit ramp had been rigged with high-yield explosives. Smack-dab in the middle was a fifth car, also packed with high-yield explosives. A sixth car had inadvertently been caught in the pile-up, but it ultimately made very little difference to the plan.

The main aim of terrorism is to cause terror. The psychological effects of inexplicable acts of violence can be far more devastating to the group mentality than strategic warfare. Sometimes, there is virtually no difference between the two. The state of mind behind the first strike of shock-and-awe warfare is not terribly distinct from the mind-set of suicide bombers. What separates them are the responses of a state actor and the acknowledgement of warfare and battlefield conditions and readiness.

The drivers on the 101 had no warning. Many woke up that morning under the delusion that combat had officially ceased several months prior. They weren't aware that for some of their fellow commuters, the war was ongoing.

The synchronized explosions were huge. They took out neighboring vehicles, causing a chain of additional explosions. Shock and panic set in quickly as people tried to escape the blast zone. Some succeeded, by sheer miraculous luck, but most did not. Shrapnel tore through windows, killing passengers where the flames failed to reach.

Soon, a stampeding crowd of people who had escaped their vehicles moved between the lanes of traffic, seeking safety in numbers. A contingency existed for this, too. Farther back in traffic, well away from the explosion radius, gunfire erupted. A four-man death squad dressed in body armor and wearing masks took flanking positions across the highway. Shooting at random, their goal was to increase the body count and incite further panic in the already heavily stressed crowds. They killed forty people, chasing them down the off-ramps, shooting into the cars stalled there, killing the men, women, and children inside. Eventually, they stripped off their armor, abandoned their hardware, and disappeared into the confused crowds.

I had not known about the shootings. The explosions were well-publicized, but the news report I'd read had been heavily sanitized. I remembered congratulating Jaime for his efforts. The memory turned sour and left me queasy. Thinking about the little girl in the marketplace, my stomach threatened to heave itself out.

I backtracked through the convergence web to find the center point from which all of the data had populated. I was searching for one particular name, and I found it. I reloaded the web for the marketplace bombing, hunting for that central spoke. Again, I found the name and face I had known would be there.

Jaime Kristoff.

I choked down the rising gorge and moved farther back through the datastreams.

I knew he had been involved in other terror attacks. I had even colluded in some, but I was slowly realizing that

I had only ever known of a small fraction of the operation parameters. Jaime and his group of freedom fighters were highly compartmentalized, and they operated in cells. Nobody ever knew more than his or her small piece of involvement, so much so that I would not have been surprised to learn that the shooters on the 101 had been as surprised by the explosions as the other drivers.

Before me loomed the enormity of all the things I did not know—and did not want to know. I had been willfully ignorant and was content to stay that way. There were hundreds of datastreams in Alice's databank, and easily twice that many convergence webs. Thousands of episodic memories, capsule recognitions, and multiple layers of complex null voids—Alice and her team of memoralists had searched for them all, hoping to fill the voids and further strengthen and add to their datasets. But I did not want to know about any more of it.

I was feeling nauseous. My limbs were heavy and fidgety. I unplugged, needing a breather.

"Your face is pale," Alice said. She was sitting across from me, leaning intently toward me.

"This is…" I didn't know how to describe it. Intense. Unbelievable. Horrifying.

I had thought of Jaime as a fighter, a patriot, somebody I could cheer for. I had done small jobs for him in an effort to further his cause. We had both been ready for the war to be over and were stuck on the losing side. I had wanted my old life back, or at least some small sense of it. But seeing a child detonate herself in the middle of a crowded square for him—and the fact that he would use a little girl to serve his own ends in such grotesque fashion—I couldn't fathom that.

Extremists have come up with a hundred excuses for their actions, a hundred rationalizations to help them cope with their choices and to shrug off responsibility for the immorality of their behavior. Two datastreams in and after a small, cursory glimpse at several others, I found myself reevaluating Jaime, my relationship with him, and even my own actions.

I had taken jobs from him. Killed for him. The *chiang* for one. I'd been hired to do that job by both Jaime and Alice. He'd wanted the PRC general dead to further his own war, while she wanted the memory chips to further her own ends. I knew without looking that I would find a datastream devoted to the general.

"You need to see the rest," she said, maybe guessing at my thoughts.

"What else is there?" I asked.

"What do you know about the Berkley massacre?"

"Not much."

She squeezed my hand, urging me back down the rabbit hole. I took a deep breath to center myself and plugged in.

I waded through the streams, working my way backward. One of the earliest-archived entries had been from during the war. The date was familiar: May 26, the day of the massacre. The memory was another long, complex, interwoven map of convergences. I searched for the *chiang*, and was surprised to find that he was but one datapoint among thousands of others. I had figured him to be a more central figure in all of this, but the convergence point, the individual at the heart of it all, was a null void. The first half-dozen spokes to come out from the central null were also voids, with the data points finally populating the web two or three layers beyond that.

Some of the null voids had been identified and had either a name, a photograph, or, in a few cases, both. This time, Jaime was not the central null void. I didn't even see him within the first few layers of faces. There were hundreds of firefighters, policemen, National Guard, and US Army. Each bore a rank designation, and somebody had done the extra legwork to uncover their years of enlistment and length of service. I rescanned the profiles and studied the faces closely, but I couldn't find his. I was sure he had to be there, though. I went through the files again, taking my time, memorizing each face, and studying the contours of jaws and cheek bones, eye and hair color, hunting for a match.

The man identified as Samuel Hodgson had a passing familiarity. The name rang a bell, too. Kaften had asked me what I knew about him. I looked closer, reshaping the angle of view and drawing the face nearer. Small creases ran below his eyes, and the shape of his nose was about right. Hodgson was younger, and his face was unscarred. I called up the protocols for image analysis and tagged Hodgson for study. I received more than a hundred thousand hits and applied a smart filter to give me viewing angles of his left side. In the post-riot images, he was wearing a short-sleeve combat shirt with armor plating over it. He was smoking a cigarette and was clearly shaken. His left arm was exposed. Remembering Jamie's outdated tattoo and the animated nanos, I tagged a second filter using my mem ident and ran a correlation.

A *Times* photographer had shot a profile capture of Hodgson. The photographer had fired off a six-shot burst of images in rapid succession, and I could see the animation forming in freeze-frame across each image file. A small puff of smoke coming from a skull grew larger in each successive image, then disappeared. Hodgson was Kristoff. Kaften had questioned me about Hodsgon, then about Jaime, asking me what I really knew about the man. I realized I knew far less than I had thought, but I was satisfied I had found what I was looking for.

I stared at the faces again, noticing more similarities between Hodgson and Kristoff. The rest were strangers united in a common cause. At the center of the Berkeley massacre's map was a small regiment of men from the US Army.

The most heavily populated data points at the outlying rings were college students. Most were anti-war protestors, but other grassroots organizations had joined the coalition to express anti-violence, anti-corporate greed, plain old anti-business, anti-technology, anti-military, and anti-nano-everything viewpoints. The gathering had grown into a large demonstration for a multitude of voices, but most of the people in the crowd had been nothing more than hangers-on needing a purpose. The groups had originally united to protest the US and Canadian governments' policies of internment for Asians populating the Western Seaboard in the wake of PRC and PRC-sponsored terror attacks across North America.

Critics recalled the Japanese-American internment camps across the West Coast following the attacks on Pearl Harbor during World War II. The military had established exclusion zones across the entire Pacific Coast and rounded up anyone with Japanese ancestry and settled them in relocation camps. Based on the need to protect the country against espionage, the Supreme Court upheld the constitutionality of the executive order that had interned more than 100,000 people. The ruling had never been overturned.

Finding itself at war against Asian aggressors once again, the military had an easy claim for forced segregation. Lawyers and advocates spoke out against the targeted discrimination, but lower-level courts were powerless to overturn Supreme Court rulings. When the cases finally worked their way up to the higher levels, it was too late.

Soldiers from the Ninth Infantry Division deployed across the campus of the University of California, Berkeley, pushing through resistant crowds that booed and condemned them.

Rioting had broken out the night before, and explosions had rocked the Oxford Research Unit, the Haas Pavilion, and the Valley Life Sciences buildings. Students ransacked the Li Ka Shing Center's stem cell research labs and destroyed as many tissue cultures and as much imaging equipment as they could. The research and nanofabrication labs housed inside Sutardja Dai Hall had not fared any better, and even the cyber café had been decimated. Rioters had taken sledgehammers to the walls and floors, stolen whatever they could carry, and started fires in the garbage cans. The entire campus from Walnut Street to Durant at the southern edge had turned into a disaster area. Students set their own housing complexes on fire and camped on the grounds, content to live like bums if they thought it would send a message to the higher-ups.

The Ninth ID set up snipers in the carillon of Sather Tower, three hundred feet above the expansive campus. When things got rough for the ground-level troops, the bird's-eye snipers were able to precisely fire high-velocity rounds into the crowds. They took a lot of lives that day, but few regarded them as heroes in the days and weeks that followed.

UC Berkeley had many foreign students. PRC citizens and second-generation PacRim-Americans accounted for more than half of the university's enrollment. The military had orders to detain all 16,000-plus students for questioning, which consisted of a long series of loyalty questions, interrogations, and intensive background checks. Nearly all of them were relocated to detention centers in Kansas, Arkansas, Montana, Texas, and New Jersey.

In a show of solidarity, many student unions banded together to harbor fellow PacRim students and oppose the military. The initial protests on campus had been organized by the Stop the War Coalition, which was known for its attempts to remove military recruiters from the campus and its regular anti-war and anti-discrimination protests. Several members of the group had also been arrested early on for attempting to provoke violence against the police and National Guard.

Many of the PacRim students had turned to the Doe Memorial and Bancroft Libraries for shelter, near the Memorial Glade green zone. A thick concentration of protestors had gathered at the Glade, thousands of students holding signs and banners bemoaning the evils of American capitalism, corporatism, and militarism. They burned effigies of the President and dolls dressed in military uniforms. They set the American flag on fire and cheered and danced around the burning embers. They were loud in their persistent shouts, their voices filled with hatred and anger toward the men and women in uniform.

"Fuck you," they yelled, throwing their fists into the air as the Ninth ID set up a line to oppose them.

The squad commander attempted to give instructions and orders, but the crowd of protestors shouted over him, drowning out his words. They yelled for America to die and for these fascist pigs to get off their campus. Tempers flared and raged, and the shouts and voices quickly turned to action. Bottles were thrown, first plastic, then glass. Bricks and chunks of concrete followed.

The soldiers were dressed for crowd control and had come prepared for the riots. A line of men stood behind thick, clear shields, watching the violence unfold through toughened smart-glass helmet visors equipped with enhanced retinal displays. They held up well against the antagonizing forces, and the squad commander tried repeatedly to calm the protestors, giving them numerous warning to disperse. On the commander's fifth attempt at reasoning with the crowd, a beer bottle flung at his head shattered against his helmet. A piece of glass cut his cheek, and he decided then that the time for reasoning was over. The crowd was growing restless, and the violence was clearly escalating.

Armed with high-pressure hoses, they shot powerful jets of water into the crowd. They lobbed canisters of tear gas into the center of Memorial Glade, but a few protesters had been wise enough to bring masks, and they refused to be cowed. Those who had been blasted with the hoses found their feet again and charged forward, angry and hurt. Rubber bullets put down a few. Protestors from other sites around the campus struck up their own agitations, and numerous melees reached from one end of Berkeley to the other as the crowds lashed out against anybody in uniform—military, police, and even campus safety.

Any notion of crowd control went out the window almost as soon as Army soldiers set foot on the Glade. The mob assaulted their front lines, and the violence grew congested and bloody in short order. Someone, somewhere, threw a Molotov cocktail into the thick of it, and flames lashed out against soldiers and protestors. More Molotovs lit the air, and Hodgson screamed as his sleeves and combat gloves caught fire. He dropped and rolled in the grass to smother the flames. A young girl rushed up to him and kicked him in the face. Then she stabbed him with a large shard of glass she had in her hand.

Hodgson was dazed, on his back, smoke curling up from his arm. She straddled him and jammed the chunk of glass beneath the safety visor, into his skin, and yanked brutally. She tore open his face, gouging a thick trail down his cheek and jaw. He screamed and punched her, hard. She fell off him, her nose broken, both lips split open. He rolled and got his knees and hands under himself. Blood rushed down his face and into the grass. It took him a few moments to collect himself and find the strength to stand up. The medichines were already stitching his face back together, but I knew it wouldn't heal properly—it would leave a long, ropey scar as a reminder of that day. By the time he was on his feet, she was gone, off to find somebody else to attack.

The soldiers had been instructed to use rubber munitions, but at some point during the confrontation, they had switched back to standard steel-jacketed, armor-piercing rounds. Even though some of the college kids had thought to bring their own gas masks, not a single one of them wore anything more protective than blue jeans and T-shirts.

Whether the change in ammunition was an order passed down the chain of command or simply groupthink seizing control of the armed forces had never been clarified. The few after-action reports that had been made public—or rather, that had been unearthed by a small group of investigative journalists—all indicated that the soldiers hadn't been consciously aware of switching over to lethal ammo. Considering the hectic state of affairs and the stress of combat, I tended to believe them. Instinct and rote maneuvers took over, and in the heat of the moment, any filled ammo magazine was a good one, even the wrong type.

I watched Hodgson eject a magazine and drive in a new one. The wound on his face had reopened, but the blood flow was minimal. Pebbles of glass caught in the fabric of his combat fatigues glittered in the dying daylight. The sun set to the echoes of gunfire and screams, and the night held the promise of more violence. Streetlights had been broken or shot out. Dancing flames of burning trash and cars and from dorm rooms set ablaze by vandals illuminated the campus.

The uniforms fought to subdue the protestors, and dead bodies lay in the memorial pool, turning the water a dark crimson that was almost black in the dusk. Corpses, mostly protestors as well as a handful of policemen and soldiers, littered the campus. Their blood had made thick puddles of the mud and stained the grass of Memorial Glade red.

Weariness seized the crowd and the soldiers. The fight had gone out of nearly everybody, but a few protestors were perpetually belligerent. They were shot down quickly, lest they inspire others.

For a moment, everything was still, as if the world were on the edge of a gasp. Weariness turned into exhaustion. The rioters gave up, their faces screwed up with confusion and defeat. Police and Guardsman ordered everyone down to the ground then went about the business of handcuffing them. Children's faces shifted and hollowed as they realized they were not quite adults prepared for the harshness of reality. Whatever light had been in their eyes before the battle was extinguished.

The military separated the Asians and tagged them for the camps. The others went to jail. The Ninth ID regrouped and prepared to storm Doe Memorial Library. With the ground secured, helicopters flew in, and soldiers rappelled down and through the library skylights while the ground-level troops hustled up the stairs and breached the main entrance.

Beneath the library was the Gardner Collection, a four-story underground structure that housed the University's collection of three million volumes. Fifty-two miles of bookshelves filled the space, and a subterranean hallway connected the Doe and Moffitt Libraries. Inflatable mattresses, blankets, pillows, backpacks, propane lanterns, and table-top grills, along with assortments of canned goods and packets of dried meat, were scattered between the aisles of books. Sleeping bags were arranged atop study tables. The foreign students had made the tunnels and stacks their temporary home while waiting for the war to end so they could resume their lives and their studies.

They watched with wide eyes as the military descended upon them. They were frightened and confused. Some didn't even speak English well and did not understand the orders being issued to them.

Soldiers tore away bedsheets, yanked off pillowcases, and kicked over mattresses. The soldiers rummaged through bags, dumping their contents on the floor, spilling papers, pencils, pens, calculators, and textbooks. They examined the food, carelessly tossing it aside. They were on the hunt for weapons or anything that could be used as a weapon: knives, forks, and maybe spoons that had been sharpened to a point.

An older Asian man and his wife strode forward, their arms extended to either side of their bodies, protecting the cluster of students behind them as they stood before the soldiers. Both were getting up in years, and the man's hair was gray. The woman had a bird-like fragility to her, although her eyes were diamond hard.

"Please," he said. "They've done nothing wrong!"

Both were vaguely familiar. Their daughter had inherited her father's eyes and nose and her mother's mouth and the severe glare. Alice's parents.

Hodgson pushed the woman away roughly. Clearly distraught at the sight of his wife being manhandled by the soldier, the man strode forward, but his reward was a punch to the ribs. He stumbled forward, and I could see Hodgson was quickly losing control.

"You must stop this," the woman said. Her voice was stern, hardened from years of teaching, I guessed.

Hodgson was done fucking around. The last few hours had run him through the wringer, and he was clearly tired. Still, his eyes were calm and calculated as he raised his gun and shot her point-blank. The bullet entered below her right eye and punched through the back of her skull. Her blood splashed against her husband, and his mouth hung open in a perfect, disbelieving *O*. Then Hodgson turned the gun on him and fired.

None of the soldiers reacted, except to lift their guns. I watched groupthink prevail again as the soldiers opened fire on the huddled mass of students. Some ran between the stacks. Soldiers gave chase and gunned them down in the aisles. So scared that she was shouting in Chinese instead of English, one girl spun to confront the soldiers. She slipped on the loose sheets of paper and nearly lost her footing. She grabbed onto the bookshelf, dislodging a row of thin volumes and old bundles of paper lined with handwritten text. She regained her balance in time for a hail of bullets to send her down on her ass.

I watched as the soldier, emotionally disconnected from his action, backed away to regroup with the others as the girl's chest slowly deflated with her dying breath.

I was fatigued and stank of flop sweat. Although what I had seen had been horrifying, a part of me was disappointed. I was used to feeling the rush of the DMT, and it had been ages since my last high. I missed it and struggled to push aside that neediness. I tried to figure out how Alice must have felt when she'd seen all this.

She looked at me expectantly, her lips slightly parted. She pushed forward in her chair. "Do you see now?"

I did. "Hodgson. That was Jaime... The burns, the scar—that had to be him."

"He's aged a lot since the war ended, don't you think?"

"He must have played around with the nanos. Reversed them somehow to cause cellular decay so that he could look years older. He did a good job, too. Took me a few scans to key in on it."

I thought about her relationship with Jaime and about the *chiang* job. It didn't jibe, and that nagged at me. He was linked in, but aside from his own memories, any correlates were void. I didn't have the energy to plug back in, but I thought maybe Alice and I were finally on the same page. I sat still for a long minute, thinking.

I'd gotten the *chiang* job through Jaime, but I knew Alice had used him as a middleman. She had wanted him dead, and Jaime had gone along with it. According to the convergence web, they were tangentially linked.

"Jaime doesn't know you're a memorialist."

"No. Very few people do."

"So you both wanted the general dead, but for different reasons."

"General Yuan was born as a US citizen. He was at Berkeley during the time of the riots, in hiding in the basement of a residence hall with a few others. They were taken into detention and put in a relocation camp in Carlsbad. As part of his loyalty test, he was offered the chance to give up his citizenship, which he took. He was turned over to the PRC as part of a prisoner-exchange program when the war ended, part of the Northern Alliance's effort toward peacekeeping and restoring stability to the region. The PRC was impressed that he had so willingly severed his ties with America that they offered him the option of enlisting and granted him a field commendation and promotion. The publicity stunt helped the PacRim ruling body turn him into a media darling.

"The celebrity went to his head though, and he thought he could do anything. He had a penchant for whores, and he enjoyed hurting them. I couldn't tolerate any such transgressions, and I certainly would not allow that type of behavior to be repeated by others."

"So you killed him to send a message to your other PRC clients," I said.

She gave me a slight downward turn of her head, which I took for a nod.

"And Jaime?"

"And Jaime wanted the opportunity to be able to claim credit for the murder of a well-regarded and much-publicized official in his little guerrilla war."

"He had no idea there was ever any intersection in their lives?" I asked.

"Even if he did, what were the odds that it would surface? Again, he had no idea I was a memorialist or of the work I was doing. Convergences are an incredibly complex tapestry. Sometimes, the data leads to important discoveries. Other times, less so."

"Did you know they had converged?"

"No. This was one of those important, and surprising, discoveries. I wanted retribution against the *chiang* for his transgressions against an employee. Being a collector, I was naturally interested in his memories, but at no point did I suspect it was linked to other matters."

"But you knew Jaime had been involved in the massacre before you hired me."

"No," she said. "With convergences..." She seemed to search for the best way to piece together her words. "Oftentimes, we have disparate events, occurrences that we believe are unrelated. On one end, I had the Berkeley massacre and a small web of convergences from the few memory stacks we were able to access. On another end were protest rallies, or maybe the events of an ordinary day in somebody who would go on to become a protestor there. Sometimes, it takes an intermediate, an outside source or occurrence, that links them and brings it all into focus. That's how it was with the *chiang*. He was a linking point, but not central to the spoke."

She paused again, collecting her thoughts. "I've had this map of the massacre for a long time now. I'd known about Hodgson, but not about Jaime, that they were one and the same. When I first met Jaime, I had felt a certain familiarity, but I did not know why. His cover story was plausible, and he was much older than Hodgson, so I dismissed any worries. Until recently, I'd had no reason to doubt him."

"But somebody made you doubt him," I said, starting to fill in some of the blanks.

She nodded.

"Kaften," I said.

"He saw it almost instantly. It was ludicrous. But then I saw it, as well. And now you've seen it. We ran algorithms to compare facial recognition and defined similar characteristic, defining features. The feedback was impossible to ignore."

"Why would you show all this to Kaften?" I asked.

"It was part of my deal with him, to keep you alive and secure your release. Sniper rifles weren't enough. He wanted access to everything I had on Samuel Hodgson and Jaime Kristoff." She leaned back in her chair and crossed her ankles. She looked tired. She pushed a loose lock of hair back behind her ear. Her small, economical movements were a nicely feminine contrast to her business-like demeanor.

When I closed my eyes, I still saw images of the girl in the marketplace. Jaime's suicide bomber. Something hard and cold unfurled in my belly as my thoughts turned, again, to Mesa. I thought about Jaime and considered what Alice had said earlier. Her words rang in my head. *He has Mesa.*

"I want my daughter back," I said.

"I want to hire you for another job," she said.

I nodded for her to continue. I knew what she was going to say before the words were out.

"I want you to kill Jaime."

I nodded again.

Her eyes shot wide, and she was suddenly alert.

"I've lost contact with my driver," she said. "Hai is dead."

Muffled gunfire erupted upstairs.

CHAPTER ELEVEN

ALICE HANDED ME A GUN.

It had a good heft and felt comfortable in my hand. A Rossi .38. Six bullets in the chamber. Copper wad cutters equipped with Honeywell Micro ElectroMechanical Systems. More black-market military-grade goods that made me wonder how far and deep Alice's reach extended. The Honeywells were smart bullets, built from muscle wire that allowed them to change direction in flight based on targeted heat signatures. Good for shooting around corners or from behind cover.

It grew quiet upstairs, but the stillness was broken by a squeak of weight on the floorboards and the sound of cautious footsteps.

"We have to go," I said.

Alice ordered the memorialists to gather their memory

chips and get ready to leave. She pushed aside a filing cabinet, revealing a recessed fingerprint scanner in the wall. She pressed her thumb, index, and little finger of her right hand to the pad. A hidden door popped loose with a soft click, exposing a tunnel. She pushed the cabinet back into place, hiding the scanner again.

Above us, raised voices pled for their lives and were answered with gunfire. Alice urged the group through the tunnel, touching the shoulders of each as they passed, quietly whispering assurances to them. Her security measures upstairs would keep the gunmen from simply opening the door and waltzing down the stairs. They would probably use detcord to blast the door out of its frame, then breach the access well.

"C'mon," she said, pointing down the tunnel with her gun.

She pulled the door shut behind us, and there was a slight pop as the seal was reestablished. Luminescent panels in the ceiling lit the way for us.

"It's an old Prohibition tunnel," she said. "This restaurant has been in my family for many generations now."

"Must have been handy."

"Oh, yes," she said with a small grin.

It had been used for smuggling alcohol back in the 1920s, but it also connected several of her family's businesses and made for a convenient passage between buildings and handy storage space.

We hustled down the tunnel. A soft thump behind us told me the basement had been breached. It was simply a matter of time before the intruders figured out Alice's escape hatch and followed us into the corridors.

The tunnel was part of a system, splitting off into other arteries that ran beneath Chinatown. I watched the memorialists split off down different pathways, heading in different directions and disappearing from view.

"Where does this go?" I asked.

"Across the street. We can come up behind the restaurant, by the alley, where the car is."

"There could be more troops there," I said. "We don't know what we're up against or how many people are after us."

"No, we don't. But we need transportation. It won't hurt to look, and if we need to, we can always retreat back to the tunnels here."

"Presuming they don't find it first."

"Nothing about this situation is perfect, Jonah, and we don't have much in the way of options."

"Damned if we do. Damned if we don't."

She nodded. "Exactly. C'mon, through here."

She pressed her right hand to another scanner, repeating the gesture she had used a few minutes before. The door opened with a soft click, revealing a small room with refrigeration units, canned goods, and cartons of chicken and vegetable stock. The labels were all in Chinese. Aside from the foodstuffs, the room was empty.

We went up the stairs and into another empty room that was badly in need of a fresh coat of paint. I figured we were in the small apartment building across the street. We stood quietly, listening for any noises. After a few moments of silence, we proceeded to the side exit to the alley—a windowless steel door that only opened from the inside.

Alice had tucked a data pad into her waist earlier. She took it out and fiddled with it. I looked over her shoulder at the display and smirked.

"Radar?"

"It's come in handy," she said.

"Like the tunnel."

"Just like."

We watched the data load, giving us a wireframe view

of the alley. Two human-shaped heat signatures glowed orange on the screen. A warm blue glow defined the weapons they carried, but did little to tell us what kind of armaments or defenses they possessed.

"It's a small squad," I said, surprised.

"It's not PRC then. They would have the streets cordoned off."

"And we probably would have heard them coming from a mile away. This is surgical."

"PRC will be here soon, though. There has to be a patrol in the area, especially after the marketplace attack. We need to go," she said.

"The car?"

Alice shrugged. "Two on two. Even enough odds. You go left. I'll go right."

She pressed herself against the wall while I pushed open the door. The soldiers had been facing the restaurant, but they responded quickly as we rushed out of the apartment complex, our guns raised. Alice and I fired several shots, letting the bullets take care of the rest as we hurried to the car.

Finding the heat signatures we were aiming for, the smart bullets sought out flesh between the gaps in the soldiers' armor. Even though they had chest plating and Kevlar shirts and pants, the bullets were able to sniff out the exposed skin of their necks and faces and blast through. One fired his assault rifle as a death spasm ripped through him, but the recoil arc pulled the gun wide, spraying the car with bullets. The bulletproof windows chipped under the gunfire, but held strong. The bullets flattened into the glass. Thick concentric circles webbed out from the point of impact.

I tore the driver's-side door open while Alice climbed into the backseat. The front window was down. Hai sat there with a spent cigarette dangling between his lips, a bullet hole squared up against his temple. Ash fell as I pushed him over into the passenger seat and used his thumbprint ident to start the car.

I had my hands on the wheel when the door flew open. I turned in reflex, my face leaning into the punch, which rocked me sideways. My vision blurred, and a loud ringing filled my ears. I was sure my nose was broken.

He grabbed the front of my shirt, jerked me out of the car, and threw me to the ground. I kicked backward, scrambling away from him. I saw the two dead soldiers. This guy must have come from inside the restaurant after hearing the shots. He came forward, gun raised, ready to shoot me. The back door of the Lincoln opened, and Alice quietly emerged. She took a quick, silent step forward, her gun leading the way. She pushed it into the back of his neck and fired. The bullet tore clean through, obliterating the soldier's data port and its delicate wiring.

I scrambled toward the other two corpses, crab-crawling across the rough, unevenly patched road. "We need to chip them."

"There's no time," she said. "More are coming."

I kept going, trying to get my feet under me, but I was still dazed as the adrenaline did fucked-up things to my body. The signals weren't getting through my sluggish brain. I tried to protest, but she shut me down quickly.

"I'll take care of it," she said, an awful edge creeping into her voice. "We have to leave!" she screamed at me.

Her panic knocked some sense back into me, and I looked between her and the bodies. Then the choice was taken away from me.

The sharp smack of boots on concrete rushed toward us. The men's voices were raised, but the gunshots had dulled my hearing, and I couldn't make out their words. Bullets tore up the concrete at my feet, and I scrambled backward. Alice grabbed my arms and helped me up.

We dove into the car. I fell into the driver's seat, keeping my head low. The rear end of the car was under fire. Automatic machine gun rounds pocked the glass and thudded into the trunk lid. I hit the accelerator hard, and the big car surged, going nowhere. Still in park. I yanked on the selector as the bullets got closer. The rational part of my mind knew the car would be fine, that we were relatively safe, but I knew that the gunfire was drawing more and more attention—and the PRC—to us.

Its wheels grinding for purchase, the car lurched forward. I peeled out of the alley, squealing the tires as they finally caught the pavement.

Alice said, "Go left, then another left at the light." Her voice was surprisingly calm and collected, but a trace of fear in her eyes betrayed her worry.

She was quiet for a moment, then she said, "I need to know the routes. Where are the checkpoints now?" She was talking to one of her contacts within the PRC. She sounded nervous as she recounted what had happened at the restaurant and reported three dead in the alley. "They weren't PRC," she said. "We don't know who they were." She looked over at me. "Go right. Right, right here. Good, keep going straight now." She was quiet for another few moments, then she directed me to make a left turn.

"I need a favor," she said, then paused and sighed. "Fine. I will consider your debt cleared." Another pause. "Two dead men have information I need. Send PRC militia to my restaurant immediately, in the alley. You have to hurry."

I drove casually, merging with the traffic. My flight reflexes were telling me to go faster, to race away from all of this as quickly as I could. My heart was a jackrabbit kicking hard at my ribs. I watched the speed carefully, fearful of drawing attention to us. My eyes roamed back and forth from the rearview and side-view mirrors, watching for a tail. I changed lanes, getting all the way over to the right, then turned and looped around several blocks, Alice guiding us. Both of us waited for familiar cars to turn with us. None did. After a few tense minutes, I let out a long, slow breath, the tension slipping away ever so slightly. I spent several long, paranoid minutes making sure no one had followed as Alice told me which streets to avoid.

"How many people know about your beach house?" I asked.

"Not many. Why?"

Alice's house overlooked the deep-blue depths of the ocean. "We have to get rid of this body."

She mulled it over, weighing the risks. She decided the attempt was worth it and contacted one of her "employees," who went to check out the property and secure it.

Sweat crept down my face. In the passenger seat, a thin stream of blood trickled from the hole in Hai's head. Below his earlobe, the flesh was pure and smooth.

"Where are his dataports?" I asked. If they had done a download, we were sunk.

"His arm," Alice said.

Every time I'd seen Hai, he was wearing the same outfit: a suit jacket, solid black tie, and a button-down shirt—the same as he still wore. His undisturbed clothes gave me a sliver of hope.

"He's not a memorialist," Alice said. "Not a DRMR."

My heart finally started to ease up, my pulse slowing. My shoulders were tight, but the pressure was finally releasing.

"What are his upgrades?" I asked.

"Nothing memory based. He had a standard encrypted comm package and monitoring software. Nothing that could be traced or recorded or downloaded."

Made sense, I thought. Given her line of work, Alice had to be careful with her employees. It wouldn't do to have the hired help committing everything to hard memory. Even this extra layer of security wasn't foolproof or impenetrable. The tracking software would warn her if he veered away from their standard arrangements, and anyone who was able to break him and make him spill whatever secrets he knew wouldn't be able to do it fast enough to catch Alice unaware.

Although we hadn't seen any indications that we were being followed, we still took a long, circuitous path through the city, absorbing the patterns of movement around us, slowly growing more relaxed, but hardly complacent. Her source had come through for us. We didn't come across any checkpoints or random patrols. However, distant wailing sirens rushing past us set us both on edge.

It had been a long time since I had driven a car this nice and responsive. It gained speed quickly, and the brakes were equally reactive, so I had to be gentle with the pedals. Even under the weight of the armor, Kevlar padding, and bulletproof glass, the Lincoln was still easily maneuverable and smooth. Sleek and black, full of muscle, the car was a shark weaving through traffic.

By the time we made it to the house, night had fallen.

I put the car in the garage, and Alice introduced me to a muscular man named Niu. She went inside and came back with a large white bedsheet, which we wrapped around Hai. She carried a bucket of heavy chains we'd found in the garage while Niu and I carried the body down to the beach and into a waiting boat.

Niu piloted us out to sea. The running lights were off, and we saw no other boaters out on the calm water. We left the engine running, dropped anchor, then wrapped Hai in the chains. It took all three of us to hoist him up and over the port-side gunwale. We held him for a moment, and Alice closed her eyes to say a brief, silent prayer. She nodded when she was finished, and we pushed him off the edge and into the water. We watched as the ocean claimed him and he sank out of view.

Alice said nothing, but she wiped away a tear and sat by herself on a bench. When I went to her, she asked me to leave, her voice soft but raw. I stood in the small pilothouse with Niu. Neither of us spoke while he took us back to shore.

We parted in silence after climbing the steps from the beach. The house was safe enough, and Alice claimed that the three of us, plus her doctor, were the few individuals who knew of this property. Regardless, we would be keeping the guns close.

In the bathroom, I washed the gore off my face and neck. The suit jacket and white shirt were both ruined, so I stripped them off and dumped them on the floor. I was too jazzed to sleep, and my mind was racing with questions.

I was on edge from the adrenaline dump, nervous and twitchy with too much energy. I stood on the deck, letting the evening breeze wash over me. My eyes adjusted to the dark, and I watched the black expanse of water shifting in the night.

The door slid open behind me, and Alice's footfalls were soft against the wooden deck. She put her arms around my waist and pressed her face into my back. Her breath soaked through the fabric of my undershirt and warmed the skin beneath. Her hands moved across my chest, down to my waist, seeking proof of life after so much death. I turned in her grip, and she stared up at me expectantly as I leaned down to kiss her. She kissed back, hard, and untucked my shirt, pulling it off.

I ran my fingers through her long soft hair, bunching it up in a fist to pull her face close to mine, then pulling her head back to expose her slender neck. I kissed her shoulder and collarbone and nibbled at the base of her neck. Her fingers pressed against my skull as she breathed heavily.

Her cotton robe fell away easily. Her small breast fit

well in the palm of my hand. I ran my tongue over the scars on her chest, sinking to my knees, kissing my way down her body as she leaned against the railing. My heart was racing, and in the wake of the day's earlier violence and the adrenaline come-down, I was spent. But we needed each other. Needed the comfort of one another. Needed to feel alive after so much violence, murder, and death.

I nuzzled against her hips, the small patch of pubic hair soft beneath my lips, and she shifted her weight, parting her legs for me and raising one over my shoulder. I could taste ocean salt in the folds of her skin, and I inhaled her scent, exploring the crevice of her body with my tongue. Her fingers gripped the sides of my head again, pulling me closer as she tilted her hips forward, moving against my face.

She came, pushing me deep against her. She breathed hard and raggedly as her legs quivered. I kissed the inside of her thighs, slowly working my way back up her body. She urged me to my feet and led me back inside and to her bedroom.

I undressed, and she sat on the bed's edge before me. She took me in her mouth and moved slowly, her tongue lapping delicately at the tip, and I had to pull away. She took my hands, pulling me down on top of her. I attacked her neck, and she arched and squirmed beneath me, her nails scratching my back, grabbing my ass, and forcing me deeper inside her. We ground our bodies tightly against one another, and I was breathless when I exploded inside her.

She kissed me hard, then wrapped her arms and legs around me, hugging me. I kissed her face, tasting her tears. When I rolled off her, she spooned against me, and we slept for a time.

I woke up cold, in a tangle of sheets and limbs. I pulled myself free and felt around the floor in the dark for my pants. I found the small tablet in the pocket and went into the living room. Naked, I sat in a plush chair and pushed the data spike into my port. It sent a small, icy shiver through me.

I played around with the menu and the setting options. I wasn't interested in the webs and the spliced connectivity maps of groups of people surrounding a single event. I wanted individual memories, and I turned off the safety settings.

The memory of the *chiang's* final moments hung over me. It felt like forever since I had done this, and I was rigid with anticipation. My mouth was dry. My lips felt chapped. I decided to go for it and let the rush of endorphins flood through me. My heart galloped, on the verge of tearing itself apart, knowing that death was imminent. I felt what he had felt, and it gave me a rush because I remembered all of it from my own perspective. The feeling of power. The control of having a life in my hands. The weight of the gun. My finger curled around the trigger, and I whimpered in anguish, begging for my life. My heart raced, tears warming my face, dizzy from all the conflicting emotions. High from the adrenaline dump, I was both fidgety and fully in control. The warmth of muzzle flash bloomed against the back of my skull, singeing my hair beneath the flush of gasses and heat. Then nothing. White light blinded me, and my body thrilled with the rush of hundreds of chemicals as my pineal gland emptied itself.

The world tipped, and I fell down the rabbit hole, into a vortex of colors. Breathing became difficult, but I was incredibly relaxed and comfortable. I sank deeper into the couch, letting the DMT flood through me. The mem ended too quickly and left my head feeling heavy. I spent the next few minutes fighting through delirium and trying to collect myself, feeling drunk and loopy.

I crashed quickly and ended up in a funk. I was beyond

worn out, but I didn't want to go back to bed. My mind was still racing, caught up in too many thoughts. I wondered how Mesa was doing and how she was being treated.

I thought about the schoolgirl turned suicide bomber and about teaching Mesa how to shoot rifles and pistols, training her to take lives, trying to force her to kill. I wondered what kind of father that made me, and I loathed myself for all of it.

I had never wanted to be a father. I didn't want to be bothered by all the bullshit parents dealt with. The crying. The diapers. Two a.m. wake-up calls. The screaming and wailing. The idea of a kid was unbearable. I never understood why people put themselves through that willingly or why some people wanted that so badly for themselves. I was intent on never letting it happen until, of course, it happened.

Selene had wanted kids, but her pregnancy was a fluke. When she told me the test was positive, there had been a nervous hitch in her voice, and she'd struggled to keep eye contact with me. She knew how I felt about kids, and she was afraid of my reaction. My life, as I knew it, was over. And that was fine. In that moment, all of my defenses crumbled away with two simple words.

"I'm pregnant," she said.

With those two words, I was a father. I couldn't hold back the smile, or the tears, and I took her in my arms. We laughed, cried, and made love. Before I even saw the ultrasound or held her in my arms, that little girl-to-be wormed her way right into my heart and brought me a joy I'd never thought was possible.

But I'd lost her. I had tried everything I could think of to earn her love and her respect, to be her father. She was fine as a child, but those teenage years had been brutal, and she'd grown to hate me. Maybe I was too authoritarian, or maybe she knew I wasn't proper parenting material. She sensed it, the way animals sense fear. She turned against me and left a void deep inside me. She'd fought to become her own person, while I'd fought to keep her in my life, which pushed her farther away.

I missed her, and I missed the life we used to have. Driving her to school. Sharing dinner at the table in our house with her mother, Selene and me helping her with her math and science homework before sending her to bed. All of that was gone, and I had never realized how badly I needed it or how much I craved that stability.

Alice padded softly across the carpet behind me. She put her hand on my shoulder then bent over to kiss me, stretching her fingers down my chest.

"You're crying," she said, surprised.

I unplugged the data spike and set aside the tablet. "Just thinking."

She sat beside me and asked me what was wrong, but I ignored her question. I found myself needing the comfort her body provided, and she let me take her again. We made love slowly, and when I was spent, she lay against me. With her eyes closed, she asked if I was feeling better.

"I don't know," I said. "I need to find her. I need to get back to the camp."

"Echo Park?" she asked.

I nodded.

"Echo Park was attacked. She's not there. Neither is Jaime."

"What?" I shot up straight, pulling her with me. "Why didn't you tell me? What happened?" I was yelling, suddenly furious. I held her between both of my hands, squeezing her arms tightly. Fear crossed her face, but I didn't care. "What happened?"

She twisted free from my grip and shoved me away, kicking herself away from me, to the other end of the couch. Whatever closeness we'd enjoyed evaporated.

"Kaften," she said. She rubbed her arms and glared at me. "Asshole."

"I didn't know. You didn't tell me."

"God," she said. "There's so much happening..." She looked away from me, down at the floor.

"Tell me what happened. Kaften attacked the park?"

"This afternoon. It was a total slaughter. They knew where all the PRC were stationed, how to get in and out. They knew the security protocols, shift changes, everything. They had a lot of inside knowledge."

A cold stone dropped into the pit of my stomach. I already knew the answer, but asked anyway, "Inside knowledge from who?"

"From you," she said. "You were their inside man. They trawled your brain, plundered you for all you had. You gave him everything. He damn near walked right into the park. He had snipers take out the guards overlooking Echo camp, while he led a ground party to take out the street-level forces."

"He went after Jaime," I said. I knew Kaften wouldn't see any difference between the PRC and the park's inhabitants. "How bad was it?"

"Bad. He turned that park into a charnel."

"But Mesa... you said she was with Jaime. They weren't at the park?"

"They escaped, somehow. Kaften was looking for him, but couldn't find him anywhere. They disappeared. My sources confirmed Jaime was not among the dead. Neither was Mesa."

"Then where are they?"

"I don't know," she said.

"He attacked the park today? Before or after we were attacked?"

She shook her head. "I don't know. Why? You think that was Kaften, too?"

I thought about Kaften's regiment, their supplies, equipment—and their uniforms. The men outside of Alice's restaurant had used guns and worn clothing that didn't match Kaften's.

"No," I said. "I think that was Jaime. He was retaliating, sending a message. Does he know you trade with Kaften, that you supply him?"

"I don't know," she admitted. Then she conceded, "Maybe."

"Did Kaften lose any troops in the attack? Somebody Jaime could have trawled?"

"Not that I know of."

I paced the living room, massaging my scalp. A headache was growing behind my eyes. "Fuck," I yelled, exasperated.

Kaften. Jaime. Mesa. This whole thing was fucked. What the fuck was I wrapped up in? Where had it all gone sideways? What was the link, aside from me? What was missing?

I couldn't focus. I had too many things running free in my head, and the pain was blistering. I was the link between all of them. I was what had fucked it all up. I knew Jaime. I did work for him. I had admitted that much to Kaften. His bullshit soldier-boy idealism, fighting for a country that didn't even exist anymore, painted us all as traitors because... I swallowed and thought about it, then forced myself to admit it. Because we were terrorists. We attacked individuals, without much distinction between soldiers and citizens, and we lived among the enemy. We blew up marketplaces and attacked innocent bystanders in traffic. I was on the very edge of a cell, a freelancer without any true loyalty to any one cause. Kaften knew this, and he had soaked up every last drop of intel I had to offer.

I had given up Jaime to Kaften. I had given up those people in Echo Park. I had given up my own daughter.

I sat back down. "Jesus," I said, running my hand against the stubble of my scalp. I was sweating, and the hairs on my neck and arm stood on end. "I did this."

Alice looked at me but didn't move. I wanted to feel the warmth of her body pressed against me, but I made no motion for her to come to me, so she stayed put, tucked into the corner of the sofa.

"I think Jaime knows you betrayed him," I said.

She looked at me sharply.

"He sent his death squad to kill you. Or to kill me. Or both of us. Maybe he knows I gave him up to Kaften, and he decided to punish us. Either way, that squad at the restaurant, that was Jaime."

I focused harder on it and ran the algos, trace summaries, and comparisons. In the end, I was fairly sure the same squad that had killed all those people on the 101 had come after us at the restaurant.

"Then I feel even less remorse over their deaths than before," she said.

"Why did you support them?" I asked.

She didn't answer for a long time. Then she said, "I am Tong, but I am also American. I was born here, raised here. I lost too many loved ones, too many friends, in the war. The PRC is my enemy as much as they are Kaften's and Jaime's. With those two men, I see equal goals, if not equals means. It is their idealism surrounding their methods that divides them, but for me, as an outsider, I see that they seek the same outcomes. They want the PRC gone, and I understand that desire. The PRC caused so many problems for all of us. They are the reason my parents are dead, even though Jaime pulled the trigger..."

She paused, choosing her words carefully. "If we removed the PRC, there would have been no chance for convergence. If we charted it all as a system of data, the PRC would lie at the center of the convergence map, the root of all this evil and division.

"Supporting Jaime and Kaften is good business, which is why I also provide an esoteric array of services to the PRC. I will not limit my customer base, even if I have moral oppositions to the systems and governments they serve, but it also allows me to learn things about those larger data sets. It gives me information, which has far more utility in the long run. Does that answer your question?"

"Maybe," I said. "I think so."

After a time, she shifted back to my side of the couch, ready to reestablish contact.

"Your parents weren't Tong?"

"No," she said. "I came into this business through my uncle. I kept it secret from my parents. They never knew. After their death, my uncle raised me. In some ways, I find it a blessing that they died ignorant."

She curled against me and looped her arm around one of mine, pulling herself close to me. She rested her head against my chest. "I would do anything to have some semblance of my old life back. To have a family again. To be a daughter again."

I kissed her forehead, and we stopped talking. We cuddled on the sofa, enjoying one another's warmth. I pulled a blanket from over the back of the couch and draped it over us, and we slept.

CHAPTER TWELVE

MEMSEQ0500188986

MY FACE WAS PUSHED DOWN into cold earth. Mesa was beside me, her eyes pleading with me, begging me to do something. I raised my head, and the butt of a rifle crashed into my temple, leaving me dazed and seeing double. My arms were pulled behind me and secured with a loop of plastic. I watched as the same was done to her, thankfully less violently. She had been pushed down roughly, and the grit and rocks had left minor scrapes on her dirty face. Her hair was disheveled, and the fight had gone out of her.

We were hauled to our feet and dragged in opposite directions. We watched one another until we were forced into the cargo hold of separate transport jets, and then she was gone. Her eyes screamed at me, asking for help, asking me to do something—anything—to fight for her. But I didn't.

I was shoved into the hold and pushed forward until I fell into a seat. The door was thrown shut, and I sat in the darkness with the others. Nobody said a word. The PRC barked at us in a language we couldn't understand, so they screamed louder, making their words even more indistinct. I had no idea what I was asked or what I was being told. It earned me two loose teeth, bruised cheeks, and a few bruised ribs that felt just short of broken. My seatmate received the same method of interrogation.

The jet rumbled, vibrating my feet, as it lifted off with a surging moment of weightlessness that made my stomach flop. I closed my eyes and tried to focus on something other than the burning pain that racked my body. Thinking about Mesa made everything ache worse.

The cargo ship landed on a rooftop helipad, and we were escorted into the building and down a freight elevator to the ground floor. We were met by more guards and more questions. Some of us answered; some didn't. Those of us who did gave our names and denied any serial numbers or military service. An older, smaller man was removed from our group and severely beaten into unconsciousness. We were asked the same questions again.

Later, we were taken to the showers and deloused. Our heads were shaved, and we were given razors so that we could shave off all of our body hair under the supervision of an armed guard. Then our group was led, nude, to the prison commissary, where we were issued clothing.

After dinner, we were allowed to go outside. I took in the view. The Golden Gate Bridge had collapsed into San

Francisco Bay, which was a graveyard of ships and boats. Below all that were the bodies. The city was a distant dying ember.

"Hell of a view, ain't it?" a voice at my shoulder said.

I shrugged. "I was looking forward to an island vacation."

He smiled, the kind that indicated he thought I was stupid. Or maybe I was the sort of stupid he favored. He stuck out a hand, and we shook. He was an older man, in his sixties maybe.

"Jaime."

"Jonah."

"Under the circumstances, I can't really say it's all that good to meet you."

We talked for a while, mostly about nothing. Nice weather. Hell of a war. You hear any news? The attacks on DC and New York had fucked things up good, and our satellites were all out of commission after that thing in Taiwan. When we ran out of bullshit small talk, we took a casual walk, not saying anything, sizing up one another in the silence.

"What're you in for?"

"Nothing."

We laughed, figuring we were officially prisoners.

"Ever been here before?"

No," I said. "Only ever saw it in the movies."

The sunset's rays refracted through the dust over the bay—the dust of bridges destroyed, a city ruined, and lives lost.

"Hell of a view," Jaime said again. He lit a cigarette, shook another one loose from the pack, and offered it to me. We smoked while the sunlight died away, then we drifted apart.

A siren bleated, and a voice over the loudspeaker ordered everyone back inside. We went through another round of inspections as our retinas were scanned and compared against their database records, and those of us who were new were assigned what our guards euphemistically called "housing."

My cell was small, barely wider than me. I watched other people fill theirs and recognized that most of the cellmates had a familiarity with one another. I recognized a husband and wife from the mountains. Mesa was nowhere to be found. I walked down the corridor, but a guard stopped me and asked me where I was supposed to be. He nudged me back toward my cell. The door slid shut and locked. A short while later, the lights went out, throwing the corridor into perfect blackness.

Sleep did not come easily, despite the quiet. I dozed in fits and starts, and when the lights came on in the morning, I rose slowly, ragged and unfit for the day.

After morning roll call, the newbies were separated. I saw Mesa, finally. She was ahead of me by several people, and when I called to her, she ignored me. I called again, louder, and got smacked in the belly with a shock stick. The guard told me to shut up, and my stomach burned. A thick wad of bile stuck in my throat. The muscles in my abdomen kept twitching and wouldn't relax, forcing me to walk hunched over.

The guards had us form a line outside an office. Grateful for the chance to relax a bit, I leaned against the wall, waiting for my stomach to settle down. One by one, people went into the office. Mesa was ahead of me, and I watched as she entered the room, stayed for a time, then came back out to resume her place in line.

When my turn came, I passed by her and nodded. She ignored me. The room was barren, save for one beat-up desk at its center and two chairs. The one behind the desk was occupied by a slim, elderly Asian man, and the other in front of it was empty. He pointed to the empty chair, and I sat.

He introduced himself as *Shàngwèi*—Captain—Song. A second officer standing beside the desk was *Xuéyuán* Yu, an officer cadet. Yu held a scanner to my eye and processed my identity. I gave him my name, and he assigned it to the number on my clothing. I could have given him any name, really. The EMP blasts had ruined the data files, and I was sure I wasn't on anybody's radar. No police record. No military service record. I was nobody, and I could be anybody. I could have lied, but I didn't. I liked who I was.

"We have brought you here to ask you if you would renounce your American citizenship and swear oath to the Pacific Rim Coalition."

"No, I would not."

Song rested the pad on the desktop, squaring it against the desk's edge.

"You are aware that the American government has dissolved?" he asked.

"I am. I have not pledged any loyalty to the Northern Alliance. Or the Free States."

"I understand that you attacked and killed several of my men."

"Your men have attacked and killed far more of mine than I have of yours."

He shrugged, looking bored. "This is war. It is true. But you have no country, and you fight for no one. Then you are a terrorist."

"Call me whatever you want."

"Where is a man to go when he has no country, no home?"

"I don't know. I kind of like it here." Drab, gray walls surrounded us. "It's soothing."

He smiled a big toothy grin, baring yellowed teeth with bits of food stuck between and to them, along with swollen, infected gums.

"The UN has demanded that any prisoners we take be treated in accordance to the rules of war. Even terrorists are to be regarded as equal to a soldier and given the same privileges. The same... hospitalities?"

"Super."

"Do not be glib. We are discussing your future."

"You're asking me to leave my home, to fuck off to Montana or Quebec."

"This is so."

"No. I'm staying here."

"This facility is set to close at the end of the year. We are setting up a camp for the displaced population under the supervision of the United Nations until such a time that we can determine what to do with you."

After the government dissolved in surrender, most of the states were repatriated under the Alliance. A few—Texas and much of the Bible Belt—held out and created their own coalitions. For those of us in California, the ones who stayed behind, we had no country and no citizenship. Although the Alliance had made it clear that we were welcome within their borders, the UN had argued forcefully that the PRC needed to establish a green zone for war refugees and political or military prisoners.

Alcatraz was one of almost a dozen such zones spread across the state's nearly 164,000 square miles. The hope was that, eventually, tensions would ease to the point where the unclassified indigenous would be granted visas or permanent residency in California, so that we would still be able to call the state home. Although PRC's public relations staffers never said it, their government's desire was to see anyone who was unwilling to swear fealty to them leave. Politically, it was going to be a long, rocky road made worse by bickering, short-sighted politicians who lacked any clear resolutions or ideas to solve the problem.

"I saw families in the other cells. I want to see my

daughter."

"Who is your daughter?"

I gave him her name. He picked up the data tablet again and searched for her. "She stated she was here alone, that she has no family."

"She's my daughter."

"I see." He thought it over, then squared the pad against the desk. "I will have her moved to your cell promptly. Is there anything else?"

"No."

A short while after returning to my cell, Mesa stomped in angrily. I was glad to see her, but when I tried to put my arms around her, she pushed away and ducked around me. She threw herself up on the top bunk.

"Are you all right?" I asked. "Did they hurt you?"

She said nothing.

"I'm glad to see you."

"You're such an asshole." Her words were broken, and she choked down a sob. When she finally faced me, tears were running down her face. "I don't want to even fucking know you. And I don't want to make bullshit small talk with you. Just leave me the fuck alone."

"What is your problem?" I shouted. Her anger was infectious, and my voice was getting deeper and louder, turning almost to a growl. "And secondly, you don't talk to me like that. I'm your father."

"You're a fucking murderer," she said. "You're a coward and a killer."

I was standing too close, and she lashed out with a swift kick at my face. I dodged it, her small foot passing a hair's breadth from my nose. When I stepped forward, she scooted away on the mattress, pressing herself against the wall, and curled up.

"Don't you come near me," she said.

I glared at her. She glared back. Her eyes were hard

and too old for her child's face. Everybody had always said Mesa had inherited my eyes, and they were right. Familiar hate and fear rested in those eyes, and that was my fault. I wondered how the hell it had come to this. How had I screwed up so much to have ruined her so badly? After a long, stupid minute I sank down to my own mattress. She cried, occasionally making long, dramatic sighs to let me know she was still pissed off.

I thought about all the ways my life had gone wrong. I was getting pissed off with her, with myself, with everything. Rage boiled inside me. I needed to move, to escape.

"That's right," she called at my back. "Run away, you coward. That's what you're good at! Just leave me here alone!"

I could feel the eyes burning into my back, that itchy crawl of my fellow inmates' gazes pressing upon me. Their eyes held concern and pity, but also anger—and blame. They were questioning my capability as a parent, and I couldn't really fault them. I wasn't cut out for that shit. I couldn't deal with Mesa. I couldn't handle her. I barely understood her half the time. She was Selene's baby girl. Selene's had been the magic touch, the one that always stopped Mesa from crying, the one that had comforted her as a small child, that had told her everything was fine. They'd always had an easier time relating and talking with one another. Mesa and I—we never knew what to say.

Fuck it. I needed fresh air and a walk.

I took to the prison grounds again and walked the perimeter, as I had the day before. I spent a long time walking slowly, my hands stuffed in my pockets, trying not to think about anything while errant thoughts and recriminations warred. I loved my daughter, but sometimes, she could be a real bitch who was impossible to handle. She got that from her mother. I missed Selene and wished she were there to deal with Mesa instead.

"Yo, Jonah." Jaime was about a yard ahead of me, sitting on the ground, resting against the fence. He patted the ground beside him. "Pop a squat," he said. "Girl problems, huh?" A sly grin curled around the cigarette in his mouth.

I shot him a questioning look.

"Word travels quick around here. Ain't no secrets, 'specially when they got a mouth like your girl there."

"My daughter. She's a handful."

"Yeah, well, she is a woman. You ever think it'd be different, you're a fool." He said it casually, with good humor, and I gave him a dry chuckle. That was just how Jaime was. His easygoing attitude made it difficult not to get sucked in by his charm.

He asked me if I believed in God, and I started to question my assessment of him. The last thing I needed was a creepy evangelist trying to extol the virtues of some bullshit religion on me.

"No," I said, putting enough edge into it to let him know I wouldn't brook anything further.

"Why not?" he asked.

I looked at him, letting him know I wasn't in the mood. Didn't work.

"C'mon. Seriously, man, why not? Look, I'm not much of a believer myself. I'm just curious why other people believe or why they don't. It's a point of interest is all."

"Never saw any evidence he was real, and I always thought the Bible's just a book."

He pointed the cigarette smoke at the port behind my ear. He seemed to mull over my words then asked, "You a dreamer?"

I nodded.

He took a chip from his pocket and passed it to me. "You ever see the snuffs?"

"No," I said. "How'd you get this?"

He looked at me as if I were a simpleton, but the expression passed quickly. "I've made a few friends here and there. Got this one on the sly."

"What's it like?"

He shrugged. "It's like becoming personally acquainted with death, what it feels like. Lets you know it's nothing to be afraid of, that it feels good."

His eyes tracked off, lost in memory. I was suddenly uncomfortable with the route our talk had taken and was preparing to stand up and leave.

"Why do you think they're illegal?" he asked, still staring off into the distance as if I weren't even there.

It was my turn to look at him as if he were the simpleton. I shrugged, not sure where the conversation was going, not really wanting to get bogged down by a debate. I figured things would go easier if I let him say his piece and move on. "Because it encourages murder?"

"No," he said, shaking his head, a spark in his eye; he was playing with me. "Because it answers the God question." He cracked a smile, warming to the discussion. "The whole point of religion is that you get a reward in the end, right? Religion was created by men who understood life sucks, so they invented God. Said he's watching you and keeping score, and if you play your cards right, you get to go to heaven. You get to leave behind all this shit and trade up for an afterlife of bliss and joy. And people buy into this shit. They kill and die for it, they believe it so bad."

He paused to take a hit off the cigarette and to make sure I was paying attention. I nodded and encouraged him along, curious despite myself.

"Then DRMR comes along. People start to wonder. Maybe they can find the truth, see if God and heaven are real. That's why the snuffs are illegal. It raised too many questions, and gave too many answers people didn't like."

He held up the chip between us, showing it to me. Smoke from his cigarette curled up and away, and he took another drag. He dropped the chip in my hand and pointed at it.

"You got God right there in your hand. You play that fucker and feel good, and you just know. Every time you hit the end, that little deathly sweet spot and the chemical flood it triggers in your brain, that's your reward for this long, drawn out shit storm of a life. You get to go out with a quick high, the best high, and that's heaven. That's it, man. The end."

I stared at the chip. A small square of metal barely the size of my pinkie nail, it was almost translucent and shiny. "So, how did you find God?" I asked him.

"I guess you could say my wife introduced me to him." He sat there, an elbow propped up against his knee while he smoked and stared off into the distance. He started to speak again, but instead closed his mouth around the cigarette and took a long drag. He held the smoke for a while before slowly releasing it. Finally, he said, "She died in the bombings. We'd gone to the shelters they'd set up in the subways—you know the ones?"

I nodded, urging him onward.

"The subways were supposed to be safe, supposed to protect us from the aerial bombing campaigns. And it did. They had some military checkpoints at the entranceways, something defensible, I suppose. National Guard, local police. Supposed to make us feel better about our odds of survival.

"PRC didn't have much compunction about targeting non-combatants, and they didn't give two shits about the UN crying foul over it. The UN was a bunch of toothless old women, though. PRC knew that much, and they knew the easiest way to win the war was to make it terrifying for all of us. Knew we'd cave when the going got rough. So they bombed the shit out of everything from above and sent in a unit on the ground, a small force that was able to do clean-up. Took our little National Guard protectors right out, quick and efficient. Then they tossed grenades down into our little hidey-hole and left.

"My wife got caught in the blast. Shrapnel tore her up, took out some of her throat. She was dead before she really knew what was happening. I was a few feet over, but it was far enough away."

He took a long drag off his smoke and slowly exhaled. "You know that saying, right? Close only counts in horseshoes and hand grenades? Well, I was fucking this close." He held his thumb a scant inch apart from his index finger.

"I was close, but she was closer. And that was that. But she was my wife, you know? My life. I couldn't leave her behind. Her soul, her heart, all those things that make her who she is. I couldn't do it. I did a back-up. Later, I'd console myself with playbacks, trying to feel her love. I learned so much about her, about the way she thought, what she believed. I learned about how much she hoped. About what a dreamer she was. She believed in God. I kinda knew that she did, but then I learned how much she really believed. She was one of the faithful, man. And she taught me. And then I got to the part where she died... that flash of light, that chemical rush. She was dead before she even knew it, but I swear a part of her did know. She knew, and she believed. So I guess I believe. What you got in your hand there, it's a simple suicide, mind you, but it has value."

He ground the cigarette on the gravel path and struggled to stand. He had to roll onto his knees, get one foot underneath, push up and get the other foot there, holding onto the chain-link fence for support as he hauled himself up. "Bum knees," he said by way of explanation.

"Don't get old, man."

I watched him walk away then looked at the chip in my hand. Our belongings had been confiscated from the campsite and were being catalogued and stored in the commissary. We were welcome to gather whatever we wanted. DRMR was considered to be a basic good, allowable under the prisoner of war provisions following a flurry of protests and petitions to the UN from the ACLU, Amnesty International, and the Occupy movements. Cybernetic enhancements were ruled to be a commodity no different from music, books, television, and computer access. They were, therefore, allowed to all prisoners in America and most other democracies. The PRC had been pressured to allow some measure of American rights to the POWs, and eventually, they relented. It had become a joke that even if the US Army lost, the lawyers would kill the PRC for sure.

I pocketed the chip and went to the commissary. An hour later, I'd found the few belongings I cared about—my DRMR unit, a data pad, a chip of images of Selene and Mesa, some paper, and a digital pencil. Photographs from another era... I spent another hour rooting around for Mesa's stuff, bagging what I could. I found her backpack, but it felt light. I undid the zippers and found a stuffed penguin. Mr. Ziggles. I smiled and zipped up the pack. Slinging it over my shoulder, I made my way back to my cell.

Mesa had cried herself to sleep, and I listened to her soft snores. I put her bag on the desk and let Mr. Ziggles have some air, then lay down. I dug out the chip, trying to decide whether or not I wanted to play it. Jaime had called it a reward, and I needed to be rewarded for something. I had that itching again, that crawling under my skin that made me long for an escape.

I juggled the chip between my fingers, contemplating it.

I hadn't experienced an actual snuff before. My knowledge of them was purely academic. Even in my art installation, the vagaries of a snuff chip were verboten, mostly so that I could stay on the right side of the law. Snuffs raised certain moral and ethical quandaries that I hadn't been ready to tackle. Various radical groups and lawyers eager to profit in cases argued that snuff chips were as legal a form of expression as gay pride marches and exhibitionism; however, the courts went unmoved. Legally, the courts said, rape was rape and murder was murder. They were among the worst travesties in a broad spectrum of human frailties, and no one should profit—either financially or emotionally—from such violent transgressions.

My art display had consisted of a wide range of human experiences. One woman had wanted to donate the memory of her rape, the emotional fallout, and recovery, but I'd declined. I understood her reasoning, but I was afraid that its inclusion would generate the wrong kind of attention and criticism. Most of the memories were donations or had been obtained from MemSpace, Episodic, and other public domain sites. I understood the laws and the rulings against snuff, but a certain curiosity surrounded it. A notion of taboo. The promise of an experience unlike any other.

I'd heard the arguments for and against. I was curious why Jaime had passed it along to me. He was a snake oil salesman, but his charisma was unmistakable, and it made him a likeable sort.

I inserted the chip then the data spike. I listened to my daughter snore, and then I pushed play. The jolt shook me to my core and left me gasping for air. I fell, even though I was lying down and hadn't moved, and the sensations were so rich and compelling that "euphoria" failed to properly define the experience. In the end, I was shaken and still as vibrant colors washed over me, numbing me. I smiled. In the wake of my high, I understood the difference between addiction and need, and I hit play again and let the download rush through me. Over and over, until I passed out.

When I woke, my pillow was soaked with saliva, and I was sleeping on my arm in such an uncomfortable and awkward position that when I moved the wrong way, the bone protested painfully and threatened dislocation. I figured out how to untangle myself and sat up.

Mr. Ziggles was gone from the desk. When I stood, I saw him on the bunk above me. Mesa hugged him close, her eyes closed. She was at peace, finally, but the horrors I had subjected her to nagged at me again. It was dark out, and the cell door was shut tight.

I had a raging headache, and I was hungry. I had no idea of the time. I paced the handful of steps between the bed and the desk, from the toilet to the cell door. In an aisle not much longer than the length of the bed, I did pushups and crunches until the muscles ached, I was soaked in sweat and unable to move, and my head throbbed in agony in time with each heartbeat.

The snuff buzz was gone, replaced by a fog that made the edges of my mind fuzzy. I fell back onto the bed, wincing from the soreness in the muscles of my stomach and back, and tried to sleep again. I was restless and physically worn, but it took me a long time to fall asleep.

Mesa had breakfast with me, but she was wary and silent. I tried to engage her in conversation, but she remained sullen. She poked at her plate of cold, thickly congealed scrambled eggs and took small bites of unbuttered toast but ate very little. She said even less. Eventually, she decided she was finished and left without a word.

I walked the grounds again, alone. It was quickly becoming my routine, and I found it comforting. Jaime was talking with a small group of men, and we waved to each other. However, I made no effort to join them, and he made no effort to invite me. A few laps later, he peeled away from them and slowly walked up to me with a pronounced limp. His knees were bothering him, and even my bones were slightly achy in the chill.

"What'd you think of the chip?" he asked.

"What makes you think I played it?"

He grinned. "You got that look in your eyes, like they ain't all the way focused. You had a good night of dreaming. I can tell."

I stopped and looked at him. I had to smile back. He reminded me of an overly eager kid begging for acceptance.

"It was good," I said. "Amazing, really."

"You find God in there?"

"I found something, sure."

We walked for a bit, more of a shuffle, really, given how slow Jaime was moving that morning.

"I see why it's illegal," I said. "I always got it from a moral perspective, but living it... I get why it has to be bottled up."

"But that didn't stop you from hitting it over and over, did it?"

"No," I admitted. "I played it a lot, until I couldn't anymore. It was fierce."

"There's a lot more out there. The circumstances are worse, maybe, but the rush is better. The feeling of it all. When you get all these different emotions wrapped up in it, all those chemical bombs... that's where it's really at."

"The war dead?"

"Sure, those are a fucking trip. You know, when you step on a landmine or have a bomb dropped on you, they say you don't feel a thing. It happens so fast, your brain doesn't know how to process it, and it sends the body into automatic shock mode first thing, to prevent you from feeling it. Fact is, though, there's all those chemicals rushing around in your body, and the DRMR picks up on it, etches it into place. Now that—that is a fucking trip."

He had a measure of awe, of reverence, in his voice. It chilled me, but also drew me in and made me curious. I had already eaten from his poisoned apple. What was one more bite?

"You got any of those?" I asked. I wondered how deep his private stash was, what sort of experiences and memories he had buried for personal consumption, and what was for sharing.

I told myself the question was purely professional curiosity. That was what I had been curating, after all—all these experiences, all those random, powerful, vivid moments that made and shaped life. Those experiences were both unique and universal.

He smiled and clapped his hand on my shoulder. "Nah," he said. "I don't."

We took our walk slowly, the morning chill quickly turning to warmth. We found shelter in the shade, and I looked around for Mesa, but she had a knack for disappearing completely when she wanted to.

"You get the sales pitch about immigrating to Canada yet?"

I nodded.

"Supposed to be, the UN is forcing PacRim to set up a refugee camp in LA, a few others spread across the old state boundaries. Truthfully, Canada or the NA Alliance, or whatever the fuck they're calling it—it won't be much better. One refugee camp is pretty much all the same. Maybe if you got to an NA state, might be you can get Alliance citizenship. Stay at the PacRim camp, probably you won't. It's going to be fucking Somalia around here before you know it."

"I'm staying," I said.

He looked me in the eye, maybe gauging my seriousness.

"This is my home," I said. "My daughter and I, we're staying put."

"Thinking about it myself," he said. "I've always been a California boy."

He shifted, trying to work his butt into a more comfortable rut on the ground. His gaze traveled across a clump of guards taking a smoke break, talking animatedly and laughing.

"Our new overlords," Jaime said. "New boss, same as the old boss. Only a little bit louder and a little bit worse."

We laughed, but without the good humor to bring it to life.

"What do you think about all this?" he asked me.

I told him about my brief turn with the so-called militia. He asked if I'd ever killed any PRC, and I told him that I had. When he asked me if I'd been comfortable with it, I said I was. I asked him about the burn, and he gave me a story about an accident with hot oil, when he had been a cook before the war. He said he had fallen in with a militia, too. Then he took a small square of fabric from his pocket and unfolded it. The edges were frayed from where it had been torn loose and burnt, but the few stars and stripes that remained were easy to recognize.

"You still believe in this?" he asked me.

I said I did. He said he wasn't sure if he did anymore or not, but he wanted to.

"I might go to that Echo Park camp," he said. "I hear it's supposed to be pretty relaxed, at least as far as refugee camps go. I might have a job or two you can help with, if you're willing."

"I'll think about it," I said.

I didn't ask what kind of jobs, and he didn't offer any details. He refolded the small square of flag and pocketed it. He seemed grateful when I helped him to his feet.

He dug around in his pocket again and pulled loose

another chip. He handed it to me before we went our separate ways. I spent the rest of the day in my cell, alone and high on DMT, playing through my small collection of snuff chips. I got jacked up on the pain of others and high off the misery and death of strangers.

It felt good.

CHAPTER THIRTEEN

IN THE MORNING, ALICE AND I drank coffee and ate bagels. It'd been a long time since I'd had a bagel, even longer since it had felt satisfying. The coffee was rich, black, and strong, not at all similar to what we were given at Echo camp.

Alice was talking, but I was tuned out. I was lost in my own thoughts, staring into the liquid pitch in my cup. She was surprised, but not offended, when I finally interrupted her.

"I need the memory chips from the men we killed at the restaurant." I was troubled by her lack of communication with her PRC contact. "Call him," I said.

She was a woman not used to taking orders, but she nodded. The ground we stood on was constantly shifting beneath me, and I thought she was still more than a bit angry at me. That was fine, though. I was still upset with her over hiding the details of the Echo Park attack from me and angry at her conflicting loyalties. She left half of her food uneaten and went into a different room. I finished mine and poured a second cup of coffee.

She was gone for a long time before water started running from the shower. She came out twenty minutes later, dressed and with her hair wrapped in a damp towel.

"PRC were able to recover the bodies," she said. "My contact will have access to the bodies this morning after they're autopsied. He can obtain a copy for us, but the originals would be too risky and would compromise him."

I gave it a moment's thought then shrugged. "That's fine, as long as the data is unaltered. Maybe we can find out where Jaime is."

"If those men were his."

"They were." The more I replayed events over in my head, the more certain I became. "They were the same team that had carried out the attacks on the 101. Jaime's personal hit squad."

"Christ," she said.

"When will we have the chips?"

"This evening, I think. He'll contact me to arrange a rendezvous."

I ate another bagel, trying to arrange the pieces. Jaime must have realized I'd been abducted during my shift on the city reclamation crew. It didn't take much figuring out that Kaften had been behind it or that I had been severely compromised. I knew about Jaime's operations and was, therefore, a liability.

My role in the murder of the PRC *chiang* made me a powerful bargaining chip if Kaften ever needed leverage. He had trawled my memories, which would have exposed Jaime and Alice's role in the affair. And if Kaften could compromise me, odds were the PRC could dig up even more information.

The big question was whether Jaime knew I was still alive and that Alice had bought my release from Kaften. The attack on her restaurant told me she was the primary target, and it was possible his hit squad hadn't known I was there prior to the attack.

Jaime was cleaning house.

"I'm taking the car," I said. "I have a few errands to run, and I need to know where today's checkpoints are."

"Well, I'm coming with you," she said.

"No. You're staying here, where it's safe."

"If my contact calls—"

"Then you'll call me and tell me where to meet him, and I'll pick up the chips."

"But—"

"No arguments," I said, cutting her off again. "Jaime obviously thinks we're a danger to him. If we're together, it's easier for both of us to be killed. If we're separated, he has to devote twice the amount of energy toward eliminating us. We stand a better chance of evading him if we don't have to worry about watching each other's backs."

"It's too risky. I don't like it."

"I don't care," I said. "You hired me to do this job, and this is how it's going to be."

She relented, perhaps surprised by my newfound authority. We agreed on a specific commNet frequency and promised to stay in touch. If the checkpoints changed or if she heard from her PRC source, she would contact me immediately with the details.

I drove down from the hills and took a circuitous route to my destination, checking for tails. I avoided the checkpoints, but found myself behind roving military convoys twice. They paid me no attention, but they moved slowly, and traffic quickly grew congested. Although I was used to the sight, the incongruity of Chinese tanks sitting in the middle of Ventura Boulevard still struck me and filled me with unease. The people who walked around it gave it a wide berth. The scene reminded me of news footage of riots in Egypt, Libya, and Iraq.

I took Ventura to White Oak. I had an odd sense of a misplaced anxiety. After so long away, I was going back home, and with that decision came a streak of trepidation over what I might find, or what might be waiting for me.

My hands were sweaty against the leather of the steering wheel when I pulled into an empty driveway. The front yard was a riot of weeds and dry dirt patches. The house was caked in grime, and wooden boards had been nailed over broken windows. The front door was a thin piece of plywood, where the words "dead inside" were spray painted in red. The markings had become a common sight over the months, and I paid it little attention. Squatters sometimes tagged houses with that message in an effort to keep the authorities or other squatters away. On my last visit here, I'd sprayed that message in hopes of deterring the homeless from seeking shelter in my house.

The wooden steps leading up the country porch were warped and rotted, and they protested loudly under my weight. I had been to the house twice since Selene's death. The first time, I'd sat on the porch and cried, waiting for Mesa. She came home confused and frightened. Her steps slowed as she realized I was alone. She saw me crying, and it may have been the first time she'd ever seen tears line my face. Between sobs, I told her that her mother was dead.

Although the inside of the house was dark, I could make out the lumps of figures sleeping on the floor. In the center of the living room, an old, rusted barrel cradled a dying fire inside. Dark streaks of soot from the curls of smoke lined the walls and ceiling. The room stank of excrement, cigarettes, liquor, and vomit.

I caught a flash of movement and turned toward

it. A man sitting on the floor was dressed in layers of rags and covered in filth. He squinted at me but seemed disinterested. As his head swiveled away, I caught shiny flashes in his eyes and a small glint of metal from the port behind his ear. Vanity bionic upgrades from another life had become cybernetic nodes that were nothing more than a reminder of the way things had been. The work hadn't been cheap. He burped loudly and fell back to sleep, a bottle of amber liquid stoppered in his lap.

A sledgehammer had been taken to the walls so that the vandals could steal the pipes and wiring. A TV that had been made useless by the EMP blast at the start of the war had been smashed to bits. The photos and their frames that we'd hung on the wall had long ago burned to ash.

I made my way to the stairs and saw that the guardrail had been chopped away. More kindling for the fire. I was glad I'd made it back before the place burned down. I wanted to be angry with the squatters for what they had done to my home, but I was too detached and lost.

I kept an eye on the bums. I wasn't afraid of them, but it never hurt to be cautious. The stairs creaked loudly under my weight. I tried not to make any more noise than I had to in order to avoid drawing any undue attention to myself. If they felt I was a threat, things could get nasty.

The upper floor was a small loft with two bedrooms on opposite ends and a bathroom in the middle. The walls were torn up in ugly patchworks where the copper pipes were missing. One of the bedrooms had been Mesa's, but I had no need to go in there. I stuck my head through the doorway anyway and was surprised to see a child in there, lying atop a natty sleeping bag on the floor. The boy was small and grimy. His long hair was thick with grease and sticking up in clumps at odd angles. He had one large blue eye. Where his left eye should have been, he had only an ugly, jumbled mass of scar tissue. That side of his face was webbed with broken flesh over sunken bone. Although he was dressed in layers, he was clearly emaciated, and the left side of his body was deflated from where he had lost his arm and leg. His right leg was bent at the knee before him, his right elbow resting on his knee. He regarded me with his single eye then mouthed hello. The scar tissue from his face continued down his neck and across his throat before disappearing beneath the collars of his shirts. I returned his greeting with a simple nod.

When I turned my back on him, he resigned himself to loneliness or boredom with a noisy huff. I treaded lightly down the hall, to our old bedroom. The mattress we had slept on was shredded and stained with black mold. Its stuffing had probably been used to line clothes or sleeping bags or burned for warmth, along with the dresser and chest of drawers. The walls and carpet were moldy, and the room smelled rank. Somebody had shit in the corner, but it was old and dry.

I pulled open the closet door, half-expecting to find a dead body based on the stink, but I was relieved to find it empty and free of any horrors. The attic entrance was closed. That didn't mean much, really, but it gave me hope. I yanked on the pull cord and caught the ladder as it slid down toward me. The climb up was short, but my eyes had to adjust to the darkness. The squatters hadn't had reason to come up this high, and the rafters were still jammed with our boxes and the detritus of life. It took me a minute to spot the gray duffel bag I had come for. I hauled it over and down the steps, then knelt on the floor, everything else forgotten.

The bag was heavy. Inside were a couple pistols, boxes of ammunition, a folding Benchmade knife, and twenty-some mem chips. Most of the chips were copies of what I'd had in my possession at Echo Park, minus the *chiang's* murder. I had maybe enough to unload on the black market to raise money for passage north or east, to the seasteaders. Other chips sat at the bottom of the bag, though, ones that were far more meaningful to me.

In this bag was my entire life—my wedding, the first time Selene and I had made love, the birth of our daughter, and her first day of school. Sending her off to kindergarten had been painful. For the first time in her life we had left her surrounded by strangers, and she had been afraid. She hadn't wanted to be separated from her mother or me, even though the teacher had seemed pleasant and smiled at her, holding out her hands for Mesa to take. Instead, Mesa had screamed and hugged my leg, tears streaming down her face as she begged us not to leave her alone. At the end of the day, she was sullen and vowed not to go back. The next morning, she put up no fight. By the third day, she was almost eager to go.

I slung the bag over my shoulder and stood. I stepped out of the closet, and instinct took over. I smelled him before he was on top of me, and I easily sidestepped the punch he threw toward me. He was slow and drunk, but his words were oddly clear.

"They're doing it," he said. "You Muslim?"

His fists were balled at his sides, and he was breathing heavily. He was fat and tired. He waited for my answer, bringing his hands up in front of his face.

"No," I said. "I'm not Muslim."

"That's good," he said, seeming to relax. "They're doing it. They're putting the thoughts out there, making people into them, into terrorists. It's them doing it."

"Okay," I said, not sure what else to say.

"I'm for Jesus. Them ones, though, they fucked up, gonna blow up. Blow up for sure. But I gots Jesus. That's good, that one. It is."

"Okay."

"Yup. You got Jesus?"

I noticed a glint from his hand. He had a knife up his sleeve.

"Yeah, sure," I said.

"Yup. That's good. Better to have Jesus in you than the other one."

I nodded. "Yeah, that's what I hear, man."

"You watch yourself. Watch out for the gooks and the Allah assholes. It's bad out there."

"Amen, brother."

"Amen to you, sir. Fucking amen."

He stepped back out of the doorway and spread his arms wide, granting me passage in sage fashion. I walked past, but made no show of my nervousness. He nodded, I nodded back, and we were copacetic.

"What happened to the boy?" I asked. The words escaped before I realized it.

"Thems was the gooks did that. Not the ragheads. Rags got me, though, once upon a time. Lost a fucking toe."

"Huh," I said.

"Yup. You go on, now. Git."

I wasn't going to argue. This was not my house, not anymore. It was from a past life, a dead life. The house shrank and receded in the distance as I drove away. Then it disappeared from view, lost to me forever.

CHAPTER FOURTEEN

I SPENT HOURS DRIVING AIMLESSLY, waiting for updates from Alice and word that her contact had been able to obtain the mem chips we needed. The car was a newer electric, a small model that had been built in Vietnam by a PRC state-run facility, so I didn't have to worry about gas. The large battery under the hood could go three hundred miles on a single charge and had a back-up twelve-gallon gas tank, which was half-full.

I wasn't planning on driving forever, and the clock was rolling past lunchtime. I was hungry, and I needed to get out to stretch my legs and get some fresh air. Walking around the city for a bit had its own set of complications. I could get stopped by roving military police, and although I didn't think that possibility posed much threat to my personal safety, arguing across a language barrier the size of the Pacific Ocean would be a long, drawn-out hassle. They would want to know who I was, why I was here, and why I had left my refugee camp. When they discovered I was from Echo Park, that would further complicate matters, and I would have to explain my displacement and face more uncomfortable questions.

I weighed my options. I'd been making a circuitous route between Figueroa and Hill, avoiding the random checkpoints along the way. I pulled into a parking garage near the Fig and took the stairs down from the third floor. Pedestrian traffic was light, but dressed in a button-down shirt and black slacks on a weekday, I blended in well enough with the crowd. I paid attention to the people around me, occasionally taking a casual glance around. Nobody seemed particularly interested in me, and I was confident no one was following me.

I walked to what had once been the Staples Center and went through the entrance off Figueroa. Before the war, I had seen Kings games here, and Selene and I had brought Mesa to see a Disney on Ice show when she was five. The crowd was thicker that day than it had been during the Center's entertainment heydays. A throng of bodies stood shoulder to shoulder, damn near chest-to-back, inching their way forward. I got in line and waited patiently to pass through the checkpoint. UN soldiers positioned on either side of the line at regular intervals randomly asked people for IDs. They largely avoided asking for idents from those of a clearly Asian background, focusing their attention instead on easier, more politically correct subjects such as small children and the elderly. I provided my ident when asked. The soldier said nothing, so I said nothing. He pressed my card against a small device, his head bobbed repeatedly between the monitor and me, then he handed back the card and moved on.

My trip to the checkpoint took nearly half an hour.

I was instructed to remove my shoes and socks and to raise my arms over my head as I was corralled through a body scanner, then wanded and patted down before being directed to stand in another line for almost another half hour.

The security procedures were artificial precautions, a well-orchestrated show to give the illusion of safety. Nano securiclouds webbed the entrances, alerting security to potential threats before the individuals were even past the main entrance hubs, giving the guards a chance to neutralize most threats before they ever made it into the central lobby.

I was asked to present my ident again. I kept it at the ready in one hand, holding my socks and shoes in the other. Eventually, I made my way up to another guard station, where I was met with a bored, blond-haired, blue-eyed man barely out of his teens. He scanned my ident card for a fourth time.

"Purpose of visit?" he asked with a heavy accent. Dutch, or maybe Swedish.

"I want to talk about political asylum for myself and my daughter. I was hoping to get some food, too."

"Where is your daughter?"

"She's staying with some friends."

"She's not with you now?"

"No," I said, slightly annoyed.

"Do you have an appointment?"

"No," I said, again. "Don't you take walk-ins?"

"We do. It may be a, uh, long wait. Lots of people. You see?"

"Yeah, I see."

"It says you are assigned to Echo Park," he said, gesturing toward the computer.

"That's right," I said. "You must have heard about the attack?"

He nodded, and I could see sympathy crack through the all-business façade he'd been nurturing.

"You are seeking asylum to where?"

"Seattle. Or the seasteaders. Wherever."

"Hold out a hand."

I did. He pressed a heavy rubber stamp against it, leaving a large purple blot of ink.

"Okay, my friend, you proceed. Amnesty and asylum representatives are in the central court. Long line today."

When I was past the guard's kiosk, the line loosened considerably as people moved off in different directions. I found a bench and put my footwear back on, then found a food vendor. Massive liquid-crystal displays hung over the center of the promenade, where paper-thin screens broadcasted satellite newsfeeds from the PRC, CBC, BBC, and Al-Jazeera.

It took the CBC's mindless talking heads fifteen minutes to get through the local weather, the latest "leaked" celebrity sex tapes, and an update on an ailing musician's battle with the common cold before they got to the assault on Echo Park. They turned the piece over to a live on-scene reporter who talked solemnly while casually strolling through the scene of burnt tents and PRC soldiers dressed in white Tyvek suits and rubber gloves, hauling out the dead soldiers and refugees. His narration continued over the B-roll footage of the camp in its prime, of our weathered but intact tents and weary refugees standing in long lines to get fresh water and food.

I wasn't surprised by the damage. I'd seen enough similar sights. During the live footage, I studied the background as best as I could, looking for people I might have known. The carnage made it impossible to tell, though. The background was fuzzy and indistinct, while the reporter and his immediate surroundings were sharp and clear but devoid of any real information. The broadcast was as close to an on-air media blackout as you could get.

When his report concluded, the correspondent sent the program back to the studio, where a panel of so-called experts continued to hash it out. Two male liberals and two conservative women comprised the panel. They all tried to speak at the same time, their conversation escalating into a shouting match, and were at each other's throats in the span of three words, trying to drown each other in righteous fury and indignation. I wondered what the point of the segment was then figured the talking heads were getting bent out of shape simply to vent, create drama, and feel really good about themselves while they basked in their on-air spotlight.

I found it curious that they had labeled this an "American" story and used figureheads from the liberal and conservative movements—ideologies that, even prior to the country's death, had long since ceased to truly represent the views of the American people.

After Al Qaeda launched a series of attacks in the Midwest and the PRC began their loud sabre rattling in the Pacific, US officials began heightening security. "Heightened security" became a euphemism for "excuse to strip you of your rights." Afraid to challenge the politicians out of fear over lost interviews and exclusive info, the press corps turned a blind eye. The dissolution of civil liberties progressed slowly, mounted over successive periods of hysteria. We stopped wearing belts to the airports, disposed of bottled liquids, and took off our shoes while government officials used virtual strip-search securiclouds to take nude pictures of us, all so that we could assure them we were not a threat. Nobody would admit that these "precautions" had done nothing to prevent the following waves of terror attacks, which had been completely unrelated to airport security, in other major cities across the country. But we submitted and were primed to submit again. National

Guard checkpoints on our nation's highways became another minor inconvenience. A necessary evil, we were told, like having our commNets tapped and e-mails read. We submitted willingly to America the Police State in exchange for the empty promise of security.

Then the PRC struck. The media, in the days and weeks that followed, speculated on the death of democracy, ignoring the fact that democracy had already been long forgotten. Dirty bombs and poison gas attacks in the nation's capital, New York, and Philadelphia had seen to that.

When people in Boston and Chicago reported to emergency rooms with mysterious illnesses and doctors found injection wounds on their backs or arms, a new wave of panic gripped the country. Terrorists had wandered American city streets, stabbing people with hypodermic needles filled with a cocktail of hearty, drug-resistant bacteria. Scores of the infected died, while others grew so sick that they needed organ transplants and amputations. The terrorists' escalation to germ warfare generated such widespread fear that hardly anybody disagreed with the President's order for the military to occupy city streets in order to help local police maintain safety and alertness.

I wondered which America Kaften was fighting for. Which ideology was he hoping to resurrect? The military-police states the major metropolitan cities had become? Or an earlier, more idealized version of America that he knew from historical downloads? When he was drafted, had they even bothered telling him about the Constitution, or had it been completely wiped from memory by then?

I thought about Mesa and wondered if the Northern Alliance was really any better. Would I be trading one dictatorship for another, forcing her under the thumb of some other demagogue run by the corporate machine and the military-industrial complex? Or would it be something similar to the life we used to know, where we could safely walk the streets or go to a movie theater without first passing through an hour-long security checkpoint to "establish our safety"?

The burger and fries on the plate before me were cold. I'd eaten a small portion, mindlessly chewing without tasting any of it. The fries were limp and soggy and glued together into a thick, gelatinous bundle of grease. The burger wasn't even real meat, but some unnaturally bright-pink artificial concoction jammed between day-old buns and hidden beneath relish, ketchup, and mustard. I doused it in Sriracha to give it some heat and flavor. If I burned off my taste buds and didn't study what I was eating, the food was edible enough.

I took my tray to the garbage kiosk and threw away the paper items, left the tray on a stack of similarly colored trays, and made my way through the promenade and seating area, down the stairs to the center court. I'd always wanted to be courtside, but not quite like this. Not jammed up against a suffocating crowd and bureaucratic rubber stamps.

A long row of tables with dividers between them gave the illusion of privacy, and each station had two chairs. UN office monkeys and Alliance reps staffed the tables and did the interviews. Dressed in expensive suits, they had the air of self-entitled arrogance that marked them as government sanctioned power whores who got off on playing with people's lives and enjoyed juggling fates in the palms of their hands.

I was annoyed by everything right then—the hackneyed farce of tables and chairs, the crowd of human cattle I was stuck in the middle of, and the denigrating presumption that I should have to ask for permission to live my life. I was expected to petition for it in order to afford my daughter safety in a part of the continent that had not been torn apart by warfare, power-hungry invaders, and in-fighting among the survivors.

These Alliance reps, with their crisp haircuts and shiny shoes, were the same as the UN and the rest of the world. They had watched America crumble and burn and had done nothing. They'd sat by, unconcerned and uncaring. Even at the height of their occupation, nobody asked the PRC to leave. There was no timetable for withdrawal. Nobody condemned them. They were given a handful of economic sanctions and trade restrictions, but even that was another farce. The world's politicians were weak and their silence made them willing participants in the destruction of the United States. They wanted to avoid war because it would be bad in the polls, and their country's citizens were weary of long, overdrawn battles that would claim thousands of their countrymen. War was almost as unpopular as America, and the weights didn't balance, so a democracy was allowed to die, and an entire nation's worth of people were deemed politically expendable. The UN was trying to place us as best as they could. States throughout the Alliance had a refugee quota, as did UN-member countries in Europe, but asylum candidates were rarely sent overseas.

Mesa had wanted to go to Seattle, through the Underground Railroad the refugee immigrants had established. We could sneak away through Nevada and find help with a host of sympathizers then apply directly for asylum in Washington. The governor had opened the state's borders in a politically unpopular decision that would probably cost him the next election. He had said he would always be American, first and foremost, and he considered it his duty to help other Americans, no matter how they found themselves in his state.

The people around me talked about rejection rates, how many times they'd applied before, the whys and hows of their prior rejections, and their hopes that this time would be different. My annoyance turned into full-on pissed off. The line moved forward a smidge. Then a message from Alice popped up on the private comm frequency. I listened to it, dividing my attention between her words and the chatter around me, as I shuffled forward with the rest of the cattle. Her contact had reached out to let her know we were good for a meet.

At the table ahead of me, a woman was crying into her partner's shoulder. The man in the suit tapped a brief message on the datapad and asked them to leave. She cried harder, and the suit asked them to leave again. No sympathy. No compassion. Not a fucking care about them.

Fuck it. Fuck them. Fuck their new world order.

I shoved my way through the throng, losing my place in line. It earned me some whispered contempt, and I could feel the stares on my back as I shoved my way back up the steps. A guard stopped me and asked if something was wrong. I told him I was feeling sick to my stomach, and it was more truth than lie.

I went out the Eleventh Street entrance. The guards left me alone, probably thinking I was another dejected soul who had been ground up and spit out by the political machinery. I wandered the streets, taking an indirect route back to the parking garage on Figueroa, where I'd left the car. Inside the garage, I did a quick once-around the floor and checked the other vehicles to see if anyone was waiting for me, maybe another one of Jaime's hit squads, for instance.

I listened to Alice's message again. Her contact wanted to meet in three hours at a sushi joint on Third Street. In prime conditions, the trip would take about a half hour on the Santa Monica Freeway. I was given a route to follow that would take me around the checkpoints, and I estimated it would take almost an hour to get his location.

Traffic was moderate, and the directions proved good.

I had plenty of time to kill, so I parked some distance away from the restaurant on Swall, along a residential block of apartment buildings. The area was nice enough. The tall tan buildings with stucco walls and balconies overlooking the street had gone largely untouched by the war. My car blended in with the other vehicles parked along Swall. I walked down Third, in front of the single-story businesses that lined the street. Most of the multi-floor complexes, such as Cedars-Sinai and Bloomingdales, had been crushed, but a lot of single-story businesses had reopened, mostly mom-and-pop shops and some restaurants. I passed a liquor store housed in glass-fronted A-frame and a bar advertising Happy Hour and half-off sake, then I turned down Holt, took Burton to Sherbourne, and went back up to Third.

Satisfied that I was alone, I took an outdoor table at a coffee shop, where I could keep an eye on the sushi joint. I sipped a spiced latte and started to relax. The tension and anger I'd been carrying around with me began to bleed away, and I was grateful for the quiet calm and the open spaces around me.

I let my guard down a bit but remained mindful of the people around me. I kept track of those who walked by then waited to see if they reappeared. A few other customers joined me on the patio, but I lingered over my drink longer than they did, and they left ahead of me. I was there for a while but not longer than would be considered unusual. I leafed through a newspaper that had been left behind on another table and tried to be as inconspicuous as possible.

The meeting was slated for five thirty, but traffic to and from the restaurant across the street had been minimal. Ten minutes ahead of the meeting time, a wiry Chinese man exited a car parked curbside and went inside. I watched for a few minutes, but nobody followed. I gave him another ten minutes, erring on the side of caution and deciding to be fashionably late, then paid my bill and left a decent tip for the waitress.

I went to a table at the back of the restaurant, near the bathrooms and away from any windows, where I found the Chinese man picking at a plate of udon with chopsticks.

"Mr. Tsou," I said, taking the seat opposite him.

He called for the waiter, fired off a rapid string of words in a language I did not understand, and poured me a small cup of hot tea. His arms we thin cords of muscle and vein, and his neck was long and slender. He wore a short-sleeve button-down with a thick blue tie. His sport coat was draped over the back of another chair. His salt-and-pepper hair was short, and he had the distinct air of a cop. When he spoke to me, his English was impeccable and softer than his Chinese.

"You are a friend of Alice's," he said. "I ordered you udon, too."

"Thank you," I said. "I appreciate your help on this."

He shrugged, his head cast down toward the bowl, his eyes closed against the steam. He seemed small and defeated, and I wondered what Alice had held over his head to ensure his cooperation.

"You're police?"

A small smile crossed deftly over his lips, and he canted his head this way and that, as if to say maybe yes, maybe no.

"I was," he said, "before all this." He made a circle in the air over the table with his chopsticks, pointing at nothing but including everything. "Now... it doesn't matter so much anymore what I am, I suppose. I am police, sure."

"You've got a hell of a lot of access to get what we needed for somebody so non-committal."

"What would you have me say? It's a job. I work for them. I do work for her. It all pays."

I thought about the nature of yin and yang and what

the battle for balance can do to a man's soul. Perfect harmony never comes without an exacting toll and a heavy penance. He had the smell of a cop, but he stank of defeat. I felt sorry for him.

I felt sorry for myself, too. I shouldn't have left Staples. I should have stayed and at least tried to get amnesty for myself and Mesa. Instead, I'd gotten petty and angry, refusing to even try, and acted like a petulant child.

By the time my noodles came, he was finished with his, so I ate quickly. He regarded me quietly, not saying a word. Obviously, he wasn't in the business of opening up to complete strangers, let alone bagmen for the crime lord he'd somehow gotten entangled with. When my bowl was empty, he passed me a folded napkin. I picked it up and dabbed at my lips, feeling the bodies of the memory chips through the thin cloth. I tucked my hands under the table and extracted the chips, then put the napkin back on the table.

"I'm guessing you viewed the data?"

He pursed his lips and tilted his head to one side. "I am lead investigator of these murders," he said, finally. I took that as a yes.

"Then you know this wasn't just some random killings."

"Do I? In some respects, depending on certain angles and one's point of view, you simply strode out of an apartment building and shot one of the men point-blank."

"And if you dig deeper, you know that these men were responsible for the freeway attack a few days ago. If you run the mems with the empath filters on, you know they were there to kill Alice. That's a whole helluva lot of cognition you're sweeping under the rug."

"It's unimportant what I do or do not know. It is important, however, that my superiors trust in my competencies as an investigator and that they do not learn the truth. For all of our sakes, I should say."

"In other words, you're sitting on all of this until Alice tells you otherwise."

He inclined his head slightly, with barely any movement at all. He looked small inside of his suit, pathetic even. Our business finished, he pushed himself away from the table and stood. He put on a hat and sport coat, cutting the profile of a dapper detective from a bygone century.

I gave him a few minutes' head start and drank a glass of water before leaving. I ran through another security check, looping around the neighborhood on an indirect path back to my car. With every step I took, I could feel the chips burning a hole in my pocket. With every second that passed, I could feel a growing uncertainty and the painful tug of time slipping away, wasted.

I feared that the information on the chips was already past its expiration date. If Jaime's location was buried in there somewhere, it was completely possible he would have moved on already. Once he'd learned of the deaths, he could have rabbited and disappeared to a new spider-hole that neither of the dead men's memories was privy to. He could have limited knowledge of the secret location to a party of one, and then he would be gone forever. And Mesa with him.

I had to find him. The memory chips had to have the answers I needed. *They had to.*

In the car, I took a deep calming breath, trying to center myself. I took the DRMR unit out of the glove compartment, organized the chips on the dashboard, and plugged in.

The chips passed the DRMR security program. No virals. No thought-bombs. No mem-wipes or Trojans. I did a quick download, uninterested in the experience of their memories. I was strictly data-hounding it, fast and easy. I dumped the mems and scrubbed them through custom filters and a facial recognition suite, hunting for Jaime-specific contexts. I didn't need to know anything about their personal lives or what they had felt at their moment of death. I cared only about Jaime and where he might be.

I let the info wash over me. Finished, I unplugged, needing time to think. Jaime had options, and in some ways, I was chasing a ghost. He was an information hound, a compartmentalization whore. He told people what he wanted them to know or needed them to believe. The chips were so rife with data, though—an odd disparity for someone who so tightly controlled the flow of information. That in itself was the trap. Addresses, phone numbers, safe houses, drop boxes, and multiple meeting points. Parking garages and malls, university centers, restaurants, coffee houses, construction sites, warehouses, and run-down vacant movie theaters. These men were part of a cell that Jaime ran directly. His elite squad. His private army. His killers.

A list of safe houses were embedded in the memories of both men, but I ruled those out because I figured Jaime would eliminate them as an option. He had to assume that his men had been bagged up by the PRC and that they would vet every memory and chase every lead. It seemed unlikely that he would know Alice had sicced her inside man, her pathetic detective, on the case and wormed her way into the investigation. All of his safe houses were exposed. His entire network was not simply compromised, but burned entirely. He would have to go to the one place only he knew about.

But where the fuck was that? Where had he taken my daughter?

I stared out the grimy, pockmarked windshield. The city's dust had left a fine film of grit in half-circles and triangles on the glass where the wipers couldn't reach. A tightness blossomed in my chest, heavy over my heart. The pressure of time manifested into physical pain made worse by the loss of precious minutes and hard-fought seconds. I had to find Mesa, and I had no idea where to even begin looking.

I couldn't face losing her. Selene's death had ruined me. If anything happened to Mesa...

Then, just like that, a small thought that had been tugging at the back of my mind lurched forward and flourished. I studied this sudden realization carefully. I remembered my time on Alcatraz, where I had first met Jaime. We'd taken long walks around the compound and had equally long discussions. I remembered his story of loss, his dead wife, and the underground shelter that had come under attack. It was impossible for me to forget.

Neither of the men had known that parcel of information about Jaime. He had not entrusted them with that detail of his life. But he had told me. He had recognized a kindred spirit. Our pain and loss made us close. In hindsight, it was easy to see that he was merely using the tools he had needed in order to recruit me, to draw me into his cause and his plans. But that little information whore had shared a piece of himself with me.

If it were true.

The Metro rail consisted of five lines and nearly a hundred stations. The red and purple lines were nearly thirty miles of subway with more than twenty stops between them. Union Station had been used as a shelter, but so had Civic Center. Jaime had said the PRC had tossed grenades down on them, so the odds favored Civic.

The subways were dead tunnels, home to the rats and the displaced who had made the underground their homes. The PRC was in no rush to get them operational and did not currently view the system as an essential part of the infrastructure. They were occupied with rebuilding the highways, establishing regular bus routes, and getting the surface and above-ground rails operational. In time, they promised, the subways would run again, when they were safe. Subways were one more avenue for the terrorists to gain a foothold in their attacks and campaigns of violence. The PRC had enough problems above ground without creating the potential for even more catastrophe below. "When it is safe" became a mantra during the infrequent press briefings they gave for the state news, but the city and its infrastructure wasn't going to be safe anytime soon. Fifteen, maybe twenty years down the line, Los Angeles could have its subways back, but only if any outlying resistance groups were completely crushed.

Jaime could be hidden anywhere in the thirty miles of tunnel, plus all the off-shoot corridors that were used for maintenance and storage. Add to that all of the other tunnels that ran above and below the subways that could have been drilled into for access, and finding him would be like looking for a needle in a haystack. Hundreds of miles of drainage networks and sewers provided Jaime with a million potential hiding spots deep off the grid. I didn't know if he was a tunnel rat, but I had to consider it. In that case, finding him would be even more difficult.

I wondered if I was looking at this the wrong way. Maybe I should be thinking of ways to make him come to me instead of trying to find him. I realized suddenly that I knew very little about him. I knew nothing of his weak spots or his pressure points. What could I do that would lure him out? What would make him peek his head up?

After several minutes of hard thought, I still came up with nothing. The fucking information whore. He would never tell anybody more than they needed to know. Never give them an inch. He was smart to do that. Don't let them have anything that could be used against you. Limit their control over you. He was a player, an operator. And I was a fucking idiot.

Mesa, you poor thing...

I called Alice. She answered almost instantly.

"Call Kaften for me," I said. "Tell him I have a business proposition and to meet me at our spot."

She started to ask why, but I cut her off and disconnected the call, not in the mood for explaining things. I needed time to make peace with this decision.

As I drove, thoughts of dead wives, murdered parents, and random bombings swirled in my head. Dead shooters. Highway attacks. Little girls with bombs stuffed in their backpacks.

Night fell, and my headlights fell upon an outdated placard. COMING SOON ALCYONE TOWERS. Large raised letters stood out against a mock holographic display of the finished complex. Back when the towers were proposed, space had been at a premium, and overpopulation had been a growing concern. Growing outward had been impossible, so growing upward was the sole alternative. The mock-up showed three thick, massive multi-legged structures that rose and twisted into a square antiprism. Only half of one tower had been finished before the attacks shut down construction.

I parked near it, shut down the car, and debated what exactly I was doing there. I wondered if I would be able to find my spilt blood, if that dark patch still stained the soil where I'd fallen. I wondered if Kaften still had spotters there. The unfinished tower was a good sniper's cove.

After a few minutes of waiting, I got out of the car and sat on the hood. The air was musty and had a peculiar dusty tang to it. It tasted coppery.

I waited for a bullet to punch through me, to obliterate my head, but nothing happened. Eventually, I relaxed. I listened for the sound of voices or movement. Nothing. Maybe this was a waste of time. Still, I waited, wondering if Kaften would show, and if he would let me live long enough to explain why I was there.

I sat for forty minutes before I spotted the yellow glow on the horizon, which resolved into headlights then a small convoy of vehicles. My eyes lingered over the numerous, half-finished tower floors, but I saw nothing.

Kaften was the first man out of the car. A loose regiment spread out behind him, surrounding me. His black skin took on a sheen in the headlights, and he puffed on a thick cigar. He looked me over, but I was sitting casually, not much of a threat.

"Thanks for coming," I said.

"I told you I'd put a bullet in you."

I shrugged. Water under the bridge. However, a tinge of phantom pain echoed in my shortened finger. "You're a man of your word," I said, trying to stay cool.

It earned a smile from him, a short stubby smile around a short, stubby cigar.

"So, what? You come for another one?" He looked around at the men flanking us and at the guns they held in a relaxed but ready combat posture. "Maybe a lot of them?"

I shook my head. "I came for your help. And to give you something, if you want it. If you're willing to help."

His smile grew larger. He was on the verge of laughter, but my words stole away his shit-eating grin, and his eyes grew serious.

"Jaime Kristoff. Samuel Hodgson. I know where he is. He's yours if you help me find him."

He chewed on the end of his cigar for a moment then spat it out. Slowly, he ground it out, his eyes never leaving my face. I met his gaze, staring into dark, deep pools, and I knew his answer.

CHAPTER FIFTEEN

WHEN THE NAZIS LAUNCHED THEIR blitzkrieg attacks against England, bombing the country into so much rubble, Londoners sought shelter in the subways. After a night of air raids and ground-shaking explosions, they climbed up out of the rubble and started their day. They went to work and bought supplies to get themselves through another day, possibly their last. They embodied that stiff-upper-lip mentality everyone talked about. The bombings were an inconvenience, a minor disruption in their daily lives, but they carried on undeterred and unbowed.

I would've liked to say my fellow Americans had shown backbone and convictions similar to that of their 1940s-era British counterparts. But I couldn't.

As a culture, we were breastfed a sense of entitlement

well past any bounds of propriety. The old American dream about working hard and people pulling themselves up by their bootstraps to become a success was vilified. Anyone who was smart, worked hard, and made lots of money was the enemy. The American dream was replaced with the American Mentality, which said everyone should be able to have whatever they want, and it should just be given to them. And if it wasn't given to them, they were encouraged to take it. No accountability. No work ethic. No sense of responsibility.

We were weaned on instant access to information. Nothing was worth waiting for, because waiting for anything was too inconvenient. Attention spans were nil, yet, perversely, we were raised by celebrity-whore wannabes who demanded constant attention, as if they were starved for it.

When the war came, we wanted instant results. When our insatiable demands were not met immediately, we cowered underground to escape the bombs, cried, and whined. Nobody got up and went to work the next day. All the PRC had to do was turn out the lights, and we were ready to call it quits. There were no stiff upper lips down there, deep below the city in the underground tunnels. Only bent backs and broken spirits.

Jaime may have been the one man on his crowded platform to stand with squared shoulders. I could almost see it—him standing still with pride among nearly three thousand people, as if he were a breaker wall standing against the tide. He was fueled by hate and scorn, and he would have called it American pride, even though the America he believed in was nearing its expiration date—if it hadn't already passed.

The underground shelters hadn't been perfect. Although the subway lines had been constructed to withstand earthquakes up to 7.5 magnitudes, bombs sometimes made it through. Occasionally, intense bombing caused streets to collapse into the tunnels, killing those inside. They penetrated the roads and the tunnels, taking out the water and sewer lines, which flooded the tunnels. While many died from the explosives and concussive shockwaves, a surprisingly high number of people drowned. Being trampled was a fairly common way to die then, too. In one instance, a pack mentality had taken over following a close call at the Hollywood and Vine stop. A group of people seeking shelter rushed down the stairs so quickly that a few missed the steps and toppled down. The crowd pushed on, tripping over one another. Almost two hundred people were crushed to death.

Nearly ten thousand bunk beds filled the stops along the Red and Purple lines. The National Guard and Red Cross worked to keep the air raid shelters supplied with first aid kits and portable toilets. Several Guardsmen were appointed as shelter marshals in an effort to keep order among the ever-growing crowds, to assist with evacuations, and give first aid.

For a lot of people, any hope they still had after the first hard day was usually gone by the second. The shelters simply became a refuge for those who were prepared to die but were unwilling to sit outside, waiting for the big one to get dropped on them.

Hope was hard to maintain. We hacked into pirated newsfeeds over the commNet for updated death tallies and watched analysts talk about how the subways were nothing more than death tubes because the infrastructure wasn't designed to support the shelters and withstand the attacks. The broadcasts were an unrelenting loop of horrifying images and despair run in depressing repetition. The journalists promised us that their hearts went out to us. But really, they were waiting for us to die. They were hoping for the body counts to increase so they could start the news off with a fresh tally and a tired examination of death.

If it bled, it led, twenty-four hours a day and with a ticker running over the commercial breaks. I promise, we bled. We fucking bled.

Those newsfeeds probably saved our lives. Mesa and I had avoided the shelters, seeking escape in the countryside, away from the densely populated urban areas. Bombing trees and scrub didn't make much tactical sense or provide any advantages when, a few klicks over, a lovely shopping mall filled with people was waiting to be obliterated. Or at least we had thought so at the time...

I slowly descended the steps at Civic Center, down into the darkness, with Kaften and a few of his men to either side of me. A fence had been dropped to prevent admission years ago, but it had become rusty with age, and hooligans had since made the stairwell easily accessible. My footsteps against the concrete echoed softly. The motionless escalators on either side of me were nothing more than an inky black mark. The subway held no semblance of life, but it had the sour stench of the unwashed, of sweat and urine, and rotting excrement. It stank of death.

At the platform, I spotted in the ceiling above a fiberglass man in flight—the remnants of an art installation called *I Dreamed I Could Fly*. Six fiberglass people had been suspended there before the war. They flyers were broken and strewn across the ground, their once-colorful bodies ashen among the ruins of broken beds, busted toilets, and moth-eaten mattresses.

The liquid displays were shattered, the support columns dashed but still standing. The blast had obliterated some of the letters on the overhead directions, so that it read: TO N RT OLLYW D. The tracks on either side of the platform were empty, save for chunks of rubble. In the center of the station, between two concrete columns, was a grouping of bunk beds with bare frames. With the subway's circulation system dead, the air was stale and warm.

I lowered myself onto the tracks, unworried about the third rail. Electricity hadn't flowed down there in a long time. The tunnel was a large, gaping maw, pitch-black before me. I shined a light down one end then the other. I could follow the lines to Union Station or Pershing Square, hoping to find Jaime somewhere along the way, stopping to investigate the nooks and crannies that passed the beam of my flashlight.

"Which way?" Kaften asked.

I appreciated that he considered me a part of the search, even though he could have easily ignored me. His trust was a very tentative step forward, and I wasn't going to goad him back toward his usually brusque attitude.

I went with Pershing Square, toward North Hollywood, for no real reason. A hunch was all I had to go on. The park there had fountains, a purple bell tower, an ice rink, and a concert square. Husbands had gone there with their wives to sit in one of the plazas and watch kids play in the streams of water while listening to the sounds of summer music. Selene and I had gone there with Mesa, and perhaps Jaime had gone there with his wife.

Kaften and I set off down the tracks with a third man. He sent a second team of three down the opposite tunnel. Spotters were stationed on the rooftops across the way, taking advantage of the few snipers peaks outside, in the hopes that they could spot Jaime coming or going. We would all be staying in touch through a private IP over the commNet.

"Guess we're too early to ride pantsless, huh?" Kaften said.

His humor surprised me, and I laughed a bit. I remembered the annual bottomless subway ride commuters held every January. Back when the Red Line was running, hundreds of people—from the punks and Goths, young men and women, and exhibitionistic thrill-seekers, to the businessmen wearing dress shirts, ties, sport coats, and tighty-whities—had taken to the subway in their underwear. Even some of the zanier elderly had gotten in on the act. I remembered sitting across from a man who had to be in his nineties and was wearing a stained undershirt and an adult diaper.

The tradition was one more thing lost to the war, I realized, and my smile died. The PRC would have considered such a display an indecent form of protest and rounded up the revelers with guns drawn while lobbing tear gas into the crowds.

My laughter gave way to the nerves I had been trying to disguise. Pre-fight jitters. I could feel the acid in my stomach churn, creeping up my throat. A hot ball of lead in my core struggled to climb up, and I fought it back down. Fucking nerves. My head was swimming. I was afraid. Afraid I was right. Afraid I was wrong. Afraid of all the potential horrible paths we were treading. Afraid of what we would find at the end of the line.

Kaften and I had come to an amicable arrangement. We both had something the other wanted. He wanted Jaime. I needed an army. Support. Help.

"What do you want with him?" Kaften had asked me earlier, as the jeeps we had been riding in pulled into camp. Although no fires or lanterns burned, I could make out the downcast eyes of those who lived there, people who were as much survivors as victims. A stab of pity for them echoed through me, as it had the last time I was there, and I couldn't help but wonder if I found Mesa alive, was this what I would be condemning her to? Shame crept through me at that thought, but I was getting uncomfortably used to that feeling.

"He has my daughter," I said.

Kaften stared at me for a long quiet moment. I didn't know if he was a family man or if he had anyone at all in his life whom he cared for, other than the small regiment of soldiers he commanded, but I sensed a familiarity pass between us. A newfound interest glittered in his eyes. Before, he had regarded me with bored disinterest, as if I were a lesser man for having his gaze fall upon me. A small measure of fragile equality, not quite a bond, but perhaps some association akin to it, existed between us, but I knew that the ground could shift away from me any moment.

"You understand that if we find him, I'll kill him."

"I understand," I said. A part of me, the part of me that was beholden to Alice Xie, had been counting on it. Despite all the things I knew about Jaime, I still regarded him as a friend. For all the atrocities he had committed, all the sins he had trespassed... The more I learned about him, the more my closeness to him became shaded by anger and disgust. But I did still care for him, and when the time came to put a bullet in his head, I would be unsure. I would not be able to approach the task with the impartiality of my previous murders. Kaften was my ace in the hole.

"You're not really Army, are you?" I asked.

He shook loose a smoke and offered me one. It was tempting, but I said no.

"We're private," he said, confirming what Alice had told me earlier. We sat around a long table, kitty-corner from one another at the head, leaving a lot of open space around us.

"Corporate," I said.

"America's gone, pretty much, and what's left ain't what it used to be. The world's moved on, and everyone's starting to recognize that in order to get on with tomorrow, we have to face today. That's the PRC, the big old elephant in the room nobody wants to talk about. But behind closed doors, in far off places, people are talking and scheming.

California's big business, regardless of which flag it's flying."

He was talking about oil—and land, lots of prime real estate that could be bought and sold for development.

"In ten or fifteen years," he said, "you'll be seeing all these little post-nostalgia places. Chinese fryer joints with retro-cool movie themes and pictures and placards of Hollywood stars that nobody remembers or has even heard of. You'll start seeing little Asian men impersonating Arnold Schwarzenegger, with little Asian Marilyn Monroes dangling off their arms. PRC, USA, it don't matter. What matters is money. The new regime wasn't expecting the uphill climb to be as steep as it is now, but that's because they're politicians and not businessmen. Now the real businessmen are stepping up. Pretty soon, this'll all be familiar again."

"Especially after the displaced are flown out to Montreal and forgotten about," I said.

He blew out a big cloud of smoke and shrugged, unconcerned. "If they want to, they'll be let back in, if they've got the funds for it. I wouldn't worry too much about it. This is still California, and the PRC is surrounded by North America over here, not Asia. They've done about all they're going to, proved what they needed to. They're holding a solid hand now. So..." His voice trailed and gave way to another shrug.

"This camp, though... you're shuttling refugees out."

"The ones that want to go, that want jobs. The UN's not cutting it, so the Brits are helping out. They feel bad about how it all went down over here, and they've loosened up on their immigration policies. Ireland, too."

"So I figure, these businessmen you're working for, they must not like Jaime too well, him blowing up everything and calling for revolution."

He smiled. "Maybe I was wrong about you. You're not so stupid, maybe. Yeah, Jaime's a problem for them.

Nobody wants to come in, spend a few billion rebuilding, and then have it all explode in their faces."

"How did you know who he is? I mean, who he really is?"

"Military ain't the only thing that's private. And Alice Xie ain't the only one with a batch of memorialists. You seen her outfit on that, right? Now imagine if you've got real money backing it up, lots of it." He let that sink in for a bit then said, "It's how we found you, you know."

"A convergence web."

"Right in one," he said. "You're a minor data point when all is said and done, but you've shown up in enough important places with enough of the key players here to be a significant piece."

"So why go around killing all these people to get to him? To me?" I wanted to be angry about it, to feel some kind of justified indignation, but I was too used up to feel anything. I didn't have the energy for moral outrage.

"We're an army, son. It's what we do. Plus, it makes for good cover. PRC sees all these attacks and thinks there's in-fighting among all the disparate groups they haven't managed to snuff out. My group, we're working behind the scenes a bit. Think of it as urban camouflage."

"When you attacked the reclamation site... I was your target, wasn't I?"

"Yes," he said.

"All those people you killed..." I thought of Hafiz's face exploding against me from a high-velocity sniper's round.

"We had to make it look good. If one person disappears, PRC would get suspicious. Jaime might have gotten spooked and rabbited. We go in guns a-blazing, round up you with a few other civvies, and leave a high enough body count... well, that's just another day in the DMZ, isn't it?"

Bile rose as I listened to his justifications, but getting angry wouldn't do me any good. I thought about all the collateral damage his so-called urban camouflage had wrought then reminded myself I wasn't here to argue morality with him. Fuck it.

He must have reached the same conclusion. He stubbed the cigarette out on the table and stood to stretch with a loud grunt. Then we got down to business.

A better part of the night was spent studying the subway lines, gathering as much information as we could. Infrastructure records weren't quite as publicly accessible as they'd been in the old days, and the PRC was slow at restoring information records. They knew that information was power, and that was something no one gave freely or readily. It took a lot of archival digging to come up with very little. The EMP attacks had decimated the public record, wiped out all those little ones and zeros we'd all become so goddamn reliant on. In the end, we came up with about as much as we already knew.

Kaften had maps—a lot of them. Schematics. Blueprints. Building plans. I was surprised, awed really. He was sitting on a powder keg of knowledge.

The Metro subway system covered more than fifty miles of rail below ground. The Red Line had been built in phases, and we were traveling through the first phase, a five-station corridor that ran from Union Station to Westlake/MacArthur Park. The tunnel was roughly four miles long, with Pershing Square almost at the halfway mark. We were a bit closer, though, since Civic Center was the second stop.

It should have been easy. A seventy-five-foot-long subway car took up most of the tunnel. I recognized the Ansaldobreda A650 from Kaften's notes. The six-car train, all electric, had gone into service back in the 1990s. Ten feet wide, twelve feet tall, it sat on the rail tracks like a metal behemoth. I spotted the signature block-style *M* inside a red circle on the face of the car. We had to pick a side to go around it. The tunnel itself had an eighteen-foot diameter, and we were able to move beside the train easily enough. But we had little room for maneuvering, and we had to walk single-file, which was not good when the bullets started flying.

The first shot pinged off the concrete wall beside Kaften's head, showering both of us with bits of stone. He dropped to his knees, and I followed suit. We pressed up to the metal side of the Ansaldobreda, trying to make ourselves into smaller targets.

"We've got a collapse on this line." The voice of one of the men who had been sent down the Purple Line came across the comms. His voice was tinny inside my skull, but the bio-fi reception was clear, despite the thick concrete and the distance between us. He started to say more, but the sounds of gunfire and a sharp scream of pain interrupted him. I lost his signal, and from the looks of the men around me, they were equally troubled by the vacant pIP broadcast.

We were being ambushed. Hot sparks splashed across my face, and I could feel the heat of a bullet that had narrowly missed me.

"Turn off the goddamn light!" Kaften shouted, his voice booming across the feed in my head.

I responded to his barked order on pure instinct and the urgent weight of command. I was blind in the sudden dark, and I hoped that whoever was shooting at us was, too. That small sliver of hope was futile. Whoever was down there probably had night vision or optical upgrades.

"I can't see a fucking thing," I said, straining to see down the tunnel past Kaften's shoulder.

He and the other man, Andersson, both had optics and could see fine. Nanos imbedded in their optic nerves would be processing the data and filtering it for thermal vision then transmitting the information for display directly in front of their retinas. The imagery would be an odd dual overlay of their vision as it normally would be, with the computer-enhanced imagery mapped against it with as much clarity and color as could be filtered in through the software. From what I'd heard, it took some getting used to, and it had taken a few software upgrades for the mapping to catch up with the real-time vision processing.

"Just stay close," Andersson said. I could feel him shuffling close to me, but his voice was oddly disconnected through the comm relay, as if he were farther away.

"Get the door open," Kaften said, firing a short three-round burst toward our attackers. "Beta, what's your status?"

"One tango down. Alvarez and Laidon are KIA," Mitchell said. That meant he was the sole survivor of Beta team.

"Son of a bitch," Andersson said. This time, his breath was hot against my ear, close enough to ruffle my hair.

"I've got maybe half a dozen out here," the voice said. Periodic gunfire underscored his message, echoed in front of me as Kaften fired again. "SITREP?"

"It's shit," Kaften said.

I needed a minute to remember "SITREP" was short-hand for situation report.

"Hard to say how many are out there. Thinking six, maybe. We're all healthy, though."

"I'm locked down in a small maintenance cubby. I don't think I'm making it out of here, Sarge."

"You stow that shit, Mitchell. You hold your ground, and you don't give one fucking inch. You understand that? We'll wrap this up right quick, and then we'll come and save your sorry ass. You hear me?"

A moment of silence ticked by, then another and another still. The commNet was dead—painfully dead.

Kaften let out another three-round burst. His voice

practically boomed through the comm. "I said, do you hear me, goddamnit?"

Silence.

Another group of bullets pinged dangerously close. A spattering of concrete. A shower of sparks. The heat of metal.

I found myself inching back, butting up against Andersson, who was fighting with the door, trying to pull them apart. I wedged my fingers into the door, one hand above his, the other below, and we fought to pull. The work was difficult from a crouched position below the doors, but if we stood up, we were dead. We didn't have the leverage. I wondered if the Ansaldobreda's doors were locked. We would never get them open. We were going to die in this fucking tunnel.

We were maybe halfway between the emergency cross-passages that ran between the Red and Purple lines every eight hundred feet. Little cubbies like the one Mitchell had been holed up in were scattered along the line, too, for maintenance or utilities access.

"What about the troops outside?" I asked, thinking of the rooftop snipers Kaften had positioned outside the station entrance.

"No," Kaften said, so quickly I figured the word was a reflex action for him. "If Jaime bolts, those snipers could be our last chance to bag him up. He runs, and I pull those men down here, he gets away, and maybe I lose a few more men. Not going to happen."

"I'm sending a peaceful their way," Andersson said.

A peaceful was, in the parlance of the military's ironic naming scheme, a sonic grenade. It did not detonate in the typical sense that most grenades do. After a short warm-up period, it would unleash a nauseating sonic wave in a small radius to cripple those it landed near.

"Do it," Kaften urged. "Everitt, you cover your eyes."

My eyes were adjusting to the darkness well enough to see Andersson wind up and throw. The grenade landed with a soft thud a few yards down from us. A surprised shout followed. I shut my eyes tight, but I still saw the bright flash of light and heard the soft whump and the high-pitched screech of the sonic field.

The peaceful grenade had been a popular mainstay among crowd control and riot police. When it went off, anyone caught in the sonic blast was shut down instantly with uncontrollable vomiting and migraines. Although it was meant to be a more measured, more rational response than simply opening fire on a crowd of people with a hail of bullets, the effects were so severe that some people claimed that being shot was far less debilitating.

We still met some gunfire, but it seemed to have diminished. The muffled retching of at least two people confirmed this. They would be the two we would try to wring some answers from if we didn't find Jaime. We had no way of knowing who might be wired for DRMR or if any of them had mem backups, so the plan was to play it as safely as possible. If we met resistance, and obviously we had, we needed some of them alive.

Kaften returned fire, keeping the tango pinned down. Andersson and I took the chance and stood, working together to pry open the train car's doors. With both of us on our feet and getting proper leverage, we forced open the doors, and I climbed in.

Bullets chased after me, pinging off the sides of the train where I had been standing. Andersson grunted and fell back a step, almost losing his balance. I knew he'd been hit, but I couldn't see how badly or where.

"Reinforcements are here," I shouted, this time vocally. It was stupid, but it was a frightened reflex. I wasn't used to the long, sustained conversations over commNet. Kaften made his annoyance clear and shoved me back with one hand while helping Andersson aboard with the other.

"How bad?" Kaften asked, firing at the opposite end of the tunnel, where the reinforcements were filtering in.

"Not very," Andersson said. "It's healing already."

I watched him as he checked his loadouts and put a fresh magazine in his assault rifle. The stupid jingle from those old medichine man adverts danced in my head. Andersson didn't seem all the worse for wear, and that was certainly a good thing. Kaften knelt beside me, ejecting a magazine and replacing it with a full one. If he gave a damn about being seriously outnumbered, he wasn't showing it.

I had my gun in hand. I checked to make sure a round was chambered and that the magazine was full. The spare magazines in my coat pocket were a reassuring weight.

"Lob some frags downwind," Kaften said. "No more peaceful bullshit."

Bullets shattered the window at the rear of the cab, coating us in small shards of glass. The munitions went high, and we were low. We had little in the way of shelter other than the walls surrounding us. The seating was club style, so the benches lining each side of the cab faced each other across the aisle. Nothing to hide behind or use as cover. We were less exposed than we had been outside, but it was a fairly even trade-off on which was worse.

Andersson remained crouched low to the floor as he went toward the back of the cab to lob good old-fashioned grenades toward the new clump of bad guys waiting outside to kill us. He peeked out over the edge, trying to get a head count in the darkness, then ducked back inside quickly, just before the explosions.

"I counted five," he said.

Kaften nodded. "Mitchell took out a few, maybe? That's good."

I remembered Mitchell saying he thought there were half a dozen. I was dubious as to how well his efforts had paid off, but Kaften was struggling to keep our morale up. I didn't think we would make it out alive. Three against six, maybe more. It seemed too overwhelming. Then again, I was nearly as blind as a bat. Kaften and Andersson could at least see what was happening, thanks to their optics. Still, it all reminded me a bit of the Alamo. Not exactly how I wanted to go out.

In gun battles, time slows down. Sometimes, reflexes go superhuman, or people become subconsciously aware of elements around them—subtle changes in the air, noises that would have normally gone unheard, and small rhythms pulsing in the world that they would otherwise never be cognizant of. Reflexes take over and drive that person forward, forcing him to do things he wasn't even aware needed doing. Evolution spent millions of years honing the mind and body's instinct for survival, and sometimes, it does what it wants.

I had no conscious reason for it but, already crouched, I dropped to one knee and spun ninety degrees to face the door I'd come through. In one fluid move, my arm raised the gun of its own accord and snapped onto an emerging face. Before I even recognized him as an enemy, I pulled the trigger. Once. Twice. In the muzzle flashes, I saw the bullets hit him, tearing apart his lower jaw then his left eye as he turned to face me. Then he fell back and out of sight.

Kaften and Andersson stared at me, but neither said anything. Kaften clapped me on the shoulder once, and I could make out the sureness of his approval.

Time caught up in fast-forward, bringing more bullets with it. We dropped to our bellies as the bullets got closer. I pictured a team of military shock troopers marching down the tunnel, fanned out across the rails, firing their rifles in a continuous, unyielding spread straight out of some old holovid. I didn't know how close to reality that was, but they were certainly moving closer and trying hard to keep us quelled, making us an easier kill.

From his prone position, Andersson lobbed a few more grenades out the window, letting them land uncomfortably close to the train car. I sat facing the door, watching the side windows, looking for signs of the approaching enemy. Kaften was across from me and over a bit, his head swiveling back and forth, waiting for the doors opposite us to be forced open and for bodies to appear. Both of us scanned back and forth, over to Andersson then back to the gaping hole that we expected soldiers to climb through any minute.

In a moment of surreal calm, Andersson risked a quick peek over the ledge, found a target, and fired. I wondered if his grenades had taken any of them out and how many were left.

Outside the door, close to me, something shuffled quickly. Then an object landed lightly against the rubber floor and rolled. It touched my shoes, and I kicked at it, sending it spinning away from me, where it smacked into the doorframe. The grenade rolled outside, but the force of the confined explosion lifted the car and deformed the doorway. I had a moment of weightlessness, and my stomach lurched as though I were in a fast-moving elevator. Then the car resettled, half off the track. The floor was canted, and I had to brace my feet ahead and beneath me to keep from sliding. I fired at the wall, hoping the bullets would pierce the metal siding. Maybe I would get lucky and kill a fucker out there.

The person had hurried down, though, to the next car ahead of us. They were forcing the door open, piling in quickly.

Andersson glanced up over the ledge again.

"That's it." He nodded toward the front of the car. "Those are the last two then."

Kaften marched forward, his gun extended, and fired

at the small windows in the door separating our two cars. They were not shy about firing back and did so liberally. Kaften went back into a crouch but had nowhere to hide. Kneeling on the hard rubberized floor, Andersson and I shot over him. We were all shooting in a chaotic exchange of gunfire, making it impossible to tell who got whom, but in quick succession, one tango went down followed by Kaften and Andersson and the second tango, almost simultaneously.

I didn't even know I'd been hit until I tried to stand and felt a sharp jolt of pain in my leg. The bullet had grazed me. Nothing serious, but still messy.

Andersson was closest, so I checked him first. My fingers went to his neck to find a pulse, but I found a thick, slippery sheen instead. He was gone. The wound was too large, and the blood was pumping out of him too quickly for the medichines to do him any good.

Kaften was in better shape, but unable to stand. He'd been hit in the leg full-on and in the upper chest, near his shoulder.

"Just need a minute or two," he said, "to collect myself. Let the nanos do their job."

He was going to need more than a minute or two, but I didn't bother correcting him. The medichines would be breaking down the bullets into tiny little atoms, mapping the wound's channels, and working to figure out the best ways to stitch him back up and save his life. They would do a quick triage for his vitals, but it would be a few days before he was a hundred percent again. We had to get moving, but I didn't think giving him the minute he'd asked for would be too detrimental. I was surprised we'd lived that long.

Over their chests, both Andersson and Kaften wore nylon webbing, which held pouches filled with field-emergency medical supplies and spare magazines. I popped open the medic pouch and dug out gauze and a packet of Quik-Clot. I doused his wounds with the powder and wrapped his leg tight enough to staunch the bleeding then did the same for his shoulder.

"Wait here," I said. "Stay off the leg."

I didn't wait for a response. I was on my feet and out the door quickly. I thumbed the flashlight on, holding it and the gun out in front of me. If we still had hostiles out there, I was as much of a target with the light as I was without. Being crammed between the walls of the subway car and the station tube, I was as good as dead if anyone was out there.

The lamp's normally wide arc was stunted by my surroundings. Once I had edged my way to the front of the train, my field of view opened. My light fell on a dead man with bullet holes in his face. The darkness carried a soft whimper down to me. Then, closer, a wet smack hit the concrete as somebody threw up. I turned quickly, splashing my light over him, and saw the gun in his lap, his arm limp and still. He was sitting on the ground, his torso twisted to the right so he could spit up. He was in no shape to use the gun, and I took it without resistance. He glared at me lamely; chunks of his partially digested supper were spit-glued to his lower lip and chin, and the vomit was a bib against his shirt. A bit farther down the line, his partner retched again.

"C'mon, stand up," I said.

He refused with a weak shake of his head, and I had to haul him to his feet. When I grabbed his arm, his shirt was sodden with sweat, and a feverish heat wafted off his body. I pushed him toward his ill friend, and after a few steps, he fell back to the ground, dazed and tired.

Neither man was chipped, so a direct download of their memory cores was impossible. We'd planned on that contingency. We had our two prisoners, but we needed an answer from one of them. I explained this to them slowly so they could absorb my words through the sickness the peacefuls had left behind.

I shined my light on one. His pale skin looked slick, and the harsh beam of light did him no favors. His body seized, his head twisting to the side to eject a long stream of vomit. The side of his body lifted under the violence, and he passed gas. When he resettled, his body slid on the seat of his pants, and he made a loud squishy sound. Then the smell hit me. My stomach lurched, and I kept myself from puking. The other tango wasn't so lucky, however, and he threw up in his lap.

I looked down on the grown men. Their skin was shiny with sweat and yellowed by sickness. Covered in puke and stinking of shit, they wallowed in their own excrement. The military's approach to peaceful measures of suppressing enemy forces was steeped heavily in irony. Law enforcement and military were always caught in a quandary when it came to protecting and defending. The politicians thumped their chests and whined about how badly the civil rights of terrorists in the Middle East were violated when the US military killed them. Then they complained that mere detainment violated prisoners' rights. To appease the politicians and the ACLU, the military devised the peaceful sonic grenades—and were then berated for violating the basic premises of human dignity and using measures akin to torture. There was certainly nothing dignified about Jaime's men in their current state, but I had no sympathy for them. A few minutes ago, they'd been trying to kill me.

"One of you is going to tell me where Jaime Kristoff is."

Neither man did. I asked again. Silence.

"I know you guys are feeling shitty. Now, you can answer me, or I can make you feel worse."

They gave me some slight attention then stared at the

ground, at the vomit around them, or in their laps. Neither of them traded glances with the other, and neither of them would look me in the eye.

"Better or worse," I said. "I'm running out of patience."

Silence.

"Okay." I raised my gun and fired two rounds into the man on the right. The shots echoed in the chamber. He sat there with his mouth open, his brains a smear on the wall behind him. I waited for the man on the left to finish evacuating himself then gave him my full attention.

"How much worse do you want to make things for yourself?" I asked him. "Because now I can go real slow on you. Drag it out. And you don't seem to be feeling up for it too much. Am I right?"

A thick rope of saliva dangled from his filthy lower lip. The sockets of his eyes were dark pools against his pale skin. Flecks of red in his cheeks, around the bridge of his nose, and around his eyes told me he'd been vomiting so hard that he'd burst blood vessels in his face.

"A hatch, maybe a few hundred feet ahead." He stopped to cough up a thick wad of phlegm. The goo dislodged itself from deep inside his chest with the noise of ice cracking. "Some stairs. You'll find him there," he said, spit hanging from his chin.

Killing him would be easy. A bullet to his sweaty head, no resistance. No fight in him at all.

I left him and went back to the subway car where I had left Kaften. The cracks and ribs of the thick rubber floor inside were filled with blood, and the harshness of the light I carried showed the battle damage in stark contrast. The doorframe was warped and blackened, and the car creaked and wobbled slightly under my weight as I hauled myself back up.

Kaften was pale, but his mood was still strong. He got his good leg and good arm under him and pushed up while

I helped lift. He was strong, his grip good and sure. The medichines must have been putting in overtime.

"Learn anything?" he asked.

I told Kaften about my conversation with the one I'd left and that we could come back for him if we found out he was lying.

"So let's go then." He shoved past me to gingerly lower himself to the tracks. Even with both feet on the ground, he was unsteady and moved slowly, limping forward. I stayed behind him, throwing the light toward the rear every few paces and checking to make sure our six was clear.

We followed the sound of coughing, which was more violent hacking than anything else, and Kaften paid the wretched man a cursory glance before trudging past. I checked a few times to make sure he was staying still as we moved farther down the tunnel, until my beam of light could no longer find him in the darkness.

After about four hundred feet, we came to a tunnel that bridged the Red and Purple Lines and was used in case of evacuations to connect the stations. We stopped before a steel door with an ancient, rusty sign that said MAINTENANCE. I reached for the handle, but Kaften grabbed my wrist surprisingly quickly.

"We gotta check it first," he said. "Make sure it's not rigged to blow."

I'd seen enough vids to know that the handle on the other side could have a trip wire looped around it. If we opened the door, the wire would come with it, yanking out the pin of a grenade that would take off our heads. I shined the light around the doorframe, finding mostly rust. With a nod from Kaften, I gripped the handle and slowly parted the door until he waved for me to stop. The door was open less than an inch, and if a wire were on the other side, the line was still slack, and we were still breathing.

He took my light and shined it inside. Then he snaked

a few fingers into the crack, feeling around the exposed edge of the frame. Slowly, he opened the door farther and reached inside.

The door opened under its own weight, and I realized that Kaften had let it. Then I realized I had been holding my breath and let it out. He shined the light across the floor on the other side of the threshold then along the walls and ceiling. The doorway led into a slightly larger tunnel that went forward maybe three feet to a stairway that led up. An electrical utility box was just inside the door, but nothing else.

"C'mon." Kaften nodded me forward. Going up the stairs would be slow and tricky for him. "Batter up."

My path of light blazed a graffiti-ridden trail up the metal steps. Dead bulbs were trapped in rusty cages, where the ribs of metal were filled by cobwebs and grime. Our footsteps echoed in the cavern as we made our way up, and the darkness surrounding our small cone of illumination and Kaften's awkward pace—*thud*, pause, *thud*, pause—up the steps behind me made me claustrophobic.

We climbed the stairs through a square opening and into an attic. We were still fifty or sixty feet below ground, but the room was expansive and easily spanned the width between the two tunnels. The ceiling was far above us; at the sides, ladders led off to ventilation shafts. Rows and rows of old electronics were stacked in heaps that looked like shoddy pyramids built of ancient computer towers and bulky CRT monitors, relics that I'd seen in computer history books and old magazines archived in cloud storage. Office desks and chairs cluttered the space, too. Wrinkled, yellowed calendars curled away from their desktop blotters. A few other calendars were still in their plastic shrink wrap, and those, as with everything else, were covered in a thick gray-brown coat of dust.

I shined my light between the aisles of computer

equipment, then Kaften nudged me and pointed downward. In the dust were the perfect impressions of shoe prints. The confusing trails of steps and shuffles, some overlapping one another and others so clear I could count the treads, almost resembled an old dance pattern.

Although the prints were muddled, they all came from the same direction, and we followed the trail back, through a long row of manila-colored filing cabinets, steel-gray shelving units, and scarred wooden desks. At the end, we found a heap of sleeping bags and an old barrel with a still-fresh fire burning inside. A man sat beside it in a battered swivel chair, warming his hands over the flame. He made no movements for the gun that sat in his lap. Kaften had him dead to rights, his gun sights lined up squarely, even though it would have been a point-blank kill.

"Hey there, Jonah," he said.

"Hi there, Jaime."

"WHY DON'T YOU PULL UP a chair then?" Jaime pointed to the cluster of office chairs nearby, and I pulled two over to the fire.

"It's all right," I told Kaften. "Take a seat."

He slowly lowered himself, never taking his eyes off the other man. I had my gun pointed at Jaime, ready to put a bullet into his belly if he made any sudden moves or said the wrong thing.

"Thanks for the welcoming party," Kaften said.

"No hard feelings," Jaime said. "You boys set off a hell of a lot of my early-warning systems, tell you that much."

I raised my eyebrow at him. "What do you mean?"

He stretched his leg and rubbed his knee, where the arthritis was bad. "Place is wired with thermals. Knew you were here the minute you got down to the subway platform.

Figured you guys split off into two groups, heavily armed, meant you were trespassing."

"Where's my daughter?" I asked, getting down to business.

Jaime was surprised, but it slowly dissolved as he understood our roles. He had his secrets, and I had mine, but they had rarely ever conflicted as badly as they did in that moment. He appeared to be honestly confused. His eyes shifted from me to Kaften then to our guns, and something inside him squared away and settled. He grew pensive.

"Now wait, Jonah. You think…" He looked around at the nothingness of the room surrounding us then held up empty hands, surrendering everything. "She's not here."

"What did you do with her?" My voice was drawn and ragged, my mouth a dry well where my tongue was too thick. A hot fuse of anger was rushing up, and I forced myself to tamp it down. I wanted to shoot him right then and there.

"I don't know what you're talking about."

"Jaime," I said, "I'm begging you. I have a mind to do some awful things here. Please tell me what I want to know."

"I'm telling you—she is not here."

I stood, lashing out before I even really knew what I was doing. Violent instinct took over. I slammed the gun down hard against his face, breaking his nose and splitting open his lips.

"Where is she?" I yelled, hammering the gun down across his face again. Something broke away in his mouth beneath the butt of the gun, and I hit him again before he could answer. I kept hitting him, again and again, until I was worn out.

By the time my arm grew tired and the gun sagged at my side, loose in my hand, his face was torn to ribbons. His medichines were slow and overworked from the beating, but they were doing their job and keeping him conscious. His eyes were far off, struggling to focus.

"She wanted out," Jaime said finally. "You fuck. What did you think? Huh? You think I killed her? She wanted out, across the border. She was talking about Seattle. I know she fucking talked to you about it. Do you remember, at the bar? She talked about it. Asked me for help because you fucking disappeared on us. You fuck."

A pool of blood grew between his feet, and he hunched over, trying to get his head between his knees because he was sick from the gore he'd had to swallow to keep talking. He spit three of his front teeth into the puddle, then used his shirt to cover his face and sop up some of the mess.

I remembered Mesa talking about Seattle and the open-door policy they were testing. "So where is she? You set her up with a coyote?"

He nodded and then looked me in the eyes. His were cold and hard, the blue of ancient ice. "Alice Xie," he said.

The name on his lips ran through me with an electrifying jolt. I stepped back, practically tripping over the chair I'd been sitting in, and fell onto the seat. "Alice?"

We stared at each other for a long moment. Jaime reached up to his nose, gingerly touching the swollen flesh and wincing in pain. "Why don't you tell me what brings you two here, and let's work on filling in the blanks. What do you say?"

Kaften shrugged. Bored. Pale. "Whatever, man," he said. "This all ends the same."

Jaime hitched his shoulders then sat back, trying to get comfortable and act cool, but it was just that—an act. He was a good performer. He had fooled me for a good long time. But I told him everything. About Kaften's attack on the reclamation site. About being turned over to Alice Xie and her memorialist shop. About the convergence web and what I knew about his time in the military. About Alice putting the green light on him and how we were there to put a bullet in his head.

Then I admitted I'd been wrong through all of it, thinking we were on the side of the angels, killing our enemies in the PRC. All we were doing was killing innocent people in massive freeway murders, and using little girls to detonate bombs in crowded marketplaces to send a message. We weren't saviors. We were monsters. I told him how badly I wanted my daughter back and how much I wanted to get the fuck out of Los Angeles with her safe and sound.

Jaime listened and even gave some nods of sympathy. Certain pieces of information were gelling for him as the dots connected. He rubbed at his arthritic knee, and when I finished my story, he asked if I would help him stand so he could move around a bit.

"Ass is getting numb from these seats," he said. He promised no funny business and was good on his word. He strolled slowly, never stepping beyond the shallow reach of the fire's glow, and stretched his legs. His face was an ugly mask, his eyes lost in thought.

"Well," he said, mulling over his words. "That's Alice Xie for you."

"What do you mean?"

"She works in layers, man. Always. There's always some kind of giant web with her, like that convergence crap she uses. She's an information broker, but it ain't ever easy." He shuffled back to his chair and sat. When he had gathered the strength to talk, his story—or maybe "confession" was more accurate—took him a long time to get through.

Yuan, the *zhong chiang* who had been at the Berkley massacre before giving up his citizenship to join the PRC, had seen Jaime, when he was still known as Samuel Hodgson, gunning down the students there. Jaime had no way of knowing that or what information was in Yuan's head. He confirmed that Alice Xie had farmed the job to him and put a green light on the *chiang*. After I went missing, when I was kidnapped by Kaften, Xie had approached Jaime with the information she had learned.

She was willing to keep the information a secret—for a price. For Mesa.

"The boy your daughter was with, he's Tong. Works for Alice," Jaime said.

I recalled the young Asian man she'd been with at Fingerling's, but his features were vague and murky. I doubted that I would recognize him if I ever saw him again. "So you handed her over."

"Alice said she would help get the girl out of here, help set her up in the northern territories."

"So you just gave her my daughter?"

"I honestly thought you were dead," he said. "And it was a small price. With what she knows now, she could have handed me over to the PRC, or even the UN, and I'd be fucked. So... yes, I gave her your daughter."

"Then what happened?" I asked, bothered by the shifting landscape of whom I could trust and whom I couldn't. Who was lying to me and using me? Jaime, Alice, and Kaften all swirled around in my head, bit players using one another, using me. And Mesa was right there in the middle of it all.

Jaime nodded toward Kaften. "Then his little band of brothers attacked the camp. Knew a hell of a lot about our layout. Think they came there to kill me, probably on Alice's orders. Huh?"

Kaften sat there, not saying a word. I knew the information he'd used to attack Echo Park had come from me, but I said nothing.

"So, after that," Jaime said, "I figured all bets were off. I know Alice plays the middle, supporting me, supporting him, and never shall the three meet. She's funny that way. But after the park got attacked, I'm thinking she sent the dogs after me to wrap up any loose ends. That's when I started thinking about the *chiang* job again."

"And you sent your men after her at the restaurant."

"And learned you were still alive," he said. "And working for her."

"What does she want with Mesa?" I asked.

Jaime said nothing, lost in thought again.

"Insurance," Kaften said, surprising both of us. "Layers, right, that's what you said earlier. You do one on her, she do one on you." He looked squarely at me. "Then she lies to you, gets you to do her dirty work, holding some cards back from the deck. Holding your daughter, making you think she's here with him."

"And what, hoping I'll put a bullet in him, no questions asked?"

Kaften thought about that point then said, "Yeah, maybe."

"No," I said. "I don't buy it."

I looked back on my time with her and thought about the high levels of manipulation these two were talking about. There was a small pang in my heart when I carried the implications all the way through. I certainly didn't love Alice Xie, but we'd definitely made a connection. Over the last few days, our relationship had deepened into... what, exactly? Friendship, maybe, or at least something more comfortable than mutual respect.

"How'd you get so old?" I asked Jaime. His face got all screwed up from the left-field question.

"Jacked up the medichines," he said. "Reverse-engineered them. They keep you young and healthy when they're working right in one direction. Tinker around with their freqs and jury-rig the programming—"

"And they do something else."

"Right."

Then it hit me. I'd been so fucking blind. The medichines coursing through my body—what had she done to them? To me? I thought about the euphoria I felt when I was around her and the heightened awareness I had when we were together. I was suddenly less sure that my reactions to her had been natural. I wondered if she had been playing with my emotions by making me dull to the world around me, more eager to believe her, and more eager to please her. Or was that paranoia taking hold? After all the talk of conspiracies and Alice's manipulations, I wasn't sure what to think or believe anymore.

"Why is she holding Mesa?" I asked. "It's not so she'd have something to hold over me to get me to kill you. She wants her for a reason. Something that's above all of this. What is it?"

I paced, drifting in and out of the pool of dying light. I could feel the weight of their eyes on me. Kaften at least seemed interested, if non-committal. I kept thinking about layers upon layers.

"Go back to General Yuan," Jaime said. "Did you look carefully at everything in that memory chip you got?"

The truth was, I hadn't. All I had cared about was the rush it gave me. I'd used it so I could get fucked up.

Alice had told me Yuan had abused her stable of prostitutes, and that part had been true enough. But those were surface details. I needed to peel back the layers of everything she had told me in order to find the truth buried at the core of it all.

"Go to that filing cabinet." Jaime pointed to a cluster of them arranged between a few desks. "Third on the left, middle drawer."

The drawer slid open with a grating, metallic squeal. I found a cluster of chips inside, including the copy of Yuan's that I had made for Jaime. My mouth watered at the thought of a drink when I recalled cashing in the mem for whiskey. When I plugged in, greedy palpitations jitterbugged through my body, anticipating the rush of DMT. One more fucking thing to choke down.

Yuan had cashed in his US citizenship to become the PRC's golden boy, the man who stood up to America and joined the future. The PacRim marketing gurus who adored him had turned him into the cover boy for what being a good soldier meant.

But Yuan wasn't just a pretty face. And he wasn't just a little man with anger issues who took to beating on whores while he savaged them. In reality, he wasn't much of a fighter, but by the time he'd nearly washed out of boot camp, he was too deeply embedded as a national idol. He had a brain, though. A big one. He might not have known which end of a gun fired, but he knew a lot about human chemistry and physiology, and during his time at Berkley, DRMR had been his pet research project. He had been intent on expanding the applications of mnemonic capture and response, and he'd written several theoretical papers on the concept of body-shifting.

I peeled back the layers, diving in even further. I could feel the convergence washing over, and through, me. Yuan. Mesa. Alice. What Alice must have learned and must have known. What I was figuring out.

Alice was a devout memorialist. They prized, more than anything else, the living memory. They catalogued every instance. Short-term, long-term—it didn't matter. The memory was God for them. But the human vessel was finite. It could retain only so much information before it degraded, withered away, and died.

I dug through Yuan's memories of his research and what he hoped to learn and expand upon. I imagined what a memorialist might do with the information and what kind of implications this so-called body-shifting would have on the living memory.

Is that what Alice was planning? To use Mesa in a body-shifting experiment? To implant herself into Mesa's body? The more I thought about it, the more it felt right. Alice had made an off-hand comment about being somebody's daughter again. It hadn't struck me as important then, but as the pieces fell into place, it chilled me to my core.

CHAPTER SEVENTEEN

WHEN I UNPLUGGED, I KNEW everything I needed to about General Yuan and, I believed, about what Alice could do with this information. It had all been at my fingertips. All of it. If I hadn't been so stupid, so fucking blind... I cursed myself and my foolishness—then Alice. She had lulled me into a false sense of comfort and complacency before leading me around in the directions she wanted or needed me to go.

Stupid.

As I opened my eyes to the darkness around me, I saw Kaften standing over Jaime, his gun held close to Jaime's head. He was almost balancing himself on one foot, a grimace on his face. His left foot was light on the ground, too painful to take any of his weight. If Jaime had a mind to, he could have pushed Kaften over and made a break for it.

I didn't know what I would do if he did that.

"You get what you need?" Kaften asked.

I nodded.

The night before, Kaften had told me that if we found him, Jamie would not be leaving with us as a prisoner. Kaften wasn't there to arrest him. I had known that before I'd even met with him about my plans. Hell, that was why I needed him. I knew I didn't have the balls to execute Jaime. Not like I had done with General Yuan. Jaime was a friend.

If I told myself you're killing a man for God or country, it hardly feels like murder. The first time I did it, maybe then I felt guilty. Then I consoled myself, telling myself I'd done it for all the right reasons. Self-defense. For the US of A. Because God wanted me to and would reward me for the blood spilt in his name. Because these fuckers invaded my home and killed my wife. People come up with reasons, and reasons carry them through the day.

But there are lines. Boundaries that can't be crossed, no matter what greater good disguises them. Putting a gun to the head of a friend, a man whom I had grown to love and who treated me as if I were his son, and pulling the trigger—that was a different story. That was a boundary I couldn't cross.

That was why I needed Kaften.

Despite all the things Jamie had done, and all of the lives he had taken, I still couldn't cross that line. The gun was a heavy weight in my hand, and although it had been warmed by my skin, it still felt cold, obdurate, and *strange*.

Jaime sat there, waiting for it, his cold, blue eyes wide open. A small measure of compassion lingered there, along with a loss of respect for me. I watched the divide between us grow, and whatever had connected us in the past was slowly chipped away. I wouldn't save him, but I wouldn't kill him, and his eyes confirmed what I already knew. I was a coward. His eyes drifted away from mine, to a point lost behind me in the darkness.

"Can I have a minute?" I asked. The words were leaden, barely more than a hoarse whisper, but Kaften seemed to relax. He gave me a quizzical look then shuffled away in sort of a hop-step, into the darkness.

I didn't know what to say to Jaime. The words had left me. He regarded me again, more closely this time, with a measure of hope. Maybe he thought I would help him get away from all of this. A last-minute rescue.

The image of him towering over a small girl haunted me. He helped her shrug into a shiny yellow backpack laden with explosives, nails, and ball bearings then sent her on her way, telling her how proud her parents would be of her, if they were there to see her. Her large smile spread across her face as she looked back up at him, her clear, bright eyes full of innocence and pride.

She reminded me of Mesa on her first day of school, with a similar look and a full smile. Both of our hearts had broken as I left her alone, truly alone, for the first time in her life. That sad fear as it dawned on her that her mother and I couldn't protect her, and we were casting her off into the unknown world by herself. She wrapped her arms around my waist and buried her face in my stomach, wetting my shirt with her tears.

Jaime had cast the yellow-jacketed little girl off into an unknown world as well, where layers buried things she had no understanding of beneath the surface, like landmines.

My arm rose, stiff and leaden. Jaime licked his lips, but said nothing. He stared at the barrel of the gun and gave me a slight nod. My heart raced, sending a deep thudding throb into my temples and into my brain. I knew that if my finger found the strength to pull the trigger, I could not wrap his death in the flag, for that flag no longer waved. I wasn't saving myself, but maybe I would be saving countless other lives. That notion did not make it easier, and still, I did not pull the trigger. I tried to be self-indulgent and thought about the direction my life had taken since meeting him, but I had to square that against the knowledge that my actions were my own. I had to take responsibility for the man I had become. He was a dark angel, but the choices had always been mine. He had fed off me easily because I had wanted to be used, to be given purpose, and to be pointed at some cause. The mistakes were mine—all of them—and I found that I could not punish him for my errors or for my self-righteousness.

"Just do it, Jonah," he said.

I found his eyes in the dimness, and he met me straight on, gave me an encouraging nod.

"If you don't, Kaften will," he said. "I'm dead either way."

When I finally pulled the trigger, it was for Mesa. She was pressed tightly against me, her tears soaking through the thin fabric of my shirt, cold against my skin beneath, leeching away the warmth between us.

The gunshot was booming in the attic. Its echo was dull but lasting. Even through that noise, the splash of liquid and pulped flesh smacking against the concrete floor was loud. His hand fluttered and twitched on his thigh, but his still-open eyes were dead. I stood over him, suddenly calm. My heart no longer raced, and my breathing had slowed to a natural rhythm.

The second and third shots were easier. I almost savored them. I waited for the room to quiet and inhaled the stink of cordite through the air thick with gun smoke. When I inhaled, I tasted warm pennies on my tongue.

I WENT THROUGH ALICE'S EMPTY house room by room, not expecting to find anything. The barrenness surrounding me took on new meaning. The spartan style of the house wasn't a fashion statement or an inability to decorate. The house was chilly and empty because it had never been home. This was a safe house, a quiet place to lay low, hidden from the world.

I stood on the deck, staring out at the ocean in the dying light of day. Even though the squad medic had told him to stay off his feet, Kaften stood behind me, propped up in the doorway. His leg was healing slowly, and the squad medic, a guy named Boyd, kept insisting that he sit down. Apparently Boyd was used to being ignored. As I watched the whitecaps rolling in toward the shore, I recalled Alice rising from the waves, her caramel-colored body slick with water, and how the creases of her skin had tasted of salt. Even though I did not love her, my thoughts of her held remorse and loss that I had not felt for Jaime.

"You should sit down," I told Kaften, pointing to the Adirondack chairs near the door.

He shrugged, but sat anyway. One of his soldiers climbed the steps up from the beach, while another came through the doorway where Kaften had been standing. His snipers, Crassen and Myer. We'd all been through every inch of the house. Every drawer and cabinet. Under the bathroom and kitchen sinks. Every nook and cranny in the garage. We searched it all, hoping for some clue, some kind of indication as to where she had gone.

Not a single fucking thing.

The house was absolutely clean. No personal information. No records. No mem chips. Nothing. One of the grunts had even gone through the place room by room with a battle forensics kit, and all he had turned up was a collection of hair—mine and hers. If he found any evidence of our coupling, he kept his mouth shut.

No sign of Alice. No sign of Mesa.

"How's the leg, Sarge?" Boyd asked.

"I'm fine," Kaften said, although his bravado was lost in his pallor.

Boyd eyeballed him, disbelief plainly on his face. He hovered, but Kaften grunted and waved him away. Watching Boyd's pathetic ministrations unmoored something in me, an errant thought that drifted through my skull, fighting through the sludge of recriminations and pity. I seized it, trying to churn the depths for his name.

What was his fucking name?

From Yuan's research, body-shifting wasn't as easy as it sounded. It wasn't simply a matter of dumping your memories into somebody else's head. DRMR did that already, with no discernible side effects, save for the intended ones. Shifting was a more arduous task that required transferring an entire consciousness and supplanting the entire core of an individual with somebody else's. Although the research was dressed up in technical language and ignored the moral implications in favor of strict science, body-shifting was akin to snuffing out an entire soul. The procedure eliminated the very essence of life and individuality, turning the "host" body into an empty husk that could be occupied by an alternate. It was the equivalent of slapping a for-rent sign on somebody's forehead.

My blood ran cold at the idea of Mesa being used that way. Alice could wipe Mesa's mind clean, reformat her brain as a blank slate, and set up residence inside her, leaving her own body behind.

I had no idea why Alice would want to do this or why she had chosen Mesa. Her plans were wrapped up in too many other layers, and I was learning how complex and confusing her motives were. She always had an ulterior motive, and she thought several steps ahead, rigging the game to the point where the players didn't even know what they were engaged in. I wasn't sure I would bother asking for an explanation if I found her.

I didn't know Alice's level of technical expertise, but I figured that the complex operations of the brain, human neurology, and the ties that bound mind, body, and soul were far beyond her. She would need help. She would need a doctor—like Dr. Sanjar Hashmi, whom I had met on this deck after spending three days in a coma. He had injected me with medichines, supposedly to save my life, supposedly for the sole purpose of helping my body speed up its blood replication and to mend my injuries.

I remembered him clearly. A chubby man in old, cheap beggar's clothes, his fat fingers probing my bullet wounds. Round face. Thin locks of wispy white hair clotting his forehead. His bulbous nose flecked with blackheads.

I told Kaften about my time there and about Hashmi. I told him everything I knew about Yuan's research and my hunch that Hashmi was helping Alice Xie carry out the dead general's research experiments.

"Did it work?" one of the grunts asked.

Yuan and a few other post-doctoral researchers had experimented with body switching on cats. They documented the personality characteristics of four felines they had adopted from the humane society. Each had distinct personalities, behavioral patterns, movements, and habits. Each was truly unique. One was proud, where another was timid but engaging. The third was shy and quiet, and the fourth was energetic and approachable. They varied in age, with the youngest being a small, two-month-old kitten, and the oldest was twelve years old.

They'd shaved the cats' heads and bored holes in their skulls to fit them with cybernetic prosthetics that would capture, record, and measure brainwave fluctuations and neurological input and output. They developed small DRMR units that were implanted into each and then set about studying the animals' cognitive functions and memory creation and storage.

The cats were divided evenly into a test group and a control group. The test group was injected with a beta-blocker called propranolol, which caused a disconnect between emotion and memory, affecting the areas of the brain responsible for memory formation, like the amygdale.

So many human memories are linked to emotion. It impacts who we are, who we become, how we behave, and how we learn. One of the most powerful emotions of all is fear. The researchers subjected the test group to frightening situations—loud noises, barking dogs, electric shocks, sleep deprivation, and blasts of icy water. They systematically abused and tortured the animals, all while keeping them amped up on beta-adrenergic receptor blockers in order to interfere with how their small brains created memories of those terrifying events.

The highly potent mix of drugs was successful, and the cats' long-term memories contained almost zero evidence of the trauma they had been subjected to. Although the DRMR records captured every instance of harm, their brains did not commit the memories to storage and showed no evidence of ability to recall the instances of fright. The researchers had shown how to prevent the felines from creating new memories, and then they moved on to eliminating the memories the cats already had.

Building on years of prior research, Yuan and his postdocs began targeting molecules in the brain, rather than specific structures. PKMzeta molecules link the different cells of the brain, creating a rapid, nearly instantaneous network for communication and dissemination of information and responses. This molecular network also controls memory recall that shapes learned behavior. By injecting the test group with another drug called ZIP, the researchers were able to begin destroying the cats' long-term memories.

Slowly and persistently—using a combination of drugs, beta-blockers, and enzyme inhibitors—Yuan's group was able to chip away at the basic fundamentals of both test cats' personalities. At each step, they recorded the changes, until virtually nothing was left. After nearly a year, the two cats were reduced to, for all intents and purposes, nothing more than lumps of fur. They were basically comatose.

Then the researchers began transferring memories from the control group into the barren landscape of the test group's brains, rebuilding the networks of PKMzeta molecules in order to strengthen memory retention. They were given booster shots to support enzyme reactions, but feedback from the brain activity registers led them to continue with mild doses of beta-blockers in order to make the body-shifting less stressful. As the experiment proceeded, the researchers noted that as the memory transfer solidified, the host bodies became more agitated. They speculated that the control-group personalities had begun to realize they were not in their own bodies and were lashing out in fear and panic. The cats had been declawed, and that proved to have been a wise precaution when one cat began attacking itself. Lacking sharp claws, it bit itself repeatedly, mangling its paws and wherever else it could reach along its flanks. Researchers sedated the cat and gave it a stronger batch of beta-blockers. Eventually, its strange behavior began to subside, and it began to behave more naturally. The PKMzeta molecules took root, and after several months, the control-group personalities had successfully implanted in the test-group bodies.

The researchers then noted that body-shifting was perhaps an imprecise term or, perhaps more accurately, that the results of their research had failed to meet their initial hypothesis. The process ended up being less of a full-scale body shift and more of a hardline replication, similar to cloning. The memory transference was such a success that researchers observed almost no difference in personality between the control group and test group. They spent months documenting behavior and individual patterns and noted no incongruities between the two groups. Each cat matched its alternate, point by point. Their eating, sleeping, and bathroom schedules were perfectly synched, as were the way they walked and behaved. Even the tonal qualities of the test cats' meows had adjusted to reflect those of the control group. Although the test cats couldn't perfectly mimic the sound of their original bodies, the researchers noticed distinct changes in tone, pitch, and frequency.

"So yeah," I said. "It worked."

Crassen let out a low whistle.

"Damn," Myer said, looking at me the way a person looks at somebody close to the deceased at a funeral, unsure of what else to say.

I considered how Yuan's research might be applied to human subjects. I tried very hard not to think about what could have been done to Mesa over the last few days. I tried not to think that maybe she was already a vegetable and that if I ever found her, she would be nothing more than an empty shell that had once been my daughter.

"All right," Kaften said, slowly dislodging himself from the lounge chair and getting one solid foot beneath him, as if the matter were settled. "We find this Dr. Sanjar Hashmi and have a word with him."

Although Kaften was bombastic, finding Hashmi was a difficult task. If the PRC was good at anything, it was limiting access to information. Much of the general population lacked access to the online datastores, and wireless hookups were virtually non-existent. In some fundamental ways, California had been bombed back to an earlier century. Net cafes had been lost to the history books, and strict prohibitions existed on the installation and upgrading of cybernetic implants. Those of us who were indigenous were lucky our new overlords hadn't forced the surgical removal of our implants. Even that was due mostly to the interference of the UN, humanitarian organizations, and human rights groups. Not all POWs had been so fortunate, and scores of people had been unable to escape the clumsy surgeries to neuter their augmentations.

Even those who were powerful enough to be considered elite had very limited, heavily monitored access to the net, and their page returns were routinely filtered, censored, and sanitized, if not entirely forbidden by the strict PRC firewalls.

One of Kaften's tech specialists created his own secure

network, covertly piggybacking the PRC's datalines, in order to reach a hacker's satellite where he could log in to the freenet. Once he was inside, the job became a matter of sifting through enormous amounts of data. What should have been a simple name search yielded hits for movies, books, unrelated public profiles for various social media networks, viral videos, shopping lists, and mem recordings. Even after some extensive filtering, we encountered data that was too recent and entries that were too new—a reminder of how much the outside world had moved on.

The vast majority of California had ceased to be. A connectivity map laid over the United States would have black holes where California, New York, DC, and maybe a handful of other cities used to be. That's what we were facing. We were looking for a man lost in a black hole, a void of information. Whatever data trails Hashmi may have once had—a webpage for his business if he was in private practice or a staff bio if he taught at any of the local universities or worked at a hospital—were buried under newer, more relevant search patterns. Unless the datastores that may have once kept Hashmi tied in to the electronic world were housed in underground server units, those records now ceased to exist. Even finding a cached page was hard—but not impossible.

Eventually, we found him. A small fragment of a ghost, lost deep in the electronic ether. We unearthed a single cached m-log, which was similar to a vlog, but devoted solely to the sharing of memories and relied heavily on advertising. The site itself was inaccessible, and we had stumbled across what was, for all intents and purposes, a screenshot of a page. At the top was a small, short video ad for a neurological clinic on Wilshire. The clinic was near the VA hospital, and it probably had survived largely on referrals from there. After extracting the advertisement, we found that the names of the staff were encoded in the video's meta tags, which was where we finally found Hashmi.

The clinic was in a commercial district, surrounded by moderately sized white office buildings on one side of the street and larger, newer, glossy-black office constructs on the other side. The Wells Fargo complex dominated one corner of the avenue, but the building was in tatters. I remembered footage from about a decade ago when, at the height of the collapse, the bankers were attacked in the street by a riotous mob and the building was firebombed by people who found themselves solvent one minute and then homeless the next, their fates sealed in between the span of a breath.

We spent more time than I had wanted on plotting our route from our makeshift fort at Alice's house to the clinic and tapping into satellite feeds to gauge PRC troop movements and checkpoints. None of us, me in particular, were eager for a confrontation with the overlords. Not when we were so close.

Time itself had become a heavy weight, bowing my shoulders, while stomach acid burned through my core. By the time Kaften authorized a plan, the darkness was infinite, and a large orange orb hung in the sky. I watched the broken reflections of the hunter's moon against the waves and tried to still my soul. If I closed my eyes for too long, I saw Mesa, her eyes blank and damning as if there were nothing left of her to save.

When we finally left, Crassen drove slowly. I sat in the passenger bucket seat while Kaften was sprawled in the back, his injured leg up on the bench while he leaned against the door. Boyd sat in the storage area all the way in the rear. Kaften had ordered Myer to stay behind in case Alice returned. He was hiding up in the bluffs, watching her house through a sniper's scope.

I was jacked into the hacker's satellite, monitoring

PRC movements and watching for random roadside stops or checkpoints that had sprouted along our pre-defined route. The ride was smooth and the road barren, save for us. Crassen stuck to side streets through largely dark and empty neighborhoods, staying away from the more common, more heavily trafficked routes. Hardly any souls were in sight, maybe the occasional bus, whose bright-yellow lights shined through the windows, empty save for the driver and one or two elderly Asians. Crassen stopped for the lights and stop signs, intent on not drawing attention to our vehicle. The curfew was lax these days, not as bad as the early days of the occupation, when it struck an hour before sundown. But it was still randomly, and oftentimes violently, enforced. So I was careful not to let my attention stray and to keep my focus centered on the retinal heads-up display of the city map.

Crassen turned down Wilshire and drove through a desolate neighborhood of empty office buildings, barely distinguishable from one another in the night. Past where Wells Fargo used to be, the pharmacy across the street was a bombed out wreck, more of a soot stain against the white structure it neighbored than anything else. I squinted past the r-HUD, into the darkness, hoping to make out an address as our tracking blip closed in on the destination marker. All I saw were dirty white buildings that would need to be torn down and rebuilt if they were to ever be occupied again.

A flash of light off to the side caught my eye, then a buzzing whine drew my attention. Before any of us had a chance to say or do anything, the missile struck the ground behind us. The force of the explosion lifted the back of the jeep off the road, and Kaften was sent tumbling forward, into the foot wells behind the front seat. The jeep crashed back down, the rear wheels gone, with a sickening, crunching squeal as bare metal skidded across concrete.

Crassen lost control of the vehicle, and it fishtailed.

They were shooting at us, but the bullets were useless. The thick munitions-proof glass stopped the rounds, leaving compressed circular fractures around flattened, copper-colored rounds.

Crassen tried to recover from the spin, but the front passenger tire popped, sending sparks flying up from the bare rim as it ground against the road. The front of a building came up on us quickly, filling the windshield.

I shot forward in my seat, the seatbelt snagging hard and keeping me from going anywhere. My collarbone and waist hurt badly, and the belt stabbed into my neck. Crassen winced in pain, but Kaften, who hadn't had time to pick himself up from the floor, seemed fine where he was.

"PRC?" he asked.

"I still don't have any readings on them. It can't be them," I said.

"Well, if it's not them, they'll be here soon. They won't ignore explosions and gunfire in the middle of the night."

"We gotta get out of here," Crassen said. He sounded calm, at least.

I pulled my gun, racked the slide back, and made sure a round was chambered. I looked back at Kaften. He was up and ready to go, a gun in his hand, too.

The gunfire was coming from the driver's side, so Kaften and I got out first to lay down cover fire, giving Boyd a chance to get out through the rear hatch and come around to our side. Crassen was climbing over the center console to get out through the passenger door. We laid down short, three-round bursts, trying hard to conserve ammo. A short bark of pain nearby meant we'd hit somebody.

"C'mon, this way." Kaften pointed toward the building. The front end of the jeep was an accordion against the thick concrete. Broken glass on the ground framed a mangled strip that had been the bumper.

Kaften shouldered his way through the front entrance, where the door was nothing more than a thin sheet of plywood under layers of graffiti, and we filed in behind him, covering one another. The building's windows were busted, and rough planes of wood had been sloppily nailed over the openings from inside. We could easily see outside through the gaps.

We were in the lobby of a small office complex, an open area with stairs to either side going up. An elevator bank sat between the stairs and what I guessed was a janitor's closet, although the door was unlabeled. The restroom doors were missing, and the rooms had been stripped of virtually everything, right down to the ceramic tiles.

We hunched down on either side of the windows, peeking out, trying to get a fix on who was out there. Gunfire peppered the building, forcing us back down and away from the windows, but nobody was marching toward us. The whining shriek of another RPG filled the air before crashing into the jeep, leaving it blackened and aflame. The heat touched my face, and I wondered if the boards over the windows would catch fire.

"PRC?" Kaften asked again, wanting an update.

"Nothing yet. This isn't them. It's Tongs," I said.

He glanced back outside. "Yeah, that makes sense."

The PRC hadn't arrived. But Alice Xie had. Right down the street. On our side of the street even. Close.

"Boyd," Kaften said, "take over satellite. I need to know where these gomers shooting at us are. Track their thermals."

"Your upgrades can't do it?" I asked.

"If they're hunkered down inside somewhere, we won't be able to pick them up. Can't see through walls. Out in the open, that's one thing, but I'm not seeing any of them. We use the eyes in the sky, though, maybe we figure out where they are."

"She's got them out there to keep us pinned down, to keep us away."

"I think I got that part, thanks," he said.

"I need to get to Mesa. I can't just sit here."

"So what're you gonna do? Run down the street, hoping you don't get your head shot off?"

"I need you guys to cover me."

"This is some bullshit," Crassen said.

"Just listen," I said. "I think I've got an idea."

They got a good laugh out of that. But I gave Kaften a serious look. He quieted Boyd and Crassen then told me to fill him in. When I was finished, his expression was sour, but he said, "Do it."

276   MICHAEL PATRICK HICKS

T HE OPERATOR ASKED ME REPEATEDLY to slow
down, but I ignored her.

"A UN convoy is under attack on Wilshire," I shouted,
trying to sound panicky, which wasn't hard with the gunfire
hitting so closely. I gave her a hurried and rough estimate
of where the action was then begged her to send help.

I was using a choppy VOIP fed through the commNet
without visuals. She asked me to repeat, but I disconnected
instead.

Crassen had a foul look on his face. We'd argued the
merits of blowing their cover to the PRC, and Kaften
decided the risk was worth it. Crassen disagreed, but once
the order was given, he kept his mouth shut.

I looked at the men around me. Kaften, Crassen, and
Boyd. If they wanted to live, they were playing along. They

weren't UN. However, Kaften was working on that, arguing his way up the chain of command through an illegal sat feed, trying to convince his superiors of the direness of his situation. We thought if he persuaded them that his death would be linked to their corporation and that the ensuing scandal and diplomatic problems generated from a group of private military grunts covertly infiltrating a foreign nation on the company dime, they might want to hurry up and buy our way into the UN peacekeepers mission.

A whining shriek pierced the sky again, and this time, the missile struck the floor above us. The whole building shook, dropping sheets of dust from the ceiling. My ears popped, and the smell of burning things fouled the air.

Kaften was shouting, but I couldn't hear him through the ocean of dead air between us. The explosion had deafened me, and his words were faint echoes. Crassen put his hand on my shoulder and pointed.

Lights flashed outside. PRC. The Tong shooters aimed some of their attention toward them, and one soldier fell back, his hand gripping his throat. Another jerked and spasmed as bullets stitched their way up his chest before he went slack and toppled over. If any of them had harbored any doubts about my emergency call, that was surely over.

My hearing was slowly returning as the gunfire grew from small pops to a full-on assault. The soldiers outside were shouting commands at one another and at the hostiles bunkered in the buildings. The PRC had taken on the full attention of the Tong, and we had been momentarily forgotten.

Kaften was still sparring with whoever was on the other end of his commNet while giving me the middle finger. Crassen punched my shoulder as if to emphasize the disgruntled mood of his commander, then nodded toward the back of the lobby.

Alice was just a few buildings away, in Hashmi's clinic,

and I needed to get out of this building and into hers. I tried the few doors that were left. Most were thin sheets of plywood, the same as the front entrance, and led nowhere. Empty office. Empty storage. I found one that led down a short L-shaped hallway, to the rear entrance of the building. Old, rusted vehicle skeletons, the meat picked from their bones, littered the parking lot.

I stood there for a moment, getting my bearings and wondering if I would get shot. When I didn't, I decided Alice must have focused the Tongs' attention on the main strip of Wilshire, or else they'd abandoned their posts to help their comrades against the PRC. Either was fine by me.

I worked my way through the lot then up and over the fence that separated it from the next parking lot. I tripped over something in the dark but quickly picked myself back up. I moved fast, in a half-crouch, taking cover behind the shells of vehicles.

I was about three buildings away from the clinic. Then two. I went up a small grassy embankment, still keeping low enough to touch the ground. The grass was soft against my fingers, and my legs were aching, but I forced myself forward, into the next parking lot. I had to climb a thick, tall concrete riser and drop down into the lot, where I found more cars, if I were still being generous enough to call them that. One was in good shape. I couldn't tell the make. Some Chinese model—a new one.

I pushed at the makeshift door to the building, but it didn't give. Something on the other side blocked it. I put my shoulder into it and shoved harder. The door yielded slightly before the barricade reasserted itself. If I pressed hard enough, I could make a small gap between the door and the jamb. I dug my fingers through, feeling for the obstruction, which was cold, solid metal, not a chain. Alice's men must have put something like a desk or filing cabinet up against the door. I rammed myself into the door with all of my weight. The door cracked under me, as loud as a blast of thunder, then I heard a scraping noise from inside. I pushed again, the palms of my hands flat against the wood, my feet set. Cords in my neck popped out, my temples throbbed, a muscle spasmed between my shoulders, and something snapped painfully deep in my back.

The door opened wide enough for me to slide through. I had to catch my breath. Despite the cold sweat breaking out against my forehead, I had no time to be old and weak. I shimmied past the tall cabinet that'd been blocking the door. The damn thing had barely moved before it had butted up against a desk and stuck.

I heard the soft murmur of voices. The people in the room had to have heard the commotion, I thought, wondering how loud it had really been. The cabinet had slid over ratty old carpet, maybe bumped the desk. It may not have been so loud. Maybe it seemed louder to me because I'd been trying to be quiet.

A dim glow at the end of the hallway offered enough light for me to see. I was in a reception area with a wall of dusty old blue file folders—a few green, a few orange—divided by alphabetical tabs. No one had gone through them in a long time, and I was surprised by this. Social Security numbers were in those files, along with dates of birth and all kinds of private information that could be used to build false identities to get out of California.

Probably nobody had gone in there because the neighborhood was protected by the Tong—and Alice Xie, who could use and sell that kind of information.

Following the light, I moved slowly, afraid of making any further disturbance that would alert them to my presence. A hallway ran the length of the receptionist's area, forming a T-intersection with the exam rooms off to the left and right. The light I was chasing spilled from a room around the corner. Somebody coughed. I snuck a look and saw an Asian man come out of a room a few doors down and turn right to continue down the stretch of hall. He carried an assault rifle. In order to get to him, I would have to pass the lit room.

I waited and watched. A shiver ran through me from the sweat puddling under my arms and against my chest, making the shirt tacky against my skin. My nerves were bothering me more than the heat, and I wiped sweat away from my brow. Coming alone had been stupid.

The guard went down to the end of the hall, to a small window that faced the side of the next building. Not much of a view. He started to come back down toward me, and I slunk back toward the opening of the reception area, out of his line of sight. It put him out of my line of sight, too...

I guessed at the amount of time it had taken him to get from one end of the hall to the other. Then I crab-walked back to the intersection and glanced around the corner to the left. He was there, his back turned to me. I checked behind me, saw flittering shadows against the wall, and made my move, fast.

Most of the time, getting hit in the head dazes a guy. He doesn't fall unconscious right away, not like in the holovids. I clubbed the man with the butt of the gun, catching him on the side of his face right as he was turning back toward me, maybe sensing I was there. He was off balance and shuffled backward, scrabbling at the walls on either side of him, trying to grab some purchase to prevent himself from falling, but I was on top of him in a hurry. I hammered the gun down onto his face and heard his nose break. I smacked him again, hard against the temple, then he was still. I didn't care if he was still breathing.

Outside, the gunfire grew louder, sounding closer since I was in the street-facing side in the building. When

I turned, Alice Xie stood there, regarding me silently. She carried a gun, but made no move to raise it.

"I wasn't sure if you would make it," she said.

She raised the gun, pointing it at my belly, as I stepped forward. I stopped.

"Where's Mesa?" I asked.

"She's inside." She nodded to the door behind her. "Drop your gun."

I knew I should have raised it as quickly as I could and taken her down right then and there, but instead, I let the gun slip from my numb fingers. I didn't know if I was fast enough or who else was in the room with Mesa.

"Raise your hands, please, Jonah." She tipped the barrel of the gun upward. I put my hands up, and she motioned me to walk past her and into the room.

I stopped at the threshold, my breath caught in my lungs. Mesa was naked and laid out on a stretch of white butcher's paper on the examination table. A host of wires ran from her to a cluster of machines and datapads. A thick group of wires had been fed into the dataport behind her ear. Under the sodium lights set up in the corners of the room, she was ghostly white.

"Don't do this," I said.

Sanjar Hashmi stood over Mesa, fiddling with the connections while glancing back and forth from her to the machine readings. He turned toward me, as calm as a still lake. No sympathy. No humor. A visage of medicinal cool.

"It's already done," Alice said. "She's gone."

I tried to stammer out some objection, but the words were clogged in my throat. My face felt swollen. My eyes and cheeks burned. My hands fell and I took two steps forward. Hashmi thought I was going for him, and darted out of the way. Alice said something in warning, but I didn't hear her. All I saw was Mesa, and I went to her.

A stray lock of hair stretched over her forehead, lying

in her eyes. I brushed it aside, surprised by how warm she was. Her chest rose and fell. No respirator. Her open eyes stared up at the ceiling, lifeless and empty. Her breath was hot against my skin, and when I pulled her close, her arms went slack against her sides.

A strong hand gripped my shoulder, and instinct took over. I lowered Mesa, then turned and launched myself at Hashmi, tackling him. I punched him once, then twice. His broken teeth cut my hand and his lips. A gun barked, loud in the small room, and a bright flare of pain erupted below my rib cage. The taste of copper filled my mouth. Alice kicked at me, forcing me off Hashmi. I didn't feel anything, but there was blood all over the doctor and the floor. I reached to my side, the contact sending a howl of pain through me, and my hand came away slick with gore.

The medichines should have been pumping painkillers into my system, working overtime to repair the wounds lancing my flank. But they weren't. Between gasps of pain, it dawned on me how badly I had miscalculated. I shouldn't have come alone. Not with Alice Xie in so much control over me. She saw the realization had hit and smiled.

I pushed myself up against the cabinet. Alice stood over me, the black bore of her handgun resting casually before my left eye.

"I've simply turned them off, Jonah. I could turn them back on if you'd like."

Her light, lilting tone was almost enough to hide the threat buried in those words. With a flicker of a thought, she could turn them on and turn them against me. The medichines were hers, and they could devour me from the inside. Those little healing machines turned into carnivorous, killing particles.

My hand pressed hard against my ribs, working to staunch the bleeding, but I was feeling lightheaded. I had come to the end of the road. I looked over toward my daughter. The lighting made the ink of her tattoos stand out harshly against her porcelain skin.

"Mesa is gone, Jonah. This is how it has to be."

Hashmi was on his feet again, using the tail of his shirt to wipe the blood away from his face and mouth. His lips were already swollen. He moved sluggishly but was cogent enough to pick up a scalpel for protection, just in case, while giving me a very cross look. He was leery, afraid of being caught by surprise again, even with Alice and her gun between us. He kept one eye on Alice and me as he studied Mesa's vitals.

I realized the tears were falling from my face when I tasted their salt. "Why?"

"I'm leaving California," she said. "Maybe the country. But I can't do it looking like this. I need a clean start, something more than a false identity and some forged documents."

I coughed up a thick wad of phlegm. "People would be looking for you."

"Exactly. I have enemies, and they could track me down. I have what you call distinguishing features. A new body, though... that could really get me places. I could start over, be somebody new. How many people have the opportunity to do something like this?"

"You killed my daughter..."

"You could have left well enough alone. I could have come back to you, in her body, and we could have left together. You could have had the best of both worlds. You could have had the chance to be a real father to her."

"To you, you mean."

"For a time. And then when I finally left you, it would have been par for the course, right? That's how Mesa always repaid you, isn't it? By leaving you. We could have been happy for a time, though."

"You are one fucked-up little bitch. You know that?"

Not my words. Kaften.

Alice was surprised to see him. I was, too. So was the doctor, who took a few steps forward, the scalpel raised before him, either as a sword or a shield, but it made no difference. Kaften raised the gun, shot Hashmi point-blank. No questions asked, Kaften blew the man's brains out in a heap of gore splattering the white flesh of my daughter's body.

Alice was fast. Very fast. She spun, bobbed away before Kaften could get a bead on her, and opened fire. Two rounds hit him center mass, knocking him off his feet. I knew he was wearing a vest, but the impact still had to have hurt and had probably cracked a few ribs.

She turned back toward me, seemingly surprised to see me back on my feet. Hell, I was surprised I was on my feet, but the adrenaline rush compelled me. I lunged toward her quickly, and she shot again, hitting me in the chest. But momentum and hate drove me forward. A solitary purpose propelled me through the blistering, white-hot pain: I wanted to kill her.

I slapped her across the face and knocked her gun away. Her fingernails raked at my face, trying to go for my eyes, but then she grabbed my ears and head-butted me. My nose shattered, and stars floated between us. I ignored the pain, nausea, and waves of dizziness, and I grabbed her hair, wrapping it around my fingers, pulled her head back harshly, and rammed my palm up into her jaw. I heard the satisfying rattle of her teeth cracking. I outweighed her easily, so I turned her around as she took another swipe at my face, her nails ripping away a long strip of flesh.

I shoved her down onto the examination table, close to Mesa's face. I grabbed a handful of wires, tore them loose from Mesa's chest and abdomen, and smashed Alice's face down against the edge of the table, working to get the length of cord around her neck.

Her fingers tried to worm through the wires, to get a grip and pull them away, but I was pulling too tightly. Her foot crashed down into my instep, and then she hammered an elbow into my side, where she had shot me. My vision dimmed to a faint, small tunnel of black, and I nearly passed out because it hurt so much. I fell backward, taking her with me, and she hit hard, knocking the wind out of me, but I didn't let go. I let her struggle. I closed my eyes and thought of Mesa.

Then a new pain erupted deep in my core. The medichines went rogue, slithering through my system, organizing into a starving beast. Metal teeth tore into my muscles from the inside of my body, my arms cramped, and my stomach twisted into aching knots. My breathing turned ragged and painful as clusters of nanomachines clogged my bronchi.

The world went gray as gut-twisting spasms shook through me, and my throat burned from coughing. I forced myself to endure the stress, promising myself I wouldn't let go. Alice's body squirmed against mine. Her fingernails groped at my face, which I twisted away from her, so all she could scrape at was my ear, but at an angle that was too awkward for her to find any purchase. A sharp pain exploded behind my navel, and the surprised gasp lodged in my throat, choking me to death while the medichines furthered their creation of a hernia, twisting my intestines and setting my entire torso ablaze with agony.

I yanked the cords tight, wrapping them around my hands so snuggly that the skin stood out in white clumps between the wires, and pulled harder. The fight was out of her, and she was back to trying to work her fingers into the wires and jerk them away, to get air into her aching lungs. I yanked so hard that I was worried the cords would snap and it'd all be over.

Her legs kicked weakly against mine, her body sliding

against me. She tugged at the wires as hard as she could with one hand then used the other arm to elbow me in the ribs and belly, anywhere she could. The sharp bone of her elbow found the bullet wound in my side, and a new wave of pain shot through me. The world went black and spun. Still, I hung on, clenching my cramped muscles to keep her from escaping. She reached back, raking my face again, and her nails came dangerously close to my eyes. Her face was turning purple, and she was, very slowly, getting weaker. Her movements grew slower, but I didn't let up. I couldn't. The plastic sheathing of the cords bit into my palms, killing the circulation to my hands and turning them into numb, frozen weights.

After an eternity, her body finally relaxed then stilled. One arm slid down against me, then the other. Still, I held on for a good long while, wanting to be sure. Slowly, the pain in my muscles subsided, and I could breathe easier. My stomach uncoiled and relaxed. The medichines stopped their onslaught as their commands to betray me died with their master.

"She's done," Kaften said, tapping my shoulder.

I forced my arms to relax, the coiled tension bleeding over into throbbing pain and stiffness. Kaften pushed her off me and helped me to my feet. I couldn't move my fingers, and the entire length of my arm was filled with sand and needles. I had to shake my arms, flex my fingers, and rotate my hands to get the blood moving again. With every infantile step, pain stabbed through me from the gunshot wounds to my torso.

A small bubble of spit bloomed in the corner of Alice's mouth. I nudged her with my foot, waiting for her to spring back up. She was still. Dead. Mesa was still, too. As good as dead, after what they'd done to her.

I stood over her and smoothed out her hair. I pulled her eyelids down to cover her blank gaze and felt the warmth of her breath against my bare wrist. Kaften pulled over a chair so I could sit before I fell over. I wanted to talk to her, but I didn't know what to say or where to even begin. Words failed me, and we sat in silence.

Kaften found gauze with the surgical equipment on the tray beside Mesa, and he did his best to patch me up. He taped gauze onto my chest and side, but his eyes said I was a lost cause. He went through the motions anyway, like a good little soldier in an impossible predicament. Having done all he could, he looked from me to my daughter then nodded at me. He left us be for a time, and I had the grim realization that I was in a room filled with the dead and soulless.

Mesa's skin was warm. I was cold and searched for something to cover her with, to keep her warm, but I found nothing.

I wanted to apologize for failing her. My mouth opened and closed of its own accord, but every time I found something to say, my tongue tripped over the words, and I decided to be quiet. I held her and cried into her hair. Eventually, I was able to tell her how sorry I was. She did not move. The world swam around me, and I was dizzy and light-headed. My vision blurred from the loss of blood, and I didn't know how much more time I had.

I held her hand, my grip loose, her fingers limp against mine. I followed the long curve of the dragon's tail tattooed around her forearm and traced upward, to the thick body and the clawed feet that gripped the stubby ends of the strong Gaelic cross in a field of flowers. A story of her heritage. Of her mother and me. Of life, death, and rebirth. Her tattoo was a construct of imagination and fantasy, but I wanted her to know the truth of it all, not merely the idealized version. I wanted—needed—to help her remember and to rebuild her mind from whatever horrible damage Alice Xie had wrought.

A sharp dagger twisted below my lungs, and the world went black for a brief time, reminding me that what I wanted or needed didn't matter. The choice wasn't mine.

Kaften came in and told me it was time to go. He said the medics would come and take care of Mesa. He said she would be fine, but we both knew that was a lie.

I was sweating and bleeding. A long stretch of red stained her white skin. My blood.

I sat still as the sound of footfalls rushed down the hall toward us. Then I said good-bye to my daughter. I squeezed her hand, hoping still for some sign that she was in there, that a piece of my Mesa still lived within that pale, fragile body. Her hand was limp and unmoving.

I closed my eyes and joined her in the darkness.

W ATCHING THE RAIN FALL OVER Seattle, I drank a
small glass bottle of Canada Dry.

Mesa slept in her hospital bed, her eyes occasionally
twitching beneath closed lids.

A dull throb beat in my chest, a small pain brought
about by the change in weather. It had been sunny and nice
a few days ago, but the forecast called for showers over the
next few days. My hand was sore, too. The phantom pain
reminded me of the missing segment of finger.

I sat in a small chair, facing a small window in the small
room. The doctors, corporate hacks more than anything
else really, said they needed more time to conduct more
tests, make more observations, and take more notes. They
said she was doing well, and the way they explained it,
without really saying anything, made it seem as though she

was okay the same way a vegetable was okay.

Earlier, when she'd been awake, the nurses had helped her walk up and down the hallways, her hands clutching a walker and slowly pushing it forward. Her muscles were fine, and her reflexes were good. If they tickled her foot, she jerked it away. Tapping her knee with a rubber hammer made her kick forward. All good signs, they said. And although her muscles were nice and toned and could support her body, she still had to relearn how to walk because that was just one more memory, an ingrained lesson at the core of her being, that had been stripped away.

"It's a good sign," her doctor, who was one of many, had said.

The PKMzeta enzymes responsible for storing memory had been utterly destroyed, turning her brain into a blank slate. Her team of doctors had been injecting her with fresh enzymes so that she could establish a new network for memory storage. While her steps were steady and unsure, we had all noticed confidence, a level of comfort with motion, beginning to reassert itself. She was relearning how to walk and storing that information so that she progressed each day.

Learning to talk was more difficult. She made mistakes pronouncing words and kept to simple things. We were teaching her names and how to say "daddy." When she was awake, I no longer appeared so alien in her eyes. I was no longer a stranger to her.

I didn't know yet who this girl would become, but I vowed to protect her. I loved her, because really, she was still my daughter, everything else be damned. She was still my Mesa.

In the closet by the entry, I had a bag full of memchips from our old house, of our old life. Good memories—clean ones that I'd avoided for too long. Maybe, when the time was right, it would help us reconnect and rediscover the lives we thought we'd lost.

The memories encoded on those chips would be shallow, though. Without the context of the life lived around and through them, they would be nothing more than superficial glances into the life of another person from another time. They might invoke feelings of warmth, but it would be nothing more than surface deep. If she wanted them, they were hers. They wouldn't rebuild her or restore her memory, but they could, maybe, be a window into her past life.

Whoever she was going to become was up to her.

Alice Xie had told me nobody gets a second chance to recreate themselves or become somebody else, somebody better. When I looked at the girl in the bed, I knew that Alice had been wrong. Mesa would recreate herself like a phoenix rising from its ashes.

I waited for that day, and I would continue to wait for however long it took. In the meantime, I sat and watched the rain. I put my feet up on the windowsill, cocking the chair back on its rear legs to make myself comfortable.

The nurse knocked lightly on the door before opening it. She plugged her datapad into Mesa's port, asking me how she was doing.

"Okay, they say. She's sleeping good."

The nurse nodded and smiled, reading off her datapad as if everything was good and fine.

Some nights, Mesa woke up crying. Most nights, I stayed awake while she slept so I could watch her. There would be a series of rapid eye movements. Occasionally, a limb would twitch, or if the dream was bad enough, flailed and flung the covers away. The nightmares came soon after they began injecting the fresh enzymes, and I was left to wonder at the horrors of her dreams. What was her subconscious mind, perhaps as new and fragile as the rest of her brain, inflicting on that blank slate? What sort of confusing tapestry had her mind created to scare her so badly that she woke up screaming, tears running down her face? She couldn't say, of course, but she calmed soon after waking and was able to slip back into sleep after a short while.

I had no idea what was going on in her head, so I would hold her and say soothing things that she couldn't comprehend, hoping that the softness of my voice would console her. After a time, it did. She would calm down and let me wipe the tears from her face as she stared at me without comprehension. On the third night, she wrapped her arms around me and held me tightly until she fell back to sleep. I kept my chin resting on top of her head, telling her everything was okay, my own tears wetting her hair until I was able to lay her back down. After these episodes, she would sleep soundly through the rest of the night.

In the morning, the nurses came to help her through her exercises, walking her up and down the hall, encouraging her every few steps, and telling her how well she was doing. When they brought her back, she looked at me furtively, a small smile on her face. She came to me and put her arms around me. She whispered my name, and it tore at me.

One of the female nurses helped her get cleaned up in the bathroom. Mesa grew agitated when the tattoos on her arm did not wash off, and we had to console her. Her wet hair soaked my shirt as I held her, calmly telling her what the tattoo meant. She lacked context for the empty words, which meant nothing to her. The representations of her heritage were lost on her. She was a woman without a mother or father, completely without history. A tabula rasa.

The temptation to load her with memories was powerfully strong, but that would have been just as false, no better than what Alice Xie had tried to do. I had no backups of her memories, only mine. If I loaded her up with what I had, she would have a skewed perspective on a lot of issues. My memories would create more damage and cause more problems for her. I convinced myself that this way was better. She'd learned all of this once before, and she could do it again. I tried to tell myself I was already seeing some of her old personality coming back up to the surface, in small snatches here and there. I tried to think back to when she was a baby. Comparing things, I decided they were the same, but different. Harder than it had been then. More painful. Less confident.

The doctors said that although she would never be able to have her past memories restored, her ability to create new ones was unaffected. There was no reason she couldn't have a perfectly normal life again, given time.

In the afternoon, I rode the bus to Pike's Market and warmed the chill from my bones over a bowl of mac and cheese from Beecher's. The place was small and crowded. The line of people waiting for food stretched back out into the rain, a line of umbrellas reaching down the sidewalk. I sat on a stool at a small counter. Packed elbows to elbows, we ate with people standing up against our backs while they ate, not wanting to go back out into the cold, damp, and rain.

I watched the fish mongers, dressed in black rubber aprons, carry thick-bodied fish between them down the street, past the flower vendors and men with stands set up to sell hand-made leather belts, belt buckles, and purses. I watched the seagulls fly over the famous big red letters of the Pike's Market sign and watched people go in and out of Starbucks.

All the life in this vibrant city amazed me. Whatever scars had been left from the war were cemented over as people moved on and the city kept going. The news reported that they were in the last stages of rebuilding the Space Needle and that a momentous reopening was slated for the next month. There would be a big ribbon cutting, probably set to some Jimi Hendrix tunes, and a city official would sign a formal declaration to make Washington State the Province of Washington, Canada, and unveil the province's new flag and arms.

I found it odd that I didn't miss California. The Los Angeles I had known was gone, dead and buried, and it would not ever be home again. Seattle, maybe. Could be, given time, same as anything else. We were there because it was where Mesa had wanted to be, and as I learned the city and walked its streets, I found it was also where I wanted to be.

My legs were sore from the steep uphill climbs required to get from one end of any given block to the next. I tried not to learn too much because I wanted to share these moments of discovery with Mesa. But I also wanted to find impressive things to show her, things she might enjoy.

Kaften's company had an apartment ready for us, bought and paid for. They'd gotten our asses out of the fryer after realizing what a public relations disaster they were sitting on. Kaften's higher ups had made it clear that our interests were their interests. Kaften got a new assignment; I didn't know where, doing what, or for how long. He'd held up his end of the bargain, though. I had given him Jaime, and he had given me my daughter. I flexed my left hand, where my index finger was shorter than my pinkie, trying to work the stiffness out of the joints, and I tried to feel something for him. I couldn't, though. We weren't friends or colleagues. We were merely two men who had the means to get something the other wanted. We had found a truce, but nothing more. I'd let go of any hard feelings I'd had for him the moment I had put my arms around Mesa. His patch job with the gauze had probably saved my life long enough to allow the doctors to do the rest.

California rarely made the news, unless a significantly nasty earthquake shook the state or a vicious attack from insurgent forces claimed a large enough number of casualties. The latter was rare, and I got the impression that riots, resistance fighters, or acts of terror didn't happen there—at least as far as the rest of North America was concerned. The state was a non-issue. Old news. The media was soft on the PRC, working hard to avoid a fight with a bully by ignoring it and giving it a free pass.

I was fine with that, though. I had what I needed.

I went back to the hospital and sat with Mesa. She was awake and watching some holovids made for kids. The characters did silly things, and she laughed along. When the vid went to intermission, she looked up at me, and I kissed her forehead. She hugged me the way she had when she was little, her arms tight around the back of my neck.

"Hey, sweetie," I said. "How're you doing?"

"Hi, Dad," she said, and kissed my forehead. The kiss was wet, her words thick and unrefined, but she was making progress.

The doctors had said she was a fast learner, maybe because something deep below the surface, some residual memories that ran far deeper than simple long-term memory, helped her along. The brain is an oddly complicated, beautiful machine. We may never really understand it, no matter how much we try to toy with it or manipulate and upgrade it.

Rehab was helping her along, though, and the doctors gave her educational uploads through her dataport—small things like the alphabet and English recitations, slowly working up to simple mathematics. They were teaching her as best as they could, at a rate she could cope with and learn from.

I lay beside her on the bed, and she curled up against me, as she had when she was small and much younger. She was, for a while anyway, a small girl trapped in a woman's body. A simpleton, almost. I hated myself for thinking of her that way.

We watched the vid together, and when it finished, I sat up, pulling her up with me.

"What do you say we practice the alphabet?" I said. She was happy enough to do it, and we started slowly.

On our fourth time through, she recited the letters in a sing-song lullaby.

I tried desperately not to think of Alice Xie and the damage she had caused or the ruin left in her wake. I tried to find peace and solace with the time I had left, which I was able to spend with Mesa. It wasn't perfect. Not yet. Maybe it never would be. But we could try.

Alice had said there were no second chances, but I was going to prove her wrong. Mesa was going to prove her wrong, too. Sometimes, people do get another shot at life. Sometimes they have to pick up the pieces of whatever is left and move on. Every ruin offers the chance of rebirth, but I would have to fight for it, to work at it, always. There are second chances, but they never come easy. Not ever.

This was a beginning. The start of something new.

A NOTE FROM THE AUTHOR

Thank you for choosing to read my book – it's greatly appreciated, and I hope you enjoyed the journey!

If would be willing to spare a minute or two, please leave a brief review of this work and let other readers know what you thought. Reviews are incredibly helpful, particularly for an independent author and publisher such as myself, and can help determine the success of a novel. They do not need to be long, twenty words or so should suffice, but their impact can be enormous.

I look forward to your thoughts, and thank you, once more, for taking the time to read this work.

If you would like to know about my future releases, and even get free advanced reader copies prior to their release, you can sign up for my newsletter at http://www.michaelpatrickhicks.com.

ACKNOWLEDGEMENTS

First and foremost, I must thank my wife, Maureen, for her endless support and enthusiasm for this project. She is an inspiration, and I would be lost without her.

I also must thank the fine folks at Red Adept Publishing for their amazing editorial support. Lynne McNamee runs a fine ship and her help was invaluable. I owe a lot to the attention of Laura Koons, Sarah Borroum, and Stefanie Spangler Buswell, and their keen eyes. They helped me at each step of the way with editing and proofreading, and worked diligently to make this book better with each draft.

Eight Little Pages was commissioned by James Anderson Foster to design the audiobook artwork for his weekly Serial Audio production of *Convergence*, narrated by Travis Baldree. Claire's artwork now graces the cover of both this revised print edition and the updated ebook, as well as the complete audiobook and 10-part serial. I liked Claire's work so much, I asked her to help me refresh the look for *Emergence*, as well, in order to keep the visual style consistent across both books. I'm very, very happy with the results! Many thanks to Claire, as well as James and Travis for their hardwork in bringing *Convergence* to life in their audiobook forms.

I should also take a moment to thank the fine folks at Amazon for hosting the 2013 Breakthrough Novel Award, and the reviewers who helped an earlier, and much less polished, version of this manuscript earn a spot in the quarterfinals. Thanks also to *Publisher's Weekly* for their glowing review of that earlier draft. Without the support and kind words from these judges and critics, *Convergence* may have been lost in the clutter of my hard-drive for good. Instead, they provided me with a much needed morale boost and allowed me the confidence to move forward with publication.

And, of course, thanks to my wonderful family and friends for their words of encouragement and praise along the way. They helped keep me sane and confident, which takes no small measure of effort.

Thanks, too, to you and the rest of my readers for making this and all of my subsequent work possible. Without you, these books wouldn't exist.

ABOUT THE AUTHOR

Michael Patrick Hicks is the author of *Broken Shells: A Subterranean Horror Novella, Mass Hysteria,* an Audiobook Listeners Choice Awards Horror Finalist, and *Convergence,* an Amazon Breakthrough Novel Award Finalist. He is a member of the Horror Writers Association and the Great Lakes Association of Horror Writers.

In addition to his own works of original fiction, he has written for the online publications Audiobook Reviewer and Graphic Novel Reporter, and has previously worked as a freelance journalist and news photographer in Metro Detroit.

Michael lives in Michigan with his wife and two children. In between compulsively buying books and adding titles that he does not have time for to his Netflix queue, he is hard at work on his next story.

To stay up to date on Michael's latest releases, join his newsletter at: http://bit.ly/1H8slIg

Website:
http://michaelpatrickhicks.com

E-mail:
mphicks@michaelpatrickhicks.com

Facebook:
http://www.facebook.com/authormichaelpatrickhicks

Twitter:
http://www.twitter.com/MikeH5856

ALSO AVAILABLE

EMERGENCE
DRMR SERIES, BOOK 2

SOME MEMORIES ARE BETTER LEFT FORGOTTEN...

Still recovering from the events that befell her in Los Angeles, Mesa Everitt is learning how to rebuild her life.

The murder of a memorialist enclave changes all of that and sets into motion a series of violence that forces her into hiding.

Hunted by a squad of corporate mercenaries, with the lives of her friends and family in danger, Mesa has no one to turn to, but she holds a dark secret inside her skull. She has no knowledge of that secret, but it is worth killing for.

The ghosts of her haunted, forgotten past are about to emerge.

The thrilling sequel to Convergence that readers are calling an "energetic," fast-paced, "roller coaster ride" is available now!

Read on for an excerpt...

A DRMR NOVEL, BOOK 2
EMERGENCE
MICHAEL
PATRICK
HICKS

Sex and death flowed freely, amped up across the nightclub's bio-fi. The emotions and sensations were intoxicating. The music was loud; the bodies, sweaty. Strangers ground against one another, riding the waves of euphoria.

Mesa Everitt felt a body press against her, and she tilted her hips back, swiveling her waist, waving her hands above her head. The response was instant, and she smiled, leaning her weight against the handsome stranger. With a sloppy-drunk grin plastered on his face, her boyfriend, Kaizhou, watched Mesa dancing. Eyes wide, pupils small, he enjoyed the show. Then he stepped up and embraced her, stealing her back from the strange man.

"This is amazing," she said.

His tongue flicked against hers, nearly in sync with the

strumming pound of an electric cello and the blasted riff of a synthetic piano. She locked her arms around his neck, staving off a wave of dizziness. Strange hands moved across her hips, but she didn't care. Couldn't care.

Watching, their friend Jade danced with an easy rhythm, her skin glistening under the pulsating lights. She disappeared briefly as a wave of artificial smoke crossed over her. Moving bodies generated air currents strong enough to part the foggy vapor before it could fully enshroud her. In those few seconds of her slight disappearance, she had found a companion.

Center stage, on a large floating platform above them, Muzyakimo Aki sang. His voice was powerful for such a slim, meek-looking man. He wore thick black frames, and his hair had been dyed multiple colors—purple, yellow, and red—against his natural black. His eyebrows were bushy, nearly a unibrow, and his gaunt face was pockmarked. But his voice... the rich timbre lulled listeners, ensnaring them in a rapture that demanded attention and seriousness. Like Aki himself, his music was a study of contrasts. Every verse, every chorus, each solo, and the chords themselves meant something different to each listener.

The DRMRs on the dance floor were transmitting freely, their lithe figures awash in the experiences of varied pasts. For the last hour and a half, Mesa had been submerged in the lives of others. Aki's music pulsed through her, and she swam through the crowd's associated memory cues streaming across the bio-fi. The sadness and joy of more than a hundred strangers pushed through her DRMR implant. She mourned the loss of a beloved pet then was caught up in the throes of a first orgasm and the loss of virginity. She felt the pride of a first A in school and the crushing defeat of a first F after the tedium of studying for a complex exam. She remembered the first time this particular Aki song came across the entertainment comm, but only a snippet had played before Mom interrupted with a list of chores. Then she shared outrage over illegal whale hunts and fishery raids by corpo suits, and Aki's music was very nearly a call to arms.

She soaked up the experiences and memories, none of them hers.

Onstage, the synthetic dancers bumped and ground, dancing against one another. They were older models, appearing human in only the most superficial ways. With slender arms and legs, as well as jointed fingers and toes, the dancers were clearly artificial. Inhuman. Their skin was shiny egg-white plastic moldings, and a cool electric-blue ring encircled their cybernetic eyes. Facial features were barely defined. Their designer had instead opted for the subtle impression of a face pressed into smooth, flat planes. The aesthetic was both undeniably beautiful and disconcerting. The dancers were logged in to the bio-fi feed, and their mimicry captures were set to resemble movements of people in the crowd. They danced with cybernetic abandon but with a computerized off-set that forced a stutter to their steps.

For a brief, halting moment, Mesa rose above the crowd, her mind soaring higher than those around her. She could see the flashes of memory, the pattern of convergence that roped through each individual soul, tying one to another. The sight was electrifying and beautiful. Their thoughts jived against the laser-light show. Bodies slammed against one another; others held embraces. Slick human machines slid against one another, exchanging kisses and sweat, running fingers through the hair of strangers. Their subconscious echoed against the synthpop of Aki's performance, the wails of electronic guitars, and the random interruptions of found noises turned into hyper-idealized artificialities. Mesa floated, briefly ethereal, long enough to see the man at the center of the convergence.

Like a hollow void, he was disconnected from those around him. A black ember burning brightly, Muzyakimo Aki united everyone around him, yet stood apart from them all. Nothing flowed from or through him. He was a jetty, an interjection in the center of the convergence.

Hands slid up Mesa's flanks, and her mouth pressed tightly against Kaizhou's, their tongues exploring one another's. He held her with a promise to never let go. Discerning the flow of his memories from the tangled current of everyone else's was impossible.

She had tried posh a year ago and marijuana the year before that. Neither was remotely similar to the rush of hundreds of souls and thousands of memories amplified through the bio-fi's feedback loop. She'd been high before, but the euphoria she felt at that moment was... exciting. She was truly high.

Jade had joined them at some point. Mesa blinked with languid slowness, taking Jade's arm and pulling her closer, so that both Jade and Kaizhou hugged her. Mesa enjoyed being between them, and she laughed as Jade's companion pressed his way in, nuzzling at Jade's long, glistening neck.

The percussions drove on, deeper and deeper, pulsing harder and harder. The concussive shockwave of sound slowly degraded into a shrill siren before giving way to pure silence. A thin skein of fog blanketed the crowd as the lights powered down, plunging the club into darkness. And then the crowd exploded in cheers, screams, and applause. The dim houselights slowly warmed up, and beneath their soft glow, Aki waved at the crowd and nodded. He turned sharply and strode offstage without a word.

"That was amazing," Mesa said again. She wiped a bright-red streak of hair away from her eyes, pushing the trails of natural black behind her ears.

She was sweaty and high, and her heart was hammering. She'd been dancing for two hours, and her throat was tight and sore from screaming along to the music and cheering for Aki. Her words were a harsh whisper, difficult to edge past her lips. She was exhausted and energized to the point of being hyper.

Fingers danced up her arm, and she met the smiling face of Jade's companion.

"Cool tattoo," he said, his index and middle finger slicking away the sweat as his digits traced the curve of a thick green dragon tail as it wrapped around a Gaelic cross.

"Thanks," she said, her throat constricting against the word in painful defiance. It came out husky and hollow. She tilted her body slightly away from him, leaning into Kaizhou enough to make it clear she didn't want this stranger touching her. More, she didn't want to discuss the tattoo.

Her arm was a sleeve of color, but she didn't remember getting the tattoo. She didn't know why she had it or what it meant. And the why of all that was a whole other story she didn't want to go into. Not there, not after Aki's performance. She was already feeling the come-down, and she knew the stranger's questions would make things worse and leave her uncomfortable.

Her fingers laced between her Kaizhou's, she said to him, "Let's go."

Jade was lost in the attentions of her companion, but Mesa nudged her anyway and tugged at her fingers.

"You coming?"

Jade's free hand was lost in the long hair of the man suckling at the joint of her neck and shoulder. She smiled and promised, "I'll catch up later." She gave Mesa's hand a squeeze goodbye then turned to face the man behind her to continue their familiarization.

The crowd was slowly thinning, but the bar and dance floor were still crowded. The club stank of sweat, spilt booze, and reefer. The floor was tacky. Mesa and Kaizhou jostled their way to the exit, shimmying between couples, gently pushing around others. Cold air blasted their hot bodies as they stepped outside. The physical force drew their breath away and frosted it in the early morning air.

In the clear sky, bright stars and a full moon illuminated Mount Rainer in the distance, and closer, the Space Needle and the Seattle skyline glowed.

"That's fucking beautiful," Mesa said.

Kaizhou followed her gaze. Neither ever tired of the view. He took her in his arms and kissed her bare shoulder. She tilted her head so that their temples touched. A small sigh of happiness blossomed into a white puff before her lips.

"You OK?" he asked.

She slipped her hand into the back pocket of his jeans, warming her palm against the curve of flesh beneath the thin fabric. "Yeah, I'm good."

She traced the outlines of the stars, making imaginary constellations, connecting them across time and distance. She was the center of that convergence, with Kaizhou beside her. Somehow, some way, she imagined it all connecting back to Muzyakimo Aki, drawing him into her web and unraveling his secrets. Onstage, the man had been an inspiring enigma, and standing in the middle of the sidewalk outside the club, she dreamed of connecting with him, pouring her hopes into him, and pulling from him all of the details of his life so that she might wrap herself in his purpose and find an aim in life.

"You sure you're all right?"

Her gaze, far-off and distant, snapped back into focus. Her eyes drew a bead on Kaizhou. She gave him a smile that washed away the troubled expression on his face, forcing a grin out of him.

Playfully, she squeezed his bottom. "I'm fine," she said.

He leaned close, nose to nose with her. Their smiles

widened, and for that evening at least, she found purpose.

Later, she quietly disentangled herself from sodden bedsheets. Warm air blew from the ducts, but by the time it reached her, it felt cool against her bare, sweat-slicked skin. She wrapped herself in a chenille blanket and curled up in the plush leather chair in Kaizhou's living room, hugging her legs close and resting her chin against the peaks of her kneecaps. She could make out the muffled sounds of his snores through the thin walls of the small apartment.

The emotional ecstasy from Aki's concert was dissipating, and she was crashing back to the baseline of normalcy. The emotional low bordered on depression simply because the highs of the night had been so far above. Such was the risk one bore for attending an Aki performance with guards willfully down to allow the bio-fi amplifiers unrestricted access to the DRMR enhancements. The memory was a powerful, jolting surge, exhausting in its exactness, and she didn't risk replaying it.

No matter how well one's memories were stored and replayed, they never captured the lived experience exactly due to the lack of amplification. Anybody who'd been to one of Aki's shows understood that risk, and all others were befuddled. The memories were a one-off, stored for enjoyment and reminiscing, but never replayed because the replay was hollow and untrue, cheapening the individual experience.

She wiped away a tear, grateful for the memory and its freshness. The memory was truly her own, even if she lacked a wealth of experiences from which to draw cues and associations while lost in the throes of Aki's music. She cried softly, but the tears were not of sadness.

She knew she couldn't go home in her wrecked state.

Her nerves needed to settle, and the jitters needed to pass.

Sporadic traffic passed below, separated by long intermissions. The dull rhythm was enough to make her eyes heavy then lull them closed.

"Hey, wakey-wakey," Kaizhou said, squeezing her shoulders. His thumbs made slow, long circles along the muscles above her collarbones. The massage was enough to wake her and pleasing enough to keep her eyes shut.

"But I don't wanna," she said, mumbling the childish mantra and exaggerating her sleepiness. The daylight surprised her. Kaizhou stood next to her, still naked. She kissed his hipbone and buried her face against his belly, breathing in his scent.

Slowly, Mesa unfolded herself from the chair, keeping herself wrapped up in the blanket, adoring its soft gentle comfort against her body. She gave him a peck on the cheek as she passed then began rounding up the trail of errant clothes.

She frowned at the previous evening's mini-skirt and halter top. The outfit was fine for a late night of clubbing but not exactly appropriate morning wear if she wanted to avoid the walk of shame.

"I'm borrowing some sweats," she called out as she pulled the drawstrings tight. Then she lost herself in one of his baggy University of Washington sweatshirts.

In the bathroom, she combed back her hair and let it fall over her shoulders. She studied her reflection, pleasantly surprised by what she saw. The smart-mirror flashed a quick "GOOD MORNING." Then the default presets loaded unobtrusively along the side and bottom: the weather forecast—cloudy, fifty-six, seventy percent chance of rain after 6 p.m.—stock reports, and a news ticker accompanied by a talking head who delivered the top news stories. Mesa turned on the water faucet, and the sink's biometrics measured her temperature and pulse rate.

The data presented itself on the bottom-right corner of the mirror, next to a pulsating, bright-red heart icon. It told her she was in excellent health for a woman in her early twenties.

Emotionally and mentally, she had reached her baseline of normalcy, and she felt surprisingly good. Her earlier breakdown after the high was fading, clouded over by the memories of better feelings. A fullness had engulfed her and made her content. The only thing missing was coffee.

The door of the flat opened with a protesting squeal. The noise was enough to wake Jonah from his stupor. Mesa met his frown with an apologetic smile.

"I was getting worried," he said, pushing himself into a seated position on the sofa. "You didn't call."

Mesa felt her cheeks flush with guilt. "I'm sorry. I got wrapped up in my night out."

"You know I worry about you, right?"

"Yeah, Dad, I know. I'm sorry."

"You need to be careful out there."

"I know. I said I'm sorry." She talked over her shoulder, moving into the kitchen, both hands wrapped around a cup of Morning Java blend.

"You need to call me when you're going to be out all night."

"Look," she said, "I told you I'm sorry. Move on."

She tossed the plastic lid in the recycler then took a deep breath of the coffee's aroma, letting the steam warm her face.

"I needed a night out. That's all. Needed to have some fun." She sat next to him, tucking her legs beneath herself.

"I get that," he said. His hunt for the next words was plainly difficult.

Mesa's therapist had suggested they learn better communication skills and encouraged them to be open with one another. Open lines of communication would be difficult for both of them, the doctor had said, but being honest about their feelings and speaking freely without worry of judgment was necessary. Jonah had taken the message to heart. Still, it never came easy. He was a buttoned-up sort.

"It's just that... before, I mean. You used to disappear a lot. You'd come and go whenever you wanted, and I don't want you to feel like a prisoner, but—God, am I making any sense?"

She rubbed his back with the palm of her hand and gave him a quick peck on the forehead. "It's cool, Dad. I get it. I screwed up."

On the coffee table were curled e-papers. Jonah's drafting pencil had rolled to the floor. She recognized the woman emerging from the thin lines and rough markings. The prominent cheekbones were defined with light shadows. Mesa knew her mother's face only from her father's drawings and the rare mem recording she kept in her bedroom.

She took a deep breath then continued. "I wasn't thinking about you. I was focusing on myself."

"You should be able to do that, though. You deserve your own space, time to yourself, whatever. Call next time, OK?"

She gave him another quick peck then pushed herself up. "I need to study."

"You're doing great, you know."

She beamed. "It feels like it. I think I'm finding my groove."

A smattering of data chips were splayed across the desktop in her bedroom, along with empty coffee cups, which she dumped into a small trashcan. Her clubbing outfit went into a hamper filled with the last few days' worth of pending laundry.

She fished the DRMR pad from a desk drawer and uncoiled the thin black cable. She scooped back her hair behind her ear and plugged the male end of the cord into the port that lay flush with her skin. An electronic chill bloomed inside her as the devices in her skull mated with the peripheral device and queued up the menu. The display came alive, splayed across her retinas. She gave the play button a mental tap, and the data began synchronizing with the installed REMINDER software.

Developed by DARPA to help brain-damaged soldiers recover from trauma, REMIND mimicked the hippocampus and aided long-term memory storage. DRMR, an earlier DARPA invention that had expanded into the civilian market, relied heavily on the hippocampus. Because that segment of her brain was severely damaged, DRMR was largely useless. However, with the addition of the REMIND prosthetics and some rewiring, her DRMR became a natural delivery system for the REMINDER protocols.

Three years earlier, she had been abducted and suffered severe trauma at the hands of a madwoman, Alice Xie. Mesa had woken in a hospital with no memory, no identity. A stranger had been beside her. Her father. He'd done everything he could to help, but any hope of recovering her lost past had vanished. Her life prior to that reawakening was gone forever.

She'd relearned many of the skills she had once had through a series of progressively difficult learning modules. With the REMINDER downloads came homework—lots of it.

The last three years had been grueling but progressive. Mesa was a quick learner, and her degree of determination, commitment, and achievement astounded her doctors and private tutors.

Her tutors believed that in another year, she would be able to pass the GED and start hunting for colleges. She wasn't sure what she would study, and she rarely thought about that aspect of her future. Although she couldn't remember her past, the void of things forgotten clung to her like a shawl. She was more interested in unearthing her previous life and learning more about her own history than worrying about what might become of tomorrow.

By the time the first tutorial was finished, her coffee was cool. Still, the acidic bitterness set off a spark of pleasure. She shut her eyes briefly, smiling to herself. She interrupted the dataflow and dislodged the chip before hunting through the rest scattered on the desktop.

She swiveled the chair around, propped her feet up on the edge of the bed, and leaned back. Mesa plugged in a new chip and let a scrap of the unremembered past wash over her.

Mesa was two years old, running barefoot through the grass. She wore purple pants and a T-shirt with a big yellow flower on it, her full belly poking out beneath the fabric. Her face was chubby, and she was constantly laughing. A smile stretched so widely across her face that her cheeks nearly pushed shut her eyes. Large and black, those almond-shaped eyes tilted upward, the clearest mark of her Japanese heritage from her mother.

Her laugh was infectious. She clung to Selene's index fingers as she and Mesa twirled around the lawn. A slight breeze ruffled their long black hair.

"Ashes, ashes," Selene sang.

Mesa's laugh built into excited shrieks. Her head tilted back toward the sun as she spun. Her favorite part was coming up.

"We all fall down!"

Mesa let go of Selene's fingers and flung herself back,

squealing as she fell. She gyrated on the lawn, kicking her arms and legs in the air, laughing and laughing. Then Selene was on top of her, tickling her ribs and grabbing playfully at Mesa's little feet, her fingers drawing more excited bouts of laughter from the child as they drew across her soles. Mesa was laughing hard, out of breath, her cheeks rosy. She stuck her tongue out between her tiny, perfect teeth.

"Ashes," Mesa said, the word too large for her mouth. "Fall down!" she shouted, rolling about in the grass, grabbing clumps of green in her tiny fist.

In her bedroom, Mesa could feel the heat of the remembered sunlight warming her. A flush of joy bloomed deep in her core, imitating the original. The memory wasn't hers, nor was it Selene's. The memory belonged to Jonah. He'd given Mesa a bag of these chips—his collection of memories from her childhood. Cherished recollections. He'd lain in the grass that day, watching his wife and daughter enjoy a perfect moment, and more than twenty years later, he'd shared that moment with his daughter, who had no recollection of him or herself. Although Selene had died years before Mesa's problems, the woman's affection for Mesa's youthful counterpart had endeared her greatly. Her mother's love swam across the ages to her, and Mesa wished for some way to thank her.

A few dozen more memories littered the desk and its drawers. Even more were scattered across the web, archived in deeply buried caches of sites such as MemSpace and Episodic. She'd found a few, posted by Selene more than a decade ago, but the search hadn't been easy. More were out there, she knew. There had to be.

She finished the coffee and unplugged, calling it quits for the day. She felt antsy and confined, stricken with a hard-core case of cabin fever.

"I need to take a walk, get out and stretch for a bit," she said.

Still dressed in Kaizhou's clothes, she said goodbye to Jonah and promised to call, but she didn't think she would be out late.

Even as the door closed behind her, she wondered how it would be to leave and never come back. To disappear. It wasn't the first time she'd had the errant thought. But she knew how much irreparable pain that would cause Jonah, and as she had before, she dismissed the idea before it could fully form. Even though her psychiatrist suggested keeping an open line of dialogue with her father and sharing her thoughts and feelings with him, she kept that secret to herself.

That and one other.

"Hicks writes like Philip K Dick and
Robert Crais combined... He focuses on
the story and never lets go."

– Lucas Bale, author of the
award-winning *Beyond The
Wall* series

PRESERVATION

A DRMR SHORT STORY

MICHAEL PATRICK HICKS

REVOLVER

MICHAEL PATRICK HICKS

"A classic example of social science fiction"
David Wailing, Author of Auto

FOREWORD BY
LUCAS BALE

"A sharp, crackling exploration of man's hubris and science gone wrong. This is Frankenstein for the new millennium."
HUNTER SHEA, author of We Are Always Watching and The Jersey Devil
MICHAEL PATRICK HICKS
BLACK SITE

THE MARQUE

MICHAEL PATRICK HICKS

ALSO AVAILABLE

THE MARQUE

The world has fallen beneath the rule of alien invaders. The remnants of humanity are divided into two camps: those who resist, and those serve.

Darrel Fines serves. He is a traitor, a turncoat who has betrayed his people, his wife, and most of all, himself. In this new world order, in which humanity is at the very bottom, Fines is a lawman for the violent and grotesque conquerors.

When the offspring of the Marque goes missing, Fines is charged with locating and recovering the alien. Caught in the crosshairs of a subdued worker's camp and the resistance cell that he was once allied with, Fines is forced to choose between a life of servility and a life of honor.

AVAILABLE NOW IN EBOOK

For more titles and news about future releases, visit www.michaelpatrickhicks.com and subscribe to the mailing list.

www.ingramcontent.com/pod-product-compliance
Lightning Source LLC
Chambersburg PA
CBHW051635180726

48284CB00006B/1742